Straws In The Wind

Straws In The Wind

By

Polly Harris

*Blackie & Co
Publishers Ltd*

A BLACKIE & CO
PUBLISHERS LIMITED PAPERBACK
© Copyright 2001
Polly Harris

The right of Polly Harris to be identified as Author of
this work has been asserted by her in accordance with the
Copyright, Designs and Patents Act 1988

All Rights Reserved
No reproduction, copy or transmission of this publication
may be made without written permission of the publisher.
No paragraph of this publication may be reproduced,
copied or transmitted save with the written permission or in accordance
with the provisions of the Copyright Act 1956 (as amended).
Any person who does any unauthorized act in relation to
this publication may be liable to criminal
prosecution and civil claims for damage.

First published in 2001

A CIP catalogue record for this title is
available from the British Library
**ISBN 1 903138 18 3
Blackie & Co Publishers Ltd
107-111 Fleet Street
LONDON   EC4A 2AB**

Cover Design by Tim Arundell

Printed and Bound in Great Britain

For Tony

who got me through it

(and also wrote this dedication)

CHAPTER ONE

Neither Bugsy Moran nor Rose Ashenby heard the car pull up, or the crunch of footsteps on the gravel. Bugsy because he was rooting out an extremely active flea from his nether regions, and Rose because she was still attacking the limp form which lay prostrate at her feet.

"You rat, Ryan!"

She kicked him. Then, snatching him up, she punched him in the stomach, so that a pathetic little wheeze of air escaped from his mouth. "You are a two-timing – slimy – evil little rat."

He sagged against her and she held him up until his eyes, glazed and lifeless, were on a level with hers then let him slide through her hands, knees buckling. She stood back, sucking her grazed knuckles, then kicked him again.

"You know something, Ryan?" she panted. "You really are a bastard. You know that? Yes, of course you do. It's your stock in trade, isn't it? Well, stuff you then. Let's see how you like this."

Wrenching open the waistband of his jeans, she seized a handful of straw and thrust it up his capacious anus.

"Well, *say* something, you –"

"Rose?"

"At least say you're sorry. But you're not, are you?"

"Rose?"

"Rats like you are never –"

"Rose! What on earth are you doing?"

"What?" She jumped then swung round, revealing a blotchy face. "Oh, ah, hi, Leo."

"I said, what are you doing?"

The woman, who had been leaning against the studio door, dropped her cigarette stub, ground it out with the heel of her cowboy boot and came over, steering a path through the mounds of steel clippings, the bale of straw and hammered-out aluminium cans. Rose abruptly let go of Ryan and he fell, sprawling on his back on the paved floor.

"Oh, I – I was just finishing off my scarecrow," she said lamely. She drew the back of a freckly hand across her brow. "Goodness, it's warm again, isn't it? I mean, much warmer than yesterday, I should think, and – and –"

"And even warmer than Friday. Yes, it is warm," the other woman agreed, deadpan.

Their eyes met, then both of them exploded into shrieks of laughter. But then, abruptly, Rose pressed her palm to her mouth.

"Oh, Leo."

She turned away, lifting the scarecrow and hooking him up by his neck to a nail in the wall.

"Hi, Bugs." Leo hitched up her mud-stained jeans and squatted down to scratch the huge black cat who, having reminded himself that this was his larder whenever Rose wasn't around, reluctantly abandoned the flea and rubbed against her legs. "Who's a gorgeous hunk, then?"

Covertly, she studied Rose, who was very carefully brushing dust off the scarecrow's T-shirt which, in letters three inches high, proclaimed that poets do it in iambic pentameters.

"That's one of Ryan's, isn't it?"

"Yes." Rose did not turn round. "And his designer jeans."

Leo expelled a long breath. "I take it that you two have – er – had a slight tiff."

"No. No tiff." Rose's voice was muffled. "He's gone."

"Gone?" Leo straightened up. "Gone where?"

"Don't know." The faintest shrug. "Nowhere. Anywhere. He's left me."

"Oh. Oh, no."

Here we go again. Leo metaphorically rolled her eyes. What was it about Rose and her men? Assholes every one – and Ryan the shittiest yet.

Rose turned round at last. "Don't say anything. I know you hated him."

"I didn't," half-heartedly.

"Yes, you did. And so did Daniel."

"Well, yes – Daniel. But honestly, it was just that we knew what a nasty little free-loading swine he is."

"Four years we were together." Tears were pouring unheeded down onto her denim dungarees. "I really thought that this time – and then – and then –"

Her voice rose, cracked and disintegrated. Shoulders hunched, she began scrubbing at her wet cheek with her arm.

"Oh, sweetie." Leo, not much given to open displays of

affection, pulled her friend to her and gave her a quick hug, then eased her into an ancient red plush chair. She moved the oxyacetylene blowtorch which lay on the arm, then gazed down at her thoughtfully. "What you need is a drink."

"Oh, no, no," Rose protested feebly. She began plucking at the wads of stuffing which oozed from the arm of the chair. "I've got to – I'm going to – I know I'm going somewhere. Oh God, I can't remember –"

Where the hell was she?

Daniel stared out of the French windows. The garden was, as always, immaculate; although to his eye, with its martial ranks of burnt-gold marigolds and scarlet geraniums, it was more like a municipal park than an English country garden in late June. On the terrace, the guests milled elegantly among the terracotta urns of petunias, in alternate pink and purple. He knew that if he went out with a slide rule every pink urn would, to a hair's breadth, be the identical distance from its purple neighbour.

The two marble nymphs beside the pool had obviously been scrubbed down for the occasion. They stood white and chilled to the bone. If that pair had nipples they'd be standing on end. But Rose's parents wouldn't have nipples in their garden – and they wouldn't have one of their daughter's sculptures in their garden either. He'd never been sure whether they genuinely didn't like her work or whether it was another subtle way of putting her down.

Beside the mossy sundial, a little family group was being captured for posterity by cameras and camcorders. The kaleidoscope of figures shifted, reformed with the grandparents, grandma holding to her bosom what he had actually heard her refer to as God's Little Afterthought; Grandpa, paterfamilias, his fair hair, even now, well turned sixty, hardly touched by grey; their elder daughter Susan, smoothly blonde; Roderick, her husband, darkly handsome, only the faintest paunch breaking the sleek lines of his suit; and the three older children, as strategically spaced as the urns: Emily, sixteen, Abigail, fourteen, and Cordelia, twelve. Was it simply a trick of the sunlight, Daniel wondered, through half-closed eyes, or did that little family group really glow? A golden circle. A charmed circle.

"Charming." A woman in a lilac suit, skirt a fraction too short, jacket a fraction too tight, appeared at his elbow. She gave a sentimental sigh. "Absolutely charming. Such a good-looking family."

Daniel made a polite noise.

The group had dissolved and was making its way towards the house, Mr Ashenby at the rear, every now and then scuffing out with the toe of his shoe another little rash of high-heel pockmarks in the smooth lawn. Just for a moment a vision, like a transparency, slid across Daniel's eyes, a vision of Rose's father in greasy overalls, probing the guts of a dead car, his wife in the little kiosk by the pumps. The vision shimmered then disappeared.

"And what a sweetie Susan is."

"She is?" The faintly sardonic note went unheeded.

"Oh, yes, an absolute darling. Jeremy, my husband, he's the godfather, you know. But of course, you do know." A fluty, girlish laugh. "The other godfather, I should say. Anyway, he's quite wild about her. And Roderick – well, Jeremy says he's going to be made up to full partner any time now. So young, so gifted." And so ghastly. "The three girls – all so pretty, aren't they? And now this darling baby boy. Yes, such a lovely family."

"Ah, Daniel dear, so here you are." A rustle of pink silk brought Mrs Ashenby alongside them.

"We were just admiring the garden," the woman said. "Perfectly lovely."

"Yes, it does look rather well at the moment, doesn't it?"

With a brief smile, the woman turned away as from another room came the protesting wail of a baby, then Rose's father's voice, distant, strident.

"Look," Mrs Ashenby's fingers plucked at the neckline of her dress, "where *is* Rosemary, do you imagine?" Her mother still insisted on Rose's given name, presumably because she had chosen it.

"I can't possibly imagine," Daniel said wryly.

He turned to her, marvelling as he always did that there was nothing of Rose in her mother. But today the face was tense; she seemed for the first time the faded blonde that she was, and that Susan would become. He saw her jump slightly as her husband's raised voice reached them again, and added more gently: "You did tell her the right time?"

4

"Of course. Her father wrote the day – and the time – down for her. Well, we all know what Rosemary is, of course." She glanced at her watch and clicked her tongue. "It's so thoughtless of her. I do hope Ryan hasn't come back early from wherever he's been. I mean –" She broke off as she caught his eye. "But then, when did Rosemary ever consider anyone beside herself?"

Rose's kitchen was even untidier than usual. Leo shook her head, half-exasperated, half-affectionate. What a slob she was. Years before, when George and Angela had decided to do up for letting the near-derelict cottage, which had been home to the coachman in more gracious days, no expense had been spared. And they'd even paid to have the coach house itself turned into a small studio for Rose.

Now though, the whole house was more often than not a tip. Just once every couple of months Rose would rouse herself and go through the place from top to bottom – but the next onslaught was clearly overdue. The kitchen was really pretty, with its pine units and yellow walls – Angela had just been to Giverny with her gardening group – but Leo, who, whether in work or play, was fastidious, wrinkled her nose, shovelled a pile of dirty crockery into the bowl and flooded it with cold water.

Then, as she went to reach down two glasses, the phone on the breakfast bar began to ring. Ryan? Fifty miles down the M40 and remembering which side his bread was buttered? It wouldn't be the first time he'd walked out on Rose then smarmed his way back. She hesitated a moment, then flicked the off switch.

Back in the studio, Rose dragged herself back from whatever distant shore her thoughts were grounded on and watched as Leo set down two bottles on the floor.

"I've fetched some glasses from the kitchen. Hope you don't mind."

"No, sure," said Rose listlessly. "Was that my phone just now?"

"Yeah. But it stopped before I could get to it."

"Oh." A faint stirring of life. "But it might have been –"

"Double-glazing," Leo broke in firmly. "Bound to be."

"Mmm. S'pose so."

As Leo picked up one of the bottles, it glowed in the sunlight shafting in through the studio door. "Apricot '96. One of my best years."

"Oh. It isn't strong, is it?"

"Naah. I was taking these round to Bob Lewis. He fixed all that dodgy guttering for me last week. But desperate remedies are called for here, I think. Bob can have some of my '97 plum."

With the toe of her boot, Leo hooked a stool towards her and sat down, then drew the cork and poured two full glasses.

"I don't know." Rose pressed her fingers to her temples. "I've got a headache already."

"That's just all the crying – and you've been doing a lot of that, haven't you?"

"Mmm. All morning." She felt a glass being thrust into her hand.

"This will do you nothing but good, I promise you. Drink up, love, then tell me all about it."

Rose lifted her glass, rolled it back and forth across her hot forehead, looked at her pale reflection in it then took a sip.

"Oh, it's gorgeous, Leo."

The golden liquid lapped her tonsils, soft as satin, sweet as red clover honey. She drained the glass and Leo bent forward to replenish it.

"Now – tell me."

"Well –" Rose was gazing down at Bugsy, who had curled himself up on her lap, "– it was this morning. I was in here, working on that, trying to get it finished." She pointed to the far corner where a long, curving metallic fish lay on the floor. "Daniel wants it this week for a Mexican friend of his."

"Hey, Rose, it's great." Leo sprang to her feet and peered down at the creature.

"Is it? I don't know – I never know about my work. It's not finished yet, of course. I've got to fix the fins, then I'm going to sheath it in metal gauze and spray it silver and gold for the scales."

"Brilliant. Daniel'll love it – and so will this Mexican guy."

"Well – maybe."

"Yes, they will." Leo gazed at her sternly. "And you will have it ready this time, won't you?"

"Oh – yes, of course."

"You don't want a repeat of last year's fiasco, do you?"

"No – no, of course not." Rose winced at the memory. "I'd have almost got it done by now if Ryan hadn't arrived."

"Good. And you're going to charge a proper price this time, aren't you?"

"Oh yes. Daniel says he'll insist on that."

"I mean – the sculpture you've done for George and Angela, you'll have barely covered your costs, the peanuts you asked for that."

"But they're friends."

"Bollocks to friends! They're my friends as well, but that didn't stop me charging the going rate for the garden I've done for them."

"Yes, but –"

"But nothing. If you don't value yourself, no-one else will. You charge people what you're worth –" she seized both of Rose's hands and shook them fiercely "– what *these* are worth!"

Expelling an angry breath, she sat back on the stool and took a long swig of wine.

"Anyway, you were telling me about Ryan."

"Oh yes, well, I wasn't expecting him back till next week – he's been at that folk festival in Norfolk."

"And?"

"And nothing." She seized Bugsy, burying her face in his black fur, and squeezed him until he squeaked. "He just came to collect his gear – books, CDs, clothes – everything, except that T-shirt and jeans which he'd left for me to wash, only I'd forgotten. Oh, Leo, it's terrible. When I got them out of the washing basket, there was the *smell* of him."

"Yeah, rats do smell pretty rank."

"No. You know what I mean – Ryan's smell. I shall never wash them, *never*."

"So he's gone, just like that. Didn't he give any reason?" Leo refilled both their glasses.

"Oh, yes. There's this girl. Julia, she's called. Julia Trebithick, I think he said. She's beautiful, Leo – and so young."

"He told you this, did he?"

"No, I've seen her. I met her, last summer, when I turned up at that festival in Newquay. You remember, I went down there specially, to surprise him."

"And you certainly did that," Leo put in dryly.

"Yes, well, anyway, he was reading his poems in a pub. There was a jazz band there as well, and this girl, Julia, she was playing the clarinet. She comes from that way, and – oh Leo, she's really lovely – long blonde hair, long blonde legs, gorgeous high cheek bones that I'd kill for."

"Or that Ryan would give up his cosy little billet here for."

"He was so cold. I couldn't believe it was him."

Couldn't you? Leo thought angrily.

"He chilled me. I couldn't be angry, or upset, not straight away. I was just frozen through. He stood there, over by the door, and told me I was a fool not to have realised we were washed up, that we'd been heading that way for months." She ran her fingers through her dishevelled reddish-brown curls. "And when I asked him why, he just laughed and – oh, Leo, it was so utterly, utterly humiliating, I can't tell you. He said to take a look at myself and then think back to Julia. And I have – and she's twenty-one and gorgeous – and I'm thirty-five, and –" her lower lip trembled, "– I've never, ever been gorgeous."

"But to be late for her only nephew's christening – and she the godmother, too. Really, that is too bad." Two fuchsia-pink spots, which perfectly matched her silk dress, had appeared on Mrs Ashenby's cheekbones. "What her father will say –"

"Edna, where is that bloody girl?"

On cue, the tall, thin, rather stooped man had appeared in the doorway, his face set in a petulant scowl.

"I – I don't know, dear."

"Perhaps she's lost track of time," Daniel interposed smoothly. "She's been working on a commission for me, for a new gallery in Mexico City. It could be a real breakthrough for her."

"Really?" There was that note of careful indifference which entered her father's voice whenever Rose's work was mentioned.

"Look, I'll give her a quick ring, if I may."

They both watched in silence as he crossed to the French eighteenth-century side table, picked up the receiver and dialled.

"No. No reply." A slight frown creased his brow.

"Well, of course," Mrs Ashenby put in, "she refuses to have an extension in that studio of hers. Says it would break her concentration, or something."

"Ye-es. I suppose, if she was running late she could have gone straight to the church. Maybe she's waiting for us there."

"Oh, of course. That's what she's done." He felt her relax with relief. "How clever of you, Daniel."

"Hmmm." Her husband sounded less convinced. "Anyway, talking of church, are we or are we not going to christen my first grandchild today?"

"Oh, John." Another brittle laugh. "Your first grand*son*, you mean."

"What? Oh, yes. My first grandson, then."

CHAPTER TWO

"Oh dear." Mrs Ashenby broke the sepulchral hush, her fingers walking round the neckline of her dress once more. "Oh dear. I – I'm not quite sure –" She glanced nervously at the oak door to the study, firmly closed. "Look – just come through to the sitting room, all of you."

She led the way back into the room they had so recently quitted and all the guests trooped after her in silence; stunned, Daniel thought, by the monumental sexagenarian tantrum they had witnessed in the church porch. He took up his station, leaning against a wall, watching as the rest of the christening party almost tiptoed in, arranging themselves around the perimeter of the room, as though delicacy forbade them to intrude on a family crisis.

"Er – well, we'd better have something to eat, I suppose," Mrs Ashenby went on as the three young village girls, attired in black dresses, white aprons and lace caps, came in with loaded trays.

When one, a pretty, dark-haired girl, appeared beside him, Daniel took a cheese puff and a glass of white wine.

"Funeral baked meats," he murmured.

"Did coldly furnish forth the marriage tables." The girl winked at him and moved on.

That would learn him. So they did still teach *Hamlet* at A Level – or had she picked it up from *Shakespeare in Love*? He couldn't remember.

"Oh, isn't it rather warm for you outside?" Mrs Ashenby fussed, as one of the guests opened the French doors.

But her words were unheeded. People slid out and Daniel watched them, their shoulders perceptibly relaxing as they escaped. Eyes, which until then had been studiously avoiding other eyes, now met, and when a little group disappeared behind an island bed of spiraea and philodendron he was almost sure that he heard stifled laughter and a definite snigger.

"Well," Roderick threw himself down into a chair, "I must say."

He expelled a long, angry puff of air. His three daughters sat in a row on the sofa, hands primly folded in their laps, impassively studying their parents from beneath blonde fringes. As the drinks tray passed in front of her, Susan reached out.

"Now, darling," Roderick put a firm hand on her wrist, "you had two before we left, and you know it will interfere with your milk." A stifled exclamation from Susan, a faint gasp from her mother at the mammarial reference, and the three girls smirked. "We can't have Tarquin turning into an alcoholic, can we? I'm right, aren't I, Edna?" as Susan turned her round eyes, still hazy with tears, towards her mother.

"Oh yes, Roddie," his mother-in-law agreed hastily. "And anyway, darling, I'm sure your father will sort something out."

Daniel looked across at Susan. She wasn't wearing well. A much prettier girl than her younger sister – that is, if you liked china blue eyes, blonde curls and a rounded figure, which he personally didn't much care for. But today there was something. In spite of being surrounded from birth by secure love and approbation, which Rose had never had; in spite of now being cosseted by au pairs and God knows what other labour-saving devices, his antennae, super-honed where this family was concerned, picked up – something. As if becoming aware of his gaze, she looked up sharply. Their glances met and for a fleeting second Daniel was horrified to see sheer naked desperation in the rather vacuous blue eyes, before she looked away again.

"I must say." Roderick began again. "A bit much, isn't it?" Appealing to the room at large. "I mean, to double-book on christenings like that, and forget *ours* to go off to some other tinpot affair at the other end of the county."

"Well, not *quite* that far, dear. But there have been one or two little mix-ups since our parish was joined with Compton Abbas and Little Swinton."

"Huh, just another way for the C of E to save money; and efficiency goes out the window. And anyway, if you want my opinion, Edna, he's past it, your vicar."

"Yes, well, he –"

"Wouldn't happen at our place, I can tell you. Richard is incredibly on the ball – for a clergyman. Even got his own web-site. I told you, darling," he frowned at his wife, slumped in one of the chairs, nibbling at her nails, (the only attribute she shared with her sister, thought Daniel inconsequentially) "we should've have had him done at home."

"Oh, Roddie, dear, of course Susan wanted Tarquin to be christened here."

But of course she did, thought the watcher in the shadows. Even though she and Roderick lived just this side of Oxford, thirty miles from the Warwickshire village where she'd grown up, Susan, with that ruthless sentimentality which no-one else seemed to be able to recognise, had wanted all her offspring to be sanctified in the same church where she herself had been baptised, confirmed, married, churched. (Were women still churched? If they were, Susan certainly wouldn't have missed out on it.)

"If he's not being christened, Daddy," Cordelia, the twelve year-old, piped up, "does that mean he's damned forever? Miss Jenkins said we're all in a state of original sin till –"

"Of course he isn't," her father broke in irritably. "For God's sake, Susie, I told you it was a mistake sending them to a church school. Ridiculous idea. Well, they're not getting their hands on Tarquin."

"Oh, no, dear, of course not." His mother-in-law was fervent. "No, I, er, well," her voice dropped, "I don't think it's a secret, darling, but Daddy is insisting that he'll pay for little Tarquin's education."

Oh bloody fucking wonderful. Daniel angrily folded his arms across his chest. Typical. His three granddaughters have to take pot luck at the local comp, but a grandson ... And worse, far worse, Rose had had to work her way through Art School because for the first time in her life she'd dared defy her father and not take the secretarial course he'd deemed appropriate for her. Bloody Victorian dinosaur.

"Well at least, this way," (had Roderick picked up something of his thoughts?) "there's still time for Rose to put in an appearance."

"Aunt Rose?" asked Abigail. "Is she coming after all?"

"And Ryan." Emily, who had spent most of the afternoon gazing morosely into the near distance, looked up, her eyes brightening with teenage lust. "Does that mean he'll be here?"

"No, thank God, he will *not*," replied her father. "You did say he was away, Edna, didn't you?"

"Yes, dear – and perhaps it is just as well."

"Too right. He damn near ruined your Ruby Wedding. Deliberately, too – turning up in those appalling deadlocks."

"Dreadlocks," Daniel amended quietly.

"What?" Roderick frowned at him. "Oh well."

Go on. Say it. *I* should know.

"Oh good." Mrs Ashenby broke into the sudden chilly silence as everyone heard the study door open and heavy footsteps cross the hall.

"Well, John?"

As her husband appeared in the doorway, she fluttered towards him.

"Well, at least Ryan's done one thing for me. Once and for all, I'm giving up on the ridiculous idea that somewhere out there," Rose's gesture took in the whole of south Warwickshire, and sent her empty glass flying, "is the guy – fellow – hunk who is going to be my life partner. I've finished with men – except you, sweetheart," dropping a kiss on Bugsy's head. "Oh, and Daniel, of course. Well, he's my best mate, isn't he?"

Leo gave her an odd look. "Yes, of course he is."

"Along with you, Leo. Whatever would I do without you both," as two maudlin tears oozed out. "Give up men forever – that's the best thing, isn't it?"

"Well," the other woman blew a quivering blue smoke ring into the air, "speaking as one whose track record is not one of the soundest – I mean, married at seventeen to a guy who turns out to be a drugs dealer, divorced at twenty, with just one appalling son to show for those three years."

But Rose knew that behind that façade of indifference Leo was desperately unhappy over her wayward son.

"Erm, how is Jamie?"

Leo shrugged. "No idea, love. I told you, I saw him on the late News a few months back being dragged out of his tree house by two hefty policewomen, but since then – zilch." She drained her glass and reached for the second bottle. "No – don't ask me about men."

Rose sighed again. "I used to have this lovely dream, you know. Me, a husband, three beautiful children –"

Leo gave a harsh laugh. "All girls have that dream at least once in their adolescence, sweetie. But then, with any luck, common sense takes over."

"Yes, but –"

"No buts." Leo was brisk. "Believe me, Rose, there are plenty of compensations – if you need any, that is. I mean, for instance, have you noticed that when you buy a pack of frozen lemon sole one is always bigger than the other?"

"Yes."

"Well, which one did Ryan have?"

"Mmm, I see what you mean."

"That's men for you – and they're all the same." Leo retrieved Rose's glass and filled it again. "You're better off without them, honest. Isn't she, Bugs?" She looked into the slitted yellow eyes. "You know, I'm convinced that cat understands every word you say to him, Rose."

"Of course he does. Don't you, sweetheart? Who's my precious baby, then?" Bugsy gave her an impassive stare. "And yet." She sighed. "I still think that he is out there, somewhere. We've all got a Mr Right, I'm sure. It's just that some of us don't ever find him."

"Well, you can keep looking, if you want, but count me out. Men of straw, the lot of them. And talking of which ..." Leo's gaze wandered to the scarecrow, still hanging from the nail. "You know, Rose, he's pretty good."

"Well, not bad, considering I haven't made one since I was at college." She reached across and nudged the figure so that he swung to and fro, a few wisps of straw drifting from his feet and hands.

"I do like his hair." Leo got up and tugged gently at the white mop head.

"It was all I could find, but it seemed to work OK."

"Ryan in his White Rasta period, I suppose."

"How did you guess?"

"Well, I'll give him that; he certainly livened up your parents' Ruby Wedding party."

Rose pulled a face. "That was their own fault. If they hadn't made it crystal clear they didn't approve of him, he would never have had that dreadlocks perm. Neither of them spoke to him all evening." She smiled faintly. "Come to think of it, though, they've never approved of any of my boy friends."

"Well, you've always gone for the most unsuitable ones, haven't you? I mean, before Ryan there was Jason, and before him Darren, and before him..."

"All right, all right." Rose put her hands to her ears. "Spare me, please."

"OK, but you must admit, love, every one of them's turned out a wrong 'un. And all your parents have ever asked from you is a walking tight-arse in a pin-striped suit with superb prospects."

Roderick got to his feet as his father-in-law came into the room.
"Well, John? Any news?"
"Yes, I think so." John Ashenby shot his cuffs as he turned to his wife. "I've just been onto the palace, my dear."
The palace? Daniel almost choked on his Chardonnay. Surely a cock-up even of this magnitude didn't quite merit royal intervention.
"The Bishop's out, at some Mothers' Union do or other," Mr Ashenby went on testily, "but his secretary was most sympathetic – most sympathetic. Promised to bring it to his Grace's attention as soon as he gets back."
"Good for you, John." His son-in-law beat his hand on the back of his chair.
"And then I rang the vicarage again. Betty was most apologetic, couldn't apologise enough, in fact. What a nice woman she is. Said that Cedric wouldn't have had it happen for worlds."
"Well, you are his longest-serving church warden, aren't you, Daddy? So you're entitled to *some* consideration."
"Yes, well, anyway, to cut a long story short, he isn't staying on for the tea party or whatever it is that other lot have got organised, but coming straight back to christen our little chappie."
So that's all right then, thought the little chappie's godfather-elect. Rather amusing, really, that he'd been asked. He hadn't been expecting it; had been astonished, in fact. All right, he'd known the family from childhood, had grown up in the same village, but even so. Of course it was the money – his money, from the Daniel Bradshaw Galleries: London, Stratford-upon-Avon, and soon, hopefully, New York. His eyes wandered round the room. Beautiful furniture, with the cherished peach-bloom of age which he always ached to run his fingers across; several good pictures – that Bonnard print which he'd found for them. The girl always reminded him of Rose.

It hadn't always been so, of course. Susan and Rose had been brought up in a black and white timbered cottage at the far end of the village, next door to him and his parents. John and Edna

Ashenby had been very lucky. They'd worked hard, but had the luck as well, which some people went all their lives and never tasted. For years they'd owned that garage on a side road to Banbury, then, in a stroke of unintentional genius, had bought the other one a few miles away. The first was now somewhere under the southbound carriageway of the M40, and the other had disappeared, even more lucratively, into the maw of that out-of-town superstore. That same month, the Old Rectory had come on the market, and the transformation had begun.

Hardly surprising, then, that the whole family had a very lively regard for money. Except for Rose, of course. Rose ... he'd never have accepted this invitation if they hadn't asked her, as well. A bit bloody late: three daughters, six previous godmothers, all well-heeled, of course, and they'd happily managed without her. But now Rose was beginning for the first time to show the potential for making what her brother-in-law would no doubt call "serious money". Had she finished that fish for Manuel? When he'd rung her, she'd sworn blind that it would be ready, but who ever knew with Rose? Rose...

"I'm going to ring Rose again." He spoke directly to her mother.

"Oh. Oh yes. There's still time for her to get here now." She gestured towards the phone.

"No, it's all right. I want to fetch something from my car so I'll ring from there."

Rose took another gulp of wine.

"Hey, Leo, this is really delicious. What did you say it was, apricot?"

"That was the other one; this is gooseberry."

"Gooseberry," Rose repeated slowly, holding the glass up so that the light turned it to a pale greenish-gold. "Wonderful colour. And not strong either."

"No more than the apricot, no. Like mother's milk for a baby."

"Baby." Rose frowned and leaned forward confidentially. "You know, Leo, there's definitely something I ought to be ..."

Daniel replaced the handset and sat gnawing his lip. Where the bloody hell was she? Maybe that little swine Ryan really had come back early. He banged his fist down on the steering wheel of his BMW, hard enough to make him wince. Well, too bad. They'd have to drag themselves out of their Sunday afternoon bliss. But Ryan wasn't due back for at least a week. Had she had an accident? Was that decrepit old Transit van of hers at this very moment lying upside down in a ditch, with her, lifeless, inside it? He'd told her, only last month, that the tracking needed seeing to. But when did she ever listen to him? He really ought to ring the police. And yet, and yet; he knew, by that instinct which always told him when Rose was in real trouble, that she was there. If he could just reach down the line and grab her.

He'd fetch her. It was only a few miles, so he could easily get them both back in time. But first, just to make sure, he'd ring Leo. She could go round there, roust Rose out from whatever she was up to, and that way she'd be ready by the time he got there. As he eased the car past the line of vehicles strung out along the curving drive, he reached for the handset once more.

"Oh, Leo. Are you sure it wasn't Ryan – on the phone, I mean?"

"Quite sure. I told you – double-glazing. Or Angela, wanting your Samurai moving yet another centimetre to the right."

Rose sniggered. "Have you finished her garden yet?"

"Just about. It'll be done in time for the party on Saturday, anyway."

But Leo was gazing thoughtfully at the scarecrow. All at once she leapt to her feet and snatched it down. "Come on, you. Let's have a look at you in daylight."

She strode off, Ryan sagging down her back, across the little cobbled yard between Rose's tiny stone cottage and studio and into the lane, where a gnarled wisteria grew out of the hedge, festooned in mauve racemes. She pulled some twine out of her jeans pocket and slung the figure up to a branch, his straw feet scuffing the verge.

"What are you doing?"

Rose, though slightly unsteady on her feet, was aghast. She cast a fearful eye at the rosy redbrick house, whose lovely barley-sugar chimneys could just be seen over the lime trees behind the studio.

"What will Angela say if she drives past? That's her hedge."

"She won't mind. Although she might not take kindly to Ryan with his flies undone." She was tugging at the figure's zip, which had stuck halfway.

"Yes, but what are you doing?" Rose repeated.

"It's obvious, isn't it? You're going into the scarecrow-making business."

"*What*? Oh, no –"

"Well, you're making one for Angela, anyway."

"Oh, no, Leo, no!"

"Yes, Leo, yes. You know how knocked out she was by that tin can Samurai you've done for her Japanese garden? Well, she's going to have a scarecrow in her new potager."

"But –"

"This do on Saturday – it's partly to show off the garden but it's also for George's birthday. And she was telling me the last time I was up there that she still hasn't got him anything."

"Well, what can you get for the man who has everything?"

"Precisely. But George really loves that veggie patch – I think he escapes there when he wants a break from Angela's latest fad – and he's going to have a scarecrow of his very own to keep guard over it."

"Oh." Rose leaned weakly against Leo's battered old white Citroen 2CV, as her friend stood back, gazing critically at her handiwork.

"Ugh. Looks a bit sinister, doesn't he?"

"I suppose he really needs a nose. I was just doing that when you –"

"I know."

Opening up the back of the car, she took out a box of vegetables.

"Your organic box. Sally delivered mine, and when I said I was coming here she asked me to bring it. Said pay her when you see her. Ah, yes."

She set the box down on the low stone wall which led into Rose's small overgrown front garden, then dug out a carrot and screwed it into the scarecrow's face.

"Yes, that's better. Hmmm. Just one more thing though. Ryan always did have a big opinion of himself."

This time she took out a large leek, ripped off the green outer

leaves and shoved it into the half-open zip, where it stood proud.
"How's about that then? Homo Erectus."
They clutched each other, shrieking with laughter.
"Oooh!" Rose sat down precipitately on the wall, holding her head. "Oh no – look."
She pointed to where the scarecrow's cock was slowly, sadly sagging.
"Homo Flaccidus," Leo amended.
"No." Rose beat her fists on her knees. "Flaccido Domingo." And she slithered off the wall and sat on the verge.
The noise made them both jump.
"Whassat?" Leo peered all round her before focusing. "Oh, hell's teeth – my mobile."
"Double glazing."
"No – better answer. Could be that new client in Worcester – I'm designing a town garden for him. Said he might ring today."
Very gingerly, she eased herself into the driver's seat and picked up the phone.
"Leo Brinkworth, Garden Design. Oh, Daniel. Hi. How are you?" Rose sank back against the wall, idly watching her. "Yes, I'm there now ... No, she can't, no ... well, just one or two ... Now look here, Daniel," Leo's normally pale face had suddenly gone very pink. "Don't take that tone with me. She *what*? ... Oh, no ... No," her gaze wandered to Rose, "no, she can't possibly ...Yes, I'll tell her. All right, *all right*."
She retracted the aerial and slowly clambered out of the car.
"Er, Rose. Promise you won't get in a state."
"What about?" Rose was wiggling the toe of her trainer in the dust.
"*Promise.*"
"Promise."
"Well, you know Tungsten, or whatever his name is –"
"Tungsten." Rose narrowed her eyes in concentration.
"Your nephew –"
"Nephew."
"Well, he's being christened today."
"Christened."
"And his godmother is nowhere to be found."
"Godmother! Oh my God!" Rose lurched to her feet. "Oh my

God." She did a little circle in the middle of the lane. "I knew it – I *knew* it. Didn't I keep telling you I had to be somewhere this afternoon? My keys – where are my keys?" She was frantically patting her dungaree pockets. "Where the bloody hell? Oh God, Dad'll go mad."

She retrieved a set of car keys and ran back into the cobbled yard. Leo caught her up alongside an old blue van, where she was fumbling at the lock.

"Rose, what are you doing?"

"Got to go. I'm late. I've done it again!" Her voice rose in a wail.

"Rose." Leo snatched the keys out of her hand and backed her up against the van. She shook her by the shoulders. "Listen to me. You're in luck – some balls-up with the vicar. So, stop biting your nails, there's a good girl. We've got fifteen minutes to get you ready. Sober you up – well, spruce you up, anyway – before Daniel arrives."

CHAPTER THREE

"Yes, well, Angela bought me this outfit for my birthday." Sympathetic smiles all round as George Smethurst, a stocky man resplendent in red silk shirt and shorts, which were engaged in savage take-no-prisoners conflict with his florid face, rolled his eyes at the little circle. "Apparently red is *the* lucky colour in this Fong Shu or whatever it's called."

Good old Angela, Rose thought with affection – discovering Feng Shui when the rest of the world was through it and out the other side. Angela Smethurst, like Mr Toad, had many passions; intense, one at a time, all of them short-lived, though long enough to make George's life a minefield of half-submerged hazards.

Rose took another sip of her bitter lemon. Its acidity bit her tongue, but no booze this evening, not after last Sunday; in fact, no booze ever again.

"Of course, I blame Leo. It's that Japanese garden of hers that's put all these oriental ideas into Angela's mind."

"Oh but, George," Jenny Fellowes, a forty-ish blonde in a cream linen dress, put in, "if it wasn't for the Japanese garden Rose would never have done that Samurai for you. It's magnificent."

Half a dozen pairs of eyes swivelled to where, guarding the koi carp pool with its little wooden bridge, stood the sculpture. Just less than life size, its red and silver helmet and black body armour glinted evilly in the mellow sunlight of a perfect June evening.

"What? Oh yes, of course; superb."

Rose smiled to herself again. George was far too nice to say so, but she guessed that, after thirty years of metal bashing in that Black Country factory of his, he had his own views on a better use for beaten-out aluminium cans.

"And don't forget my other present. I really love it, Rose." He patted her arm. "And Angela thought of it all by herself. I was really touched, I can tell you."

The eyes moved towards the far corner of the garden where the scarecrow towered above Leo's elegant new vegetable potager. In Rose's opinion, a two-metre high Wolfie, the Wolverhampton Wanderers' mascot, complete with gold shirt, black shorts, black baseball cap and grey trainers, clashed as stridently with the pure lines of the dwarf lavender and box hedging and the antique redbrick paths as George's shirt did with his face. But, through all the years which had brought him from the back streets of Wolverhampton to a successful car components factory and finally, after a take-over bid that not even he could resist, to the splendour of Manor Farm, George had never lost either his Black Country accent or his passion for his club. So Angela's choice – or rather her own suggestion – had been perfect. Good old Wolfie. He'd be providing the down payment on a new washing machine to replace her ancient one, which didn't so much wash clothes as mug them.

"I'm glad you like him, George. I enjoyed making him."

She smiled warmly at him, then felt the smile slip. Past his shoulder, over in the little knot garden which Leo had laid out within the two remaining arms of the 'E' of the original Elizabethan house, she saw Daniel, in cream chinos and black polo shirt, being greeted by Angela. She hunched her head down into her shoulder blades. Was it too late for her to make her excuses and leave, now? She winced yet again at the memory.

He'd said very little – been ominously silent, in fact – when confronted with the still-unfinished giant fish. The Mexican, Gomez, had done all the talking, expressed his desolation that he would not be able to include a Rose Ashenby sculpture in his new show – he had heard so much about them. But, well, she would understand, he was sure, he had a deadline to keep. Even his Viva Zapata moustaches had drooped, as if to match his anguish. Then they'd left for Heathrow.

Three hours later, though, Daniel was back. His face was flushed, his brown eyes had that almost black, opaque quality which, though seldom seen, always made her quake inside. "You've let me down, Rose – let yourself down – totally unprofessional – I *told* you, I'd all but sold you to Gomez before he'd even set eyes on one of your pieces. All you had to do was have it ready." He jerked his thumb towards the fish, which still lay beached in the farthest corner of her studio. "You've *blown* it, Rose. You always blow it."

She couldn't stand more of the same tonight. Could she escape? Perhaps he hadn't seen her. But escape to what? An empty bed, an empty house, silent except for one of Ryan's haunting tapes, which would bring the tears fast enough. When she'd switched the radio on the previous evening, there'd been a phone-in on Radio WM on what makes a perfect marriage. An old lady from a nearby village was talking about her marriage: "...Give and take, dear, and what my mother said the day Fred and I got married – never let the sun go down on your anger ..." No, they hadn't been blessed with children, but her Fred had been the best of husbands. He'd died last year, just six months short of their diamond wedding... Rose's eyes were so blinded by tears that she'd had to fumble for the off switch, and she hadn't put the radio on since.

Daniel had seen her the moment he arrived. Although Leo had promised him that she'd arm-twist Rose into coming, he'd made a detour on his way here, just to make sure. But the little cottage was silent, with only Bugsy basking in the evening sunshine, idly scratching himself.

He was still furious with her, of course – and with himself for ever trusting her to finish the commission on time. He should have learnt from last year when, for the autumn show in his London gallery, he'd reserved pride of place, even set up a scarlet-draped plinth, for her black Camargue fighting bull. He'd covered up for her at the preview party, of course: "Yes, I'm terribly sorry," as would-be clients peered querulously at their catalogues, "it's been sold already and shipped to Japan," when he knew full well the hessian shape still languished, half-finished and minus its bitumen coating, on her studio floor. But he would not, ever, cover up for her again.

"Chardonnay for you, I think, sir."

"What? Oh, yes thanks." He became aware of the dark-haired girl who was holding the tray of drinks towards him, hazel eyes twinkling mischievously. "I know you, don't I? Oh, of course, you were at the christening."

"Got it in one."

"So you make a habit of this, do you – waitressing, I mean?"

"Well, a girl's got to live," she showed a rather delicious dimple. "Between A Levels and uni, anyway."

"Yes, of course."

"But," she gave him a glance from beneath her lashes, "you don't really remember me, do you? Oh, not from last week. Jane, my sister, she had a holiday job in your gallery after her A Levels four years ago, and I sometimes came in to see her."

"Good heavens, of course. Jane Smith. And you are?"

"Lucy."

"That's right. Yes, I do remember you." But at fourteen, four years was a long time. What had happened to those teeth braces, that puppy fat? "How is Jane?"

"Oh, she's fine. She's working in Bristol now, at the Museum. Yes," another glance, "I used to ask her when you'd be in. I had a real crush on you, you know."

"Did you? Good grief." He was rather taken aback. Nothing made him feel all of his thirty-five years more than the self-possession of modern youth. "Oh well, that's a stage we all grow out of, thank God."

"Of course. But," as he went to move away, "talking of holiday jobs, I don't suppose there's anything going this year?"

He hesitated for a moment. "Well, there just might be. One of my part-time staff told me last week that she's off to Manchester with her boyfriend."

"Oh, great." For a fleeting instant he saw the fourteen year-old again.

"Don't count your chickens – but come into the gallery Wednesday, no, I'll be in London till then – Thursday morning, and we'll have a chat."

"I'll be there. Thanks, Daniel." And with a last brilliant smile, she moved off.

He watched her go for a moment, a slightly bemused expression on his face, then made his way among the clusters of chattering guests, weaving through the newly laid-out herbaceous beds, with their lupins billowing up against the drifts of phlox, the tall white lilies and rose peonies, and the humps of white ox-eye daisies – one of Leo's trademarks was to mix, on occasion, garden and wild flowers – towards George's group.

"Hi, George. Happy birthday."

"Daniel, lad, good of you to come. Oh, great," as a whisky-shaped parcel changed hands. "Thanks, you're a pal. How are you?"

"Fine. Hi, folks – Adrian – Roger – Jenny."

So he was ignoring her. That meant she wasn't forgiven.

"How's business, Daniel?"

"Oh, can't complain, Adrian."

"Still fleecing the wool off people's backs?" put in Roger.

"Something like that," Daniel replied coolly.

"Leave him alone, you two. Daniel," Jenny put a hand on his arm, clunking her heavy gold bracelet, "where *did* you find that gorgeous red and gold enamel pillbox? I saw it in your gallery window last night, and it's just what I've been looking for."

"Yes, it is rather nice, isn't it? She's just out of college, the girl who made it; I spotted it at her graduation show. She's very talented, I think – and she's got the drive to succeed, as well." Did Rose imagine it, or was there a sidelong glance in her direction? "I'll put it on one side for you, if you like."

"Oh, God, Daniel, do you mind, please." Roger Fellowes, heavily-built and quite rapidly running to seed from too many liquid lunches entertaining his favoured accountancy business clients, gave a heart-felt groan. "You're not supposed to encourage her."

"Shut up, Rog. You spend enough on your flash cars." And your women, was the unspoken addition.

Rose, who had known them both for years, often wondered why they stayed together, in spite of frequent infidelities on both sides. Of course, you needed things in common, a bond. Their latest venture to supplement Roger's fat income was to move into the tumble-down redbrick mill on the outskirts of the village, do it up in classic English Country House style and run it as an up-market bed and breakfast. They'd been three years on this project so far and now it was just beginning to produce the money, and the beautiful things – cars, enamel boxes, people – that money can buy. Maybe that was enough.

"That's marvellous, Daniel. I'll give you a ring tomorrow, if I may. Will you be at the gallery?"

"No, I'm going back down to London tonight."

Oh great. Rose, who had been stirring a floating ice cube round and round in her glass with the tip of her finger, drowned it, spurting the bitter lemon over her jade-green voile dress. Conveniently forgotten that I invited you to lunch tomorrow, as a thank-you after the christening. Across a clump of blue-spike delphiniums, she saw Leo waving to her and went to slide away.

"Have you seen my scarecrow?"

"No, George, I haven't."

He had, of course. When he'd arrived with Manuel Gomez she was stuffing the bloody thing.

"It's brilliant. Rose must have worked on it for weeks. Where is she? Ah, yes." George's hand fastened on her arm. "Get her to show it you. You'll love it."

"Hello, Daniel." She met his eyes for the first time, forcing a smile.
"Rose."

He nodded, not returning the smile, and they walked the length of the garden in silence, under the long rustic pergola, where the air was heavy with the sensual perfume of Gloire de Dijon, Lady Hillingdon and coppery-pink Albertine. She loved the old-fashioned roses and would usually have plunged her nose into one after another of them, until she was almost drunk on the scent. Tonight, she barely saw them.

Wolfie was keeping watch beside the white picket gate leading to Leo's potager. On either side of his papier-maché snout, his silver ball-bearing eyes glowered menacingly at the guests scattered across the striped lawns, as if on a search and destroy mission against any lurking West Brom supporters. A few wisps of straw were sticking out through the thick grey lisle tights which covered his legs and Rose picked them off one by one.

Daniel studied her half-averted face. She looked pale, and rather wretched. There were dark thumbprints under her grey eyes and he guessed that she wasn't sleeping. That evil little git Ryan. Not that Rose had said a word. In fact, she'd barely got out a word throughout the entire ceremony or the rest of that appalling afternoon, when no-one seemed to be speaking to anyone else – and least of all to Rose – and at the earliest opportunity the non-family guests had dumped their silver rattles and Teddy Bear cutlery and silently fled. But when he'd rung Leo next morning she'd told him. He'd experienced two intense emotions simultaneously: the desire to hunt down Ryan and very slowly chop him into tiny pieces, and to leap up to the moon in elation.

She was stooping down now, retying one of Wolfie's laces. Rose. His Rose, yet not his Rose. He always had this pain in his heart, always would have, he knew, at the mere thought of her. His first distinct memory, though she always insisted he couldn't possibly remember that far back, was of two solemn-eyed one-year-olds in woolly hats, sitting up in their prams, studying each other across the garden fence. His second memory was of Rose having a tantrum and beating her teething ring against the side of her pram, as he looked on in stupefaction.

"Do you remember when you painted me?" he asked suddenly.

"What?" She brought her thoughts back from wherever they had been. "Of course."

She smiled, and he felt her relax slightly. These days it was always safer for them to go back into the past. The present was a dangerous country, the future even more so.

"How old were we?"

"Oh, three I should think. Yes, I had those acrylic paints for my third birthday."

She looked at his bare arms. Beautiful brown satin, the product of a Jamaican father, Marcus Bradshaw, then a lecturer at an Oxford college, and a white mother, Elaine, who had worked in the college library. It had always fascinated her – it was such a contrast with her own pale gingery-freckled skin. So it was only natural that one day, armed with her birthday paints, she had persuaded him to strip off in the den in the spinney behind their gardens and, as a change from Doctors and Nurses, painted him all over.

Daniel had often thought since, that, for anyone with the *nous* to see, this had been the first flowering of Rose's artistic talent, for instead of the crude reds and blues of a child's taste, by the time their mothers had arrived he had been covered in endless flowing spirals of cream, chocolate and black. Only on the tip of his small penis had Rose painted a tiny pink rosebud. He'd been dragged away to be scrubbed and scolded, while Rose's paints went in the bin. They'd been kept apart for three whole days, but at that time no-one could separate them for longer.

Looking back, she'd seemed so utterly single-minded when they were little. But it had all changed. Oh, the talent, that readiness to think big, to take risks, that unerring eye for the quirkiness that somehow paid off and which lifted her work so way above the ordinary, was still there – you could see it even in something as in-your-face as this scarecrow – but now, she was drifting, totally lacking in any sense of self-worth, so that whenever success came near her, she blew it.

Of course, she couldn't help herself. It was the result of parents who had never, to his knowledge, given their younger daughter one single word of praise. If nothing negative could be said, then nothing would be said, and unlike acrylic paints, those indelible marks could not be scrubbed off

He sometimes wondered if it wasn't the same with her men. She went, every time, for trash, because she didn't deserve any better. He couldn't do anything about that, of course, he told himself savagely, not a bloody thing, but if he simply stood by and watched her destroy her professional career...

"I've finished it." She still wasn't looking at him. "The fish, I mean."

"Oh?"

"It's quite good, I think." She straightened up. "Well, Leo says it is."

"Of course it's good. All your work is good – when you finish it."

She winced. "Do you still want it then?"

"Whatever for? I'd promised it to Gomez, and he's back in Mexico City."

"Oh. Oh, well. It doesn't matter."

"Yes it does." The hurt look in her eyes made his voice harsh. "Look, Rose, when the hell are you ...?"

"Hello, Rose, Daniel."

Rose jumped. "Oh, hello, Mrs Wilson. How lovely to see you. I haven't seen you for ages." In the relief at her rescue, she smiled warmly at the dumpy little woman, in a white blouse and floral cotton skirt. "How are Sally and Mike – and the twins, of course?"

"Oh, they're all fine." Hannah Wilson smiled. "The twins are a bit of a handful, though. I think Sally will be glad when they start school."

"Yes, she looked a bit frazzled last time she brought my box. Said she and Mike should've stuck to raising organic veg; it's easier than children."

"Oh, she doesn't mean it," the proud grandmother said quickly. "And you mustn't let her put you off, dear. Isn't it about time you were thinking about it, you and Ryan? I haven't seen him tonight. I suppose he's away on one of his – er, jigs."

"Yes, that's right."

"No, he's not."

Daniel and Rose spoke simultaneously. Their eyes met for a moment, she flashed him a look of silent gratitude, then went on stiffly, "Ryan's not here tonight because he's gone."

"Gone?" Hannah Wilson's eyes opened wide.

"Left me."

"Oh, my dear." She put a hand on Rose's arm. "I'm sorry, I really am. Dear, dear – and after all this time. And he was so fond of you."

"Was he?" She could not keep the bitterness from her voice.

"Of course. But, Rose," she patted her arm, and Rose knew what was coming, "there are plenty more fish in the sea, just waiting for a nice girl like you."

"To gobble me up, you mean?" Rose snapped. But she'd known the woman for years, and would not be angry with her.

"Oh, no. You tell her, Daniel."

"Yes – yes, of course there are," he said woodenly.

"Mind you, Rose dear, I always say the best cure for a broken heart is work," the older woman went on comfortably, "and I wanted to ask you something."

"Oh, yes?" Rose asked stiffly.

"The thing is, I'd like to order a scarecrow. For Bob, you know."

She did not miss Daniel's frown. "You want me to make you a scarecrow?" Robert Wilson was an ex-copper – an Inspector, actually, and far more of a Pascoe than a Dalziel, so that for the life of her she could not see him shouting himself hoarse on the terraces at Molyneux. "A Wolfie, you mean?"

"Oh no, dear." Hannah Wilson laughed out loud, as they all looked up at the scowling figure. "No, Bob is taking over as President of the Golf Club next month, and it's his sixtieth birthday soon, so I suddenly thought – he's become really keen on his vegetable patch since he left the Force, so perhaps you could make him a golfer."

"Two birds with one stone, as you might say," remarked Daniel.

"Ye-es." She looked at him doubtfully, before going on, "The thing is – I'm not sure how much you charge."

"Well," Rose was horribly conscious of Daniel, "if I decide I can do it, I'll, er, drop an estimate in next week."

"I can give you one of his old bats – clubs, I mean. And I think I could smuggle out one of his old golfing suits."

"Well, I'd like the club. But I'd rather dress him myself – if I do it, that is."

"Oh, wonderful. Thank you, Rose. And now I must go and admire Angela's herbaceous border, or I shall never hear the last of it."

"Are you really going to do it?" Daniel's tone was repressive.

"Probably."

"Well, congratulations," he said tightly. "Looks like you've got yourself a whole new career."

"Maybe I have at that. At least it'll pay the bills. And if it gives people pleasure ..." She knew she was being defensive and the little fires of tension and irritability which had been banked down all evening burst into flame. "You're not my keeper, Daniel, so get off my back, will you?"

For a long moment they stared at one another, angry-eyed.

"All right," he said finally. "I'll do just that. I'm off now, in any case. Oh – sorry about lunch."

"Are you?"

"We've been having problems with the temperature control in the London gallery. I want to get back to check it tonight."

"Well – another time."

"Yes. Another time."

"Drink, sir?"

"Not for me, Lucy. I'm leaving."

"Oh dear, so soon?"

Rose saw the girl treat Daniel to a flirtatious smile. She was the one he was getting on so well with earlier ... Lucy? Surely she knew her – she'd certainly seen her somewhere before.

"Another bitter lemon, madam?"

"No, thank you. I'll have a gin, please – a large one," she added, as she saw Daniel frown again.

"But of course. I'll fetch you one, madam."

All these madams were making her feel positively ancient – but that was no doubt the intention.

"Thank you," she said frigidly.

"George is over by the drinks table, so I'll walk up with you, Lucy, and make my apologies," said Daniel. "Goodbye, Rose."

"Bye, Daniel. I hope the temperature's all right," she called after them, but the girl was talking to him and he did not hear her.

She watched him go, tears blurring her vision so that he seemed to leap and jerk his way back up the garden. How could they have come to this? Like strangers – no, worse than strangers. And if Daniel turned his back on her, what would she do? A huge lump of self-pity lodged like a stone in her chest, and she had to fight the urge to sink down at Wolfie's feet and howl with misery.

Over her head, the scarecrow stared with sublime indifference.

CHAPTER FOUR

Half-hidden by the red trellis archway in her Japanese garden, Leo watched Daniel stride off, and saw Rose, just standing where he'd left her. Poor Rose – and poor Daniel, too.
"Yes. *Rather* dishy, that one, wouldn't you say, Leo?"
"What? Oh, hi, Zoë." Leo greeted the woman who had appeared at her elbow.
"Pity he's gay, though. Such a waste, I always think."
"Gay?" Leo laughed. "Really, Zoë, don't be ridiculous."
"Oh, he's very discreet, I grant you that."
In fact, there had been affairs. Leo knew of several – though not of the kind Zoë was imagining – and yes, all of them *very* discreet, and even more ephemeral.
"But I mean," Zoë's eyes were still following Daniel, "that beautiful milk chocolate body – he'd melt in the mouth not in the hand, that one." She gave a throaty giggle. "And all that beautiful money – can you think of another reason why he hasn't been gobbled up long ago by some undeserving female?"
Yes, one very good reason, actually. Leo's gaze flickered back to Rose, who was now talking – very unenthusiastically, to judge from her body language – to a man, a stranger, certainly no-one that she'd ever seen before. But if Daniel didn't care to wear on his sleeve a heart that had been spoken for since the age of two, well, who was she to put her oar in?
"Anyway, Angela's sent me down to admire this absolutely Amazing oriental garden of yours."
"Well, here it is. Hot from the Leo Brinkworth production line."
"Hmmm."
The other woman, pale blonde, ultra-chic, ultra-slim, her small features ravaged less by time than by face lifts, looked around at the carefully landscaped boulders, the huge terracotta urn lying on its side, the newly planted maple trees. She lifted one hand and rippled a finger across one of the wind chimes, setting it tinkling.
"It's great, Leo. I feel positively tranquil already."
"Good." The two women, old friends – and, occasionally, old adversaries – grinned at each other. "Can't I tempt you to indulge? That shady area at the end of your garden would be perfect."
"Well ... you know, I just might, at that."

"Of course, I don't come cheap. And neither does Rose." She patted the gleaming Samurai.

"Mmm." Zoë pursed her lips dubiously. "I've heard Rose Ashenby is unreliable."

"Who told you that?" Leo bridled sharply.

"Oh, no idea." A lift of a silky, tanned shoulder.

"She's perfectly reliable – and she's good. So how about it, Zoë?"

"Well, I must admit I rather fancy having a spot like this to do my meditating in."

"You do a lot of that, do you? Meditating, I mean."

Zoë grinned. "On occasion. I'll have to get round Gavin, of course. Shouldn't be too difficult – his latest affair is just coming to the boil." She spoke indifferently. "So I'm in the market for another sweetener. A trip to Hong Kong last time, a Japanese garden this – perfect balance, wouldn't you say?"

"Perfect. Zoë, aren't you ever – well, just a bit nervous that, well–"

"That he might go off for good? Naah. Oh, Gavin isn't a bad lad, it's just that he's welded to a cock who's a serial adulterer. And besides," she gave a feline smile, "my brother is just about the meanest divorce lawyer in London. Gavin knows that Trevor starts every day eating men twice his size and still has room for a Full English Breakfast."

In the pool beside them, one of the huge koi carp was watching them, gulping air through its rubbery mouth.

"Hmm. Reminds me of somebody. Can't think who, off-hand. Here you are, my ducky." And leaning over, Zoë poured in some of her pale, blonde drink.

"I'm sorry?"

"Ms Ashenby?" The man – about forty, with greying hair and horn-rimmed spectacles – was regarding her rather uncertainly.

"Yes," she replied brusquely, then pulled herself together sufficiently to manage a wan smile. "Yes, I'm Rose Ashenby."

"Stefan Barshinsky." He put out a large hand – he was a large man altogether, over six feet, although with his slight stoop he did not seem heavy. "Great to meet you, Rose."

She put her hand into his paw. "Goodness, that's quite a name.

You're Russian, er, Stefan?"

"Most people call me Steve, actually. No, I'm from the States – Virginia – though my grandfather was Russian."

"Goodness, how romantic." Rose, the fumes of gin swirling through her brain, heard herself all but simper.

"Not that romantic, I'm afraid," he answered wryly. "He starved for the first year and shined shoes in New York for the next five. I think he'd have been a shoeshine all his life if he hadn't met Grandma."

"Oh?"

"Well, he was a shoemaker before he left St Petersburg and she realised what a good one he could be. All he needed was a break. So, there was this wealthy guy whose shoes he shined and she, er, persuaded him –" he grinned suddenly and his plain, rather slabby face lit up, "– I don't know how. It's wisest not to look into your family past too closely, don't you agree?"

Rose, who simply could not imagine any of her family doing anything between sheets which did not belong to them, and only then if they had been crisply laundered, said, "Oh, certainly."

"Anyway, this guy bankrolled Granpa so's he could open his first shoe store. He made a go of it, and then my father carried on. When Pop died last year, Mom sold out. She's English, which is why I'm here."

"She – your mother – moved back to England?"

"Oh, no. She'd never do that. She's lived in Virginia for over forty years and all us kids, and my sisters' kids, are round her. But she still misses the old country, of course."

"Of course." Rose, who could never live permanently in any country but England, agreed fervently.

"But to occupy herself since Pop went, she's bought an old farmhouse out in the wilds – not quite as old as this one, of course–" that crinkly smile again, "with a garden and paddocks that haven't been touched for years, and I'm helping her create an English garden."

"How lovely. What a great idea."

"Yeah, we're planning it between us." He took off his glasses and began polishing them on his sleeve. "She's reading all the books she can get hold of and I'm over here looking at gardens – stealing their best ideas." He grinned again. His eyes were a deep, intense blue, fringed by black lashes.

"And where have you been? Which gardens?"

"Well, I started off down south. Sissinghurst – Mom told me I must see that white border. I think we shall do something like that. And Mottisfont – that was neat, too."

"Mmm – all those lovely roses."

"Sure. They quite knocked me out, I can tell you. And I'm looking at other collections too, because for her seventieth birthday we – my sisters and me – we're buying the plants to stock this new garden. So I've been across to Norfolk to see that lavender nursery. Mom loves lavender, so we shall have a whole garden of that, maybe mixed with roses – I saw a beautiful rose and lavender garden in a village near here last Sunday."

"Ilmington, you mean?" In spite of her mood, his unaffected enthusiasm warmed her.

"Yeah, that's it. And I'll be going across to that place in Herefordshire which has all the pinks in existence, so I hear. Mom loves them too. Funny thing – the quickest way to make her cry is give her a bunch of shaggy white pinks. I guess they're so English."

Bending down, he snapped off a Mrs Simpkins in the bed beside them and as he held it out to her, Rose sniffed deeply at its sweet, spicy scent.

"Yes, they're beautiful. So, what brings you here?"

"Well, I met up with Angela at Chelsea and happened to mention that I needed a base while I looked round this way and she recommended Jenny and Roger. They're a great couple, aren't they? Those breakfasts, wow!" He patted his stomach.

"Yes." Rose managed a slightly more natural smile. "They do have quite a reputation."

"And this place has given me several ideas, I can tell you. It's great – and they tell me you're the genius behind it all."

"Me?" Rose was taken aback. "Oh no. I only made that Samurai. And him." She gestured up at Wolfie. "The designer's over there." All at once she was tired of talking, tired of smiling. "The one in the navy dress – Leo."

"Oh, right. I'll go and have a word. Well, it's been great talking to you, Rose."

He put out his hand again, then they both jumped as a loud 'clang' broke through the waves of laughter and talking all round them. They turned and saw Angela about to strike for a second time the large Chinese gong she was holding.

"Hello, everyone." She waved across to the side of the lawn where a group of youthful cooks in natty little uniforms of white T-shirts and navy jeans had been labouring all evening over a line of barbecue grills. "You'll be glad to know, I'm sure, that supper is ready."

"Oh, great. Shall we?" Steve seemed about to take her arm in an old-fashioned gesture and Rose drew back.

"No – thank you. I'm really not hungry."

"Oh, but you must. The food smells great."

"No, really." It came out far too abruptly, but she couldn't bear that concerned look which had all at once come into his eyes. "I – I'll have some later."

"Well, if you're sure," he said reluctantly. "I think maybe I'll just say hello to – Leo, did you say her name was?"

As he went, Rose was conscious of a tight band settling down over her forehead, an ache rapidly developing between her shoulder blades. She should never have allowed Leo to bully her into coming tonight. Hannah Wilson was a terrible gossip. Ryan's departure would be all round the village by tomorrow – it probably was already. Was it her imagination or was every single person giving her sympathetic glances?

Perhaps she could leave now, while everyone was crowding round the barbecues. At least she'd stayed longer than ten minutes ...

"All on your own, Rose?" George, raising his voice above the hubbub, was at her elbow. His round face had deepened from red to vermilion.

"Oh, hello, George." She gave him a pallid smile.

"Can't have my favourite girl all on her own – and not eating."

So the good news really had started its rounds. Or was it just that George had somehow picked up on her silent despair and with his usual kindness was cherishing the lame dog?

"I'm not really hungry," she said. "In fact, if you don't mind, I think –"

"Nonsense. Of course you're hungry. Come on."

And putting an arm round her, he steered her towards the food. When her plate had been loaded, she smiled her thanks and moved away. But where to go? Over to her right Rog and Jenny were deep in conversation with Zoë and Gavin. To her left, chatting animatedly, were two other couples she knew. Couples, couples, everywhere couples. The pain welled up in her again, but then was dissolved by anger. A beautiful evening, a lovely garden, evening sunlight lying on it, thick and golden as heather honey: a quintessentially English summer scene – and as false as hell. Rog and Jenny, Zoë and Gavin, how many more of these loving pairs were stuffing the living daylights out of other people, like rabbits in a burrow?

Leo caught her gaze through the crowd. But she was with that American – what was he called – Steve? And sweetie though he was, she couldn't face any more stilted 'great gardens I have known' conversation tonight. Down towards the paddock was a green and white canvas gazebo, and inside was just one solitary figure. Lettie Johnson. Rose slipped across the lawn and into the shade of the awning.

"Hello, Miss Johnson. Mind if I join you?"

The elderly woman, who had been wielding her knife and fork with swift precision, jerked her head in the direction of another chair.

"Evening, Rose. Take a pew."

"Thanks." She dropped gratefully into it.

There were plenty in the village who swore that Letitia Johnson would have been burnt as a witch three centuries ago. Whatever the truth of that, she certainly inspired nervous apprehension in many a local breast, with her sharp tongue and disconcerting habit of telling things the way they were, not the way people wanted them to be.

She speared a piece of pork fillet, held it suspended on her fork then said, "So that young man of yours has been making a damn fool of himself."

Rose flinched as if the woman had struck her. The bush telegraph wires *were* already humming, then – unless she really was a witch. Oh, what the hell – what did it matter?

What did anything matter?

"He's left me, yes."

"Think he'll be back?"

"No."

Chewing ferociously on the fillet, the woman sat back and regarded Rose, not unkindly. No-one knew how old she was. Her face had been heavily lined as long as Rose could remember, crow's feet at her eyes from chain-smoking, while her hair, a dingy yellow at the brow, had been grey all her life, as far as Rose knew.

"But if he does," she went on hesitantly, "do you think I should take him back?"

"Not up to me. But I think you know the answer to that one already."

Having demolished the fillet, she drained her glass of red wine then started in a business-like fashion on a chicken kebab.

"Like your scarecrow."

"Thank you."

"Don't much care for the other chap, though."

"Well, I suppose cans aren't ..."

"Nothing to do with the cans, Rose. As good a use as any for them, I should think. But I lost my brother in a prison camp in Burma in '43. Haven't much cared for anything Jap since then, to tell the truth." She cleared her throat, then jabbed her fork at Rose's untouched plate. "For heaven's sake, dig in. Food's no good when it's cold."

"Oh, right." And Rose, who had eaten almost nothing for the whole of the past week, after first tentatively picking at her grilled tuna, realised that she was in fact very hungry.

When they had finished and were sitting side by side in an amicable silence, Rose covertly studied her companion. An ancient tweed skirt, old trainers; her only concession to the heat and the occasion a blouse with embroidered poppies which looked as if, years before, it had come from some anonymous Eastern European state. Rose didn't suppose she'd bought anything new to wear in twenty years. She spent all her spare money on her greyhounds; past racing and brutally kicked out to fend for themselves once their earning capacities had gone.

"How are your dogs?"

"Oh, fine, most of them." The rather craggy features softened. "Lost a couple last week, though."

"You mean they ran away?"

"No," she said gruffly. "Had them put down. They'd had so

much ill-treatment, poor little sods, I couldn't persuade them that they wanted to live."

"I'm so sorry." Rose's eyes filled with tears.

"Well, can't be helped. And at least the dogs help me fill my time."

"But aren't you still lecturing?" Lettie Johnson had for years taught in the horticulture department of a nearby college.

"Nope. Said I was too old. Pensioned me off."

"Oh, but that's ridiculous." Rose was indignant.

"Well," she pulled a face, "I must admit, I do miss it. I still do some part-time though, and next month I'm giving a talk to the Gardening Club. Which reminds me – must have a word with Angela later."

"Ah, so here you are. Miss Johnson, Rose."

Rose started as their hostess, tightly swathed in a cerise dress and exuding a distracted – no, distinctly hot and bothered – air, appeared, as if conjured up, at the entrance to the gazebo. Her usually elegant apricot soufflé of hair looked as though someone had left the oven door open, and a stray lock had fallen limply in front of one ear.

"Now, I do hope you're both having enough to eat? There's absolutely loads left."

"I'll have one of those champagne syllabubs, if I may." Lettie began to heave herself up out of her chair.

"No, you stay right there. I'll get one of the waitresses to bring you one. What about you, Rose dear?"

"I'll get my own, thank you."

"Well, if you're sure."

She was about to turn away when Lettie held up a hand. "While you're here, Angela; something I wanted to ask you."

"Oh yes?"

"Mind if I come over some time and take snaps of those apple trees over there?" She gestured towards the orchard. "Want to use them in my next talk – it's on pruning fruit trees."

"But of course, Miss Johnson, we'd be delighted. Mr Perry – our gardener, you know – he's such a treasure."

"Thought they were his handiwork. They'll be perfect for showing people how not to do it."

Hiding her smile, Rose got to her feet and headed towards the trestle tables of lavish puddings.

"Hi, Rose." Leo waved a spoon in greeting. "These lemon creams are gorgeous."

"Oh, right, thanks." Rose took one, and together they strolled across the lawn. "That Steve seems a nice guy."

"Yes; and incredibly knowledgeable. He was telling me about a couple of plants I've never heard of. Mmmm, delicious." She rolled a cool lemony spoonful around her mouth, then swallowed it and smiled sideways. "Actually, I think he'd quite like to be more knowledgeable on the subject of a certain Rose Ashenby."

Rose groaned. "Oh, please, no. What did you say?"

Leo lifted a shoulder. "Only that you're a great person, but you're just coming out of a long relationship and you're not looking to start another one."

"Thanks, Leo." Rose heaved a sigh of relief.

"Talking of relationships, have you been to the loo yet?"

"No. Why?"

"Well, when you do," Leo dropped her voice to a conspiratorial whisper, "just put your head round the sitting room door and take a look at Angela's Relationships Corner."

"Her what?"

"It's the Feng Shui, apparently. You fill your Relationships Corner with photos of all the people who are hassling you in your life. So Angela's got about a thousand pictures of – guess who?"

"Not Miranda?"

"Yeah, the ghastly Randy Mirandy."

Rose sighed. "Poor Angela – and poor George."

"Why does anyone ever have kids, I ask myself." Leo's face twisted. "Maybe I should have a Relationships Corner of my own."

"Er, Leo."

They both swung round and saw Angela, looking more harassed than ever, trotting down the path from the house towards them. Behind her, Rose could see a tall, gangling young man, his shaven head gleaming in the evening sunlight. He was wearing shabby combat fatigues and an old army greatcoat which, made for a shorter man, just brushed his knees.

"Oh, God." Leo was very pale. "Oh, my God. I don't believe it."

"Leo? Are you all right?" Rose put a hand on her arm. "Whatever's the matter?"

And then, as the pair came nearer, she saw that the young man was Jamie Brinkworth.

CHAPTER FIVE

Leo lived in a neat one-storey house which had been the west lodge of a Georgian mansion. In the 1970s the lovely old redbrick house had been demolished and the two beautiful cedars in the grounds chopped down and burned, to make way for a development of five bedroom, three bathroom neo-Georgian 'residences' called, as a cynical *in memoriam*, Cedar Grove. All that remained was Leo's lodge and one shaky gatepost with a moth-eaten stone lion clinging grimly with blunt claws to the top and, on the far side of the estate, the remains of the walled garden, where Sally and Mike grew their fruit trees and brought on the baby plants for their organic smallholding in the field next door.

Rose propped the sack she was carrying against the low stone wall and went up the brick path. She walked slowly, running her hand along the tops of the old lavender bushes, releasing their perfume into the warm morning air. The garden was, as always, very pretty. She suspected that it was in revolt against the modernistic designs, which Leo spent so much of her working life with, that her own garden should be of the old-fashioned cottage kind, all the plants jumbled up together – marigolds, California poppies, larkspur, mallow, foxgloves – to make a patchwork quilt of colour.

The back door was open. She went in through the rear lobby, where the washing machine was humming softly, and saw Leo at the kitchen table. Several large sheets of graph paper were spread out in front of her, but she was sitting, chin propped in her hands, staring at the blue plume of smoke rising from the cigarette which lay in the ash tray.

"Um, hi, Leo."

Leo lifted her eyes. "Hi, Rose. Grab a chair."

The washing machine switched off and there was silence, apart from the soft tock-tock of the old clock. It hung on the wall, its face covered with faded pansy faces. Dave, that had been for ... or was it Rob? Whenever one of Leo's short-lived relationships broke up, she treated herself to a present. There were quite a few dotted around the house.

She cleared her throat. "How's Jamie? Is he still in bed?"

"No. No, he isn't."

As Leo took a long pull of her cigarette, then slowly exhaled,

Rose glanced around the kitchen, with its Shaker-style wooden units colour-washed in sea-green. It was as immaculate as ever. Leo was an almost obsessively tidy person. She couldn't possibly live with her. It would be too nerve-racking; she'd hardly dare move her elbows or walk on the geranium quarry-tiles.

"Er, would you like me to make some coffee?" she asked tentatively, when the silence seemed that it would never break.

"What? Oh sorry, Rose." Leo finally roused herself, stubbed out the cigarette and pushed back her chair. "I'll do some."

Rose watched as she took down two mugs from one of the units and spooned coffee into the brown pottery coffee pot. Leaning her hands on the sink, her back to Rose, she said in a flat voice, "He's out for a walk, so he won't hear me. He's been in prison."

"Oh, no." Rose's hand went to her mouth, her eyes on her friend's hunched shoulders. "Oh, Leo, what did he do?"

"God knows." Leo busied herself with the milk and sugar. "I haven't asked, and he certainly won't tell me."

"Then how do you know? You might be imagining it."

"No, I'm not. When Kevin was put away for drug dealing, I visited him – just at first, you know. Jamie was a baby, and, well, he was his father ... In the end, though, I asked myself if this was what I wanted for the rest of my life – and for Jamie, poor little bugger. Seeing him arrested, put away, coming out, starting all over again – because that's what it would have been. So I divorced him. But one thing you don't forget is how they look. They all have it, that look. Prison pallor – but it's more than that, somehow. And Jamie's got it, that same look. Oh Rose, where did I go wrong? What did I *do*?" She gave a great, shuddering sigh. "I did *try*, but somehow ..."

"Oh, Leo."

Rose got up, put her arms round her friend and hugged her. Just for a moment, Leo allowed herself to lean her head on Rose's shoulder, then she gave herself a little shake.

"Coffee's ready. Want a bikkie?"

And Rose, who knew Leo very well, and understood that there were jagged boundaries around her territory which even good friends could not cross, said, "Yes, please," and sat down again.

"It was a good party," Leo broke her digestive biscuit in half and dunked it.

"Yes," Rose agreed noncommittally.

In fact, the moment she got home she had burst into tears, floods of them, cried for an hour, then retreated to bed, clutching Bugsy like a talisman. She had snivelled into his black fur until she at last fell asleep and he could escape to slink off through the hedge and into Angela's Japanese garden, where he had already staked out the koi carp.

"Anyway, what are you doing here? You should be getting on with Hannah Wilson's scarecrow."

"Oh, I shall do, don't worry," Rose said earnestly. "And I'll pop into Stratford sometime this week, go round the charity shops and see if I can find a golfer's outfit." She screwed up her eyes. "I see him in sort of Bertie Wooster plus fours and a Fair Isle cardie."

"Sounds perfect. But what about his arms? You can't have him holding his club out at right angles – if you see what I mean."

"No, I know. But instead of a cross post, I'm going to use industrial wire. That way I'll be able to, you know, articulate them."

"Brilliant." Leo nodded approvingly. "So you've really been thinking about it?"

"Well, a bit. And I may be making some more."

"Oh?"

"I had two phone calls this morning – one definite, one maybe."

"Great. Who from?"

"You know that ghastly friend of Angela's, Sybil somebody, who has that country antiques barn near Moreton? She was at the party, and she wants a scarecrow as part of a display of Victorian garden implements – rhubarb bells and so on – that she's doing in September."

"What will you do for her, then?"

"Oh, she knows already." Rose pulled a face. "A Victorian head gardener – mutton chop whiskers, bowler hat, waistcoat. I wonder where I'll find gaiters ... Oh, and woolly long johns."

"Oh, Rose." Leo laughed for the first time. "Nobody will see his underwear."

"I know. But I want my scarecrows to be absolutely right."

"And the other one?"

"That's Jenny's sister-in-law. She hasn't quite decided yet. I'm supposed to be going to see her this week – with my portfolio." She rolled her eyes. "I mean, can you imagine – a portfolio of scarecrows?"

"For any relative of Jenny's, yes, I can." Leo gave a throaty chuckle. "Anyway, congratulations. A whole new dazzling career."

"That's what Daniel said."

"Oh?" Leo raised her brows ironically. "Don't tell me he's over the moon about it."

"Not so's you'd notice, no. But if it takes off, well," she set her chin defiantly, "too bad. It's all a bit strange, though, isn't it? I mean, what is it all of a sudden about scarecrows?"

"All part of this sudden urge for gardening, I imagine. You know: you've tarted up yourself and your house, so now you move onto the garden. And gardening is the new sex, apparently – and I don't mean people pricking out baby leeks on telly with their tits hanging out."

"Yes, I was reading the other day – I forget how many, exactly," Rose wrinkled her nose, "but about seventy per cent of women prefer gardening to sex."

"Well, of course. I mean, unloading a trailer full of luscious horse manure or a quick tumble in the hay?" Leo smacked her lips. "No contest."

The phone interrupted Rose's laugh.

"Leo Brinkworth Garden Design. Who? Oh hi, Steve." She gave Rose a meaningful look. "How are you? Good ... Yes it was, wasn't it ... Yes, I can let you have her number, but," another look, "she's right here, as a matter of fact. Hold on."

As she silently held out the receiver, Rose scowled at her, then took it.

"Er, hi, Steve ... Yes, it was, wasn't it. ... Thank you. I'm glad you liked them ... Oh, well, I'm not sure."

She pressed the Secrecy button and turned to Leo, her face dismayed. "Jenny's lent him her Yellow book and he's found a garden near Banbury with modern sculptures in it. He says it's open on Tuesday."

"Oh, yes, I saw that." Leo gestured towards a line of books on the dresser, where a yellow spine was visible. "I meant to tell you about it myself."

"But he wants me to go there with him."

"Sounds like a great idea."

"No, it doesn't," Rose hissed, forgetting that Steve could not hear them. "You know you as good as told him I'm off men. For good."

"Oh, for heaven's sake, Rose, be your age. You can still be civil to the buggers, can't you? And Steve's harmless, I'm sure – certainly not the type to throw you down among the love-lies-bleeding and roger you unmercifully."

"I suppose not," Rose muttered, and reluctantly clicked the button. "Steve, sorry. I think we were cut off. Yes, I'd like that, thank you." She glanced across at Leo who, after her little spurt of animation, was slumped in her chair again, tracing a knot in the table round and round with her finger. "And Leo would love to come, too … Yes, yes, that would be nice. Thank you. See you Tuesday then. Bye."

She hung up, and turned back to Leo. "We're both of us invited out to lunch on Tuesday, then the garden."

"But he doesn't want me."

"Of course he does – he sounded really pleased. And you're quite right. A nice, uncomplicated garden with a nice, uncomplicated man will do us both good, I'm sure."

"That's my girl."

"Mind you, what's a nice man like that doing not married? Maybe he's got two wives and six kids tucked away back in Virginia."

"He's a widower, actually. His wife was killed in a car crash. She was six months pregnant at the time."

"Oh, how terrible. Did he tell you?"

"Yes. We had quite a heart-to-heart at Angela's last night. It was fifteen years ago, but I don't suppose you ever get over something like that."

"No, I'm sure you don't." Rose sat silent for a moment, but then the pansy clock began to chime twelve. "Heavens, I must go. Seeing Lettie last night reminded me that I've got a sack of old silver foil for her."

"I've saved some for her as well, if you want to take that."

"Well, I'm walking." She pulled a rueful face. "I thought it would clear my head after last night."

"I thought you were off the booze."

"I was – until Daniel was mean to me."

"Oh Rose, love, he's never mean to you."

"Well, he was last night." She stood up abruptly. "Steve says he'll call me about Tuesday, so I'll let you know. Bye – and try not to worry about Jamie. I'm sure things'll be all right, honestly."

Leo looked gloomy. "I suppose so. Trouble is, I did happen to mention that Jack Greig has been blocking the footpaths across his land with barbed wire again, and now my wire-cutters seem to have gone walkabout."

Rose saw Jamie from quite a distance. Although it was a warm morning, he was still huddled in his fatigues and greatcoat, as if he was irrecoverably chilled. His thin shoulders hunched, he was leaning on a gate, oblivious to her approach down the rutted track, and when she came up to him she could see why. The entire field was blazing with poppies, as though a giant hand had unfurled a bale of exotic scarlet silk, turning an English meadow into something from the Arabian Nights. She gasped involuntarily and Jamie turned his head.

"Hi, Rose."

"Hello, Jamie. Isn't it lovely?"

As she leaned on the gate beside him, she saw that the back of one bony hand bore the tattoo 'LOVE' while the other declared 'WAR'.

"Yeah." He held up a single poppy, blotched with sooty black, and twirled it. "Perfect. This whole place, I mean. You know, Rose," he suddenly smiled at her, and the rather strained lines of his face softened so that he became the young lad he was, "I know Mum doesn't approve, but when I see a field like this, I know I'm right."

"To be an eco-warrior, you mean?"

"Yeah. And it's the only thing I want to do."

Rose's sigh was silent. She wouldn't tell him that this field and its neighbour were the next target for the silver-haired thug of a developer who had been responsible for Cedar Grove. He'd already had two planning applications turned down but these were just temporary setbacks. He'd get there in the end; he always did. And what would this small, very select, estate be called? Poppy Meadow, no doubt.

"But don't you ever lose heart?" she asked tentatively. "I mean, you see all the destruction going on, and you don't in the end manage to stop it. That by-pass – it's going ahead, isn't it?"

"Yeah. OK, we lose some battles; but we're going to win the

war. We've got to!" he exclaimed fiercely, and when she looked at him his pale blue eyes were burning with a fanatical light which made her stomach lurch.

"Jamie," she put her hand on his arm, "listen to me. Your mother gets very frightened about you. She worries dreadfully."

"Oh, sure." He gave a cynical laugh. "You can't have seen her face when I arrived last night."

"But that was just the shock. She wasn't expecting you."

"Yeah. Of course."

"She does care about you." Rose said desperately. "Truly she does."

"Does she say anything?"

"No, never. Honestly. But I know she does. Promise me you won't do anything to really worry her. You know – violence. Please."

"I'm sorry, Rose." He moved his arm, releasing her grip. "I can't do that. Direct action – that's all those bastards understand. But OK, I'll try not to do anything to hurt her. After all," his mouth contorted in a spasm of pain, "she's all I've got." He broke off then continued rapidly. "Don't tell her, but last year I found out where my dad was –"

"Oh, *Jamie*."

"Well, I wanted to see him," he said defiantly. "So I went. He was living in Nottingham with a woman – or maybe they were married, I never found out – couple of kids, poor little buggers. The whole place stank of drugs." He stopped again.

"And?" Rose was terrified of what was coming.

"And nothing. He shut the door in my face. Told me to fuck off back to my mother, and not bother him again."

"Oh, Jamie."

Rose put her arms round him in a wholly involuntary action. Beneath the greatcoat he was so thin, so fragile, that it was like hugging a frail old man, and her heart gave a painful squeeze. For a moment he let her hold him then he pushed her away, quite gently.

"It's all right, Rose." His face was blank. "Don't bother about me. I don't ever want to see him again. Just tell me this. How could Mum ever have got mixed up with a shit like that?"

"Well," looking at his young, wounded face, Rose felt about a hundred years old, "we don't always know, really know, I mean, the people we think we do, if you see what I mean." What a mess she was making of it. "I'm sure your Mum thought he was a decent man or she would never have fallen in love with him." But had Leo thought at all? Did one think at seventeen? Did one always think at thirty-five?

"I must go, love." She picked up her sack again. "I'm taking this foil to Miss Johnson."

"I'll come with you." He shook the poppy and its petals drifted to the ground like tiny drops of blood. "She's all right, Lettie." He took the sack from Rose. "She said last night to go round any time and see the dogs. I helped her sometimes, when I was a kid."

"Yes, I remember. I used to say you should be a vet."

"Yeah. I wanted to be, until the biology teacher told me I had no chance of getting any A Levels."

"Mmm. I remember that, as well."

She herself had told him: Jamie, I promise you, you can do anything you want, if you *really* want to. Funny, how she was so much better at dishing out advice on Life Management skills than taking it. Quite the little Aunt Rose she'd been. Had she been right though to encourage what she knew in her heart was an impossible dream? But in any case the damage had been done.

Miss Johnson's cottage was at the end of the track, well away from any other houses. As they approached, they could hear the dogs barking.

"Must be dinner time," Rose remarked, but Jamie did not reply.

As they dragged the gate open, on a broken hinge, a greyhound ran up to them.

"Hello, Smokey." Rose bent to pat the silky coat. This was Lettie's oldest resident, whose loving, gentle disposition wholly belied the vicious treatment he had suffered. The dog licked their hands, then barked and ran off a few paces, came back, barked again.

"Something's wrong." Jamie was looking round him. "Go on, Smokey." And the dog ran off.

When they followed him round the side of the house, they saw Lettie half-lying, half-propped up against the trunk of an old plum tree. Her eyes were closed, her face drawn.

Rose gasped with horror. "Oh, God. She isn't dead, is she?"

Jamie knelt beside the old woman, and as he gently shook her shoulder, she opened her eyes.

"No, she bloody isn't dead." She scowled up at them. "My leg hurts. I fell, you see."

Rose took her hand, all the while watching as Jamie ran his hands over her hip and leg. "But what were you doing?"

"Being a silly old fool, that's what. Taking out that dead branch up there. Aaah!" as Jamie experimentally moved her ankle. "What? Yes, that bloody well did hurt, my lad."

He sat back on his haunches. "You've broken it, I'm afraid."

"I can't have. It was just a little fall."

"Rose, go in and ring for an ambulance."

"She'll do no such thing. I tell you, I'll be all right if you just give me a few minutes." She went to sit up, gave a gasp of pain and lay back, sweat breaking out on her brow. Her face had taken on a greenish hue. Rose ran.

CHAPTER SIX

The phone was ringing as Rose unlocked her back door.
"Oh, hell." She gave a groan but then picked up the receiver.
"Hello."
"*Rosemary.* So *there* you are. *At last.*"
Rose gave another groan, this time silent. When her mother spoke in italics, there was always a storm brewing. But tonight she was simply too tired.
"Hello, Mum." She leaned up against the sink.
"I've been trying to get you for *hours.* Where *have* you been? Do you know what *time* it is?"
"No idea." Rose glanced down at her watch and saw with astonishment that it was almost half past eight. "I'm sorry. I've been out since this morning." She ran her hand wearily through her hair, struggling to gather up her scattered thoughts. "Um, did you have a nice time?"

After the christening, even Mr Ashenby had realised that his wife was near exhaustion and the next day they had gone off for a few days' R and R in Bournemouth, very much in the style of Sir Walter Eliot departing for Bath to take the waters.

"What? Oh, yes. Yes, it was very pleasant, although your father thinks the town's gone down sadly in the last few years. But as he said, what can you expect when you have Socialist Party Conferences in the place?"

"Oh, well, I'm glad it went all right anyway. Look, Mum, can I ring you tomorrow? I'm very tired. You see, Lettie Johnson fell out of a tree this morning and she's in hospital with a broken ankle and a bit of concussion, and –"

"Fell out of a tree? How ridiculous, a woman of her age up a tree."

"She was cutting out some dead wood, actually," Rose said tightly.

"But if she must do her own gardening at her age, why not stand on a ladder like any normal person? But then, when was Letitia Johnson ever a normal person? Really, I do wonder about her. Your father always says –"

"But you see, I found her – that is, Jamie and I found her."
"*Jamie?*"

"Jamie Brinkworth," Rose said, and as she heard her mother draw in a breath, went on hurriedly. "He was marvellous. I couldn't have coped on my own." Idly, she wondered whether to tell her mother that the last broken ankle he'd had to deal with was when his best mate fell off a rope ladder when being pursued by three security guards. He'd told her this as they'd waited for the ambulance ... And that was just before the unfortunate chain of events which had led to the Magistrate's court, and beyond ... No, better not. "But by the time the ambulance came and I'd gone with her, then Leo fetched me in her car, once Lettie was comfortable, and we went back to help Jamie with all the dogs, it was tea-time. Honestly, Mum, I don't know how she manages it all on her own. It's amazing."

"Yes. Anyway, Rosemary, what I rang you for is, we called in on Susan and Roddie on the way up this morning. We thought it would be nice to have Sunday lunch all together."

"Yes, of course. How's, er," Although Rose was quite definite that she'd been present when her godchild was christened, Tungsten was the name which stuck like superglue to her mind. *Think otters*, Leo had urged her, while trying to sober her up before Daniel arrived ... Tarka? Taki? What the hell *was* he called? "the baby?"

"Oh, the little darling. Do you know," her mother's voice had softened to a dove-like coo, "he smiled at me. Susan said it was wind – he'd been curling his lip like that at everyone – but we grandmothers know better. He recognised his Grandma."

"How nice."

Rose hooked a kitchen stool across and slumped down on it, gloomily studying her filthy nails. She supposed her mother would get around to the point of the conversation; for there was, somewhere, a point. Her mother never rang, as other mothers did, for a little chat; at least, not with her younger daughter.

"And how is Susan, and Roddie?"

"Well, actually, we didn't see Roddie."

"Oh?"

"No. He was out for the morning, playing golf." Was there the faintest tinge of disapprobation in her mother's voice?

"Well, it's probably good for business. You know, being seen on the golf course, in the club house."

"Ye-es, you may be right."

"And how's Susan?"

"Not at all her usual bright self, I'm afraid." Mrs Ashenby lowered her voice as if afraid of being overheard.

"Well, of course, with four children now –"

"Oh, I don't think it's that. She has that lovely girl, Birgitta. Such a nice girl." In fact, Rose did not care for Birgitta; she disliked the cool self-possession, and that small smile, which was less friendly and outgoing than secretive. "That young woman is a tower of strength. While we were there, she bathed dear little Tarquin –" of course, that was his name "– made the girls go up and do their homework, prepared coffee for us and a delicious open sandwich. I got her to give me the recipe. I shall try it at the next church meeting we have at home –"

"So you didn't stay for lunch?" Rose began to feel the first stirrings of interest.

"No, well, as I said, Susan wasn't – well, she –" Mrs Ashenby cleared her throat. "That's why I'm ringing. I want you to go and see her to find out what's wrong."

"*What*?"

Bugsy, who had just squeezed in through the cat flap, stopped dead. Rose wiggled her fingers at him, then said, "You want *me* to go and find out what's wrong with Susan?"

"Well, you are her sister."

"But –" Rose stopped. How could she say: yes, but she's always been closer to you two than to me. Not that she'd minded, seeing some of the other sister pairs at school. Just lately, she'd occasionally thought how nice it would be to have a close relationship with a sister. But then, she'd always had Daniel, and so she'd never needed anyone else – up until now, at least. Daniel ...

"I'm sure you're wrong, Mum," she went on slowly. "There's never anything wrong with Susan."

"That's what your father says. And she insisted that she was perfectly well. She got quite snappish with me, in fact, which is not like our Susan, as you know. But she just didn't do anything. Just sat, took no notice of any of the children, even darling Tarquin. And –" her voice sank even lower. "And –"

"And?"

"Well, although I'm absolutely sure I'm wrong, I did just wonder, when we arrived, if she'd been, well, drinking. She went out of the room once for a few minutes, just before we left, and came back much brighter, but when we said goodbye I could smell peppermints on her breath."

"Oh, Mum." Rose could not keep back the laugh.

"It isn't funny, not in the least," said Mrs Ashenby irritably, then, "What's that, dear?" She raised her voice. "I told you, it's in the fourth drawer of your tallboy in the bedroom ... the tallboy. Now, where was I?"

But Rose had a reluctance, almost an aversion, to interfering in Susan's life – to taking a stick and stirring the pond of what was almost a stranger's life. After all, she and Susan had nothing whatever in common except the same parents.

"Well, I'm quite sure she's fine. Unless, perhaps," she clutched at the straw gratefully, "maybe she's got a touch of post-natal depression. What do they call it – baby blues?"

"Depression! Susan, depressed? Oh, what nonsense." Her mother gave a small laugh. "There's no such thing as depression."

So that was all right, then. Susan wasn't depressed.

"In any case, Mum, I'm really quite busy at the moment. I'm going back with Jamie to Lettie's house tomorrow to sort out what to do with the dogs."

"Well, of course, if you think more of a pack of scruffy animals than your only sister ..."

"And besides, I've got two new commissions to be getting on with."

"More of those sculptures, I suppose."

"Well, scarecrows, actually."

"*Scarecrows?*" The italics were an inch high this time. "What on earth are you talking about?"

"I'm making scarecrows now. You know, for people to put in their gardens." Rose heard the defensiveness in her voice. "I did one for Angela, and people seem to quite like it," she ended lamely.

There was a short silence.

"I see. So a troop of pathetic dogs and some silly toys for people who ought to know better are more important than your own sister. Well, all right then, Rosemary."

Susan's house, large, mock-Tudor, was at the end of a cul-de-sac on a piece of land which had once held the local filtration plant, so that Daniel always maintained that the mini-estate should have been called, not Peartree Close, but Flushing Meadow. Today, it looked as usual, except that only part of the long front lawn had been treated to its usual weekend trim, the immaculate stripes ending abruptly in mid-row.

Crossly, she pressed the doorbell again. She had no illusion that Susan would take a blind bit of notice of anything her younger sister might say. So, why the hell was she here? To keep her mother sweet, of course; plus curiosity, a kind of mean desire to know what was going on. And it wasn't too much out of her way. There'd be no problem in keeping her lunch date with Leo and Steve.

Heavens, it was hot. Although still early, the peonies in the border were already drooping their heads. And they weren't the only ones who could do with a drink. Where the hell was Susan? Or Birgitta?

The door opened.

"I'm so sorry to keep you waiting."

"Uh?"

Rose gaped at the apparition smiling down at her. Not Birgitta. Not Susan. A young man, mid-twenties, in black trousers, a cream shirt and butcher's apron. Tall, dark-haired, lovely eyes, a sweet smile. A young Hugh Grant, in fact.

"You must be Rose. Do come in. Mrs Sinclair is expecting you."

"Uh?"

"I heard the doorbell." What a voice. Warm, seductive. Really, more of your Kenneth Branagh. "But I was out in the garden selecting herbs for lunch." He held up a bunch of green leaves. "The correct choice is so vital, don't you agree?"

"Oh, yes." Rose, who barely knew sage from parsley, nodded in fervent agreement.

"Mrs Sinclair wasn't sure if you'd be staying for lunch. You are, I hope."

He stopped, halfway down the hall, and turned the full force of his smiling gaze on her.

"Uh?" Rose felt rather like a chimpanzee watching a banana being peeled in a wholly different way. "Oh, oh, no. No, I have a date. That is, I'm meeting two friends for lunch in Banbury, then we're going on to look round a garden."

"Oh, what a pity." He paused, his hand on the sitting room doorknob. "But I'm sure you'll have a wonderful time. Ah, yes, Mrs Sinclair is in here. Your sister has arrived, madam."

And Rose heard the door close quietly behind her.

CHAPTER SEVEN

"Oh, it's you."

Susan barely looked up from the Victorian nursing chair where she sat slumped, her hands cupped round the glass of water on the arm. Rose suppressed the irritation which all too easily took over when she was face-to-face with her older sister.

"Hi, Susan."

She crossed the deep pile carpet, dropped a kiss on the smooth cheek, and at the same time contrived a sniff, as her mother had instructed. Had she been? Rose couldn't be sure.

"Wow, it was a hot drive. Mind if I have a swig?"

"*No.*"

As she went to take the glass, Susan jerked her hand away, spilling a few drops on the pink velvet. Their eyes met, and Rose saw a faint blush creep over her sister's cheeks.

"Well," she said bracingly, "you're looking well, Susan."

There was a soft knock and the young man came in, carrying a tray.

"I thought you'd like coffee now, madam." As he set it down on the small table beside Rose, he gave her another smile which made her toes twitch. "I do hope you'll try these." He gestured towards a plate of delicious-looking crumbly biscuits. "I promise you, people have been known to pine away when deprived of my ginger oatmeal cookies. Tarquin's awake, madam. I'll give him his bottle, shall I?"

"Oh, yes, thanks, Josh," Susan replied casually.

As the door closed behind him – and Susan's glass, Rose realised a moment later – she leaned forward.

"Susan, who *is* he?"

"What? Oh, Josh. He's the new au pair."

"The *what*?" Rose's eyes goggled. "But where's Birgitta?"

"Gone."

"But she was here on Sunday when Mum and Dad called."

"Yes." Susan's face was forbidding.

"Anyway, he's absolutely gorgeous."

"Is he?" Susan said indifferently. "I hadn't noticed."

"But where on earth did you find him?"

"Through the agency, of course."

"I'm sure I've seen him somewhere before."

"Could be. He's been on telly."

"What?"

"He's an out-of-work actor. He was in some police series or other but they killed his character off."

Of course, thought Rose. He's playing his new part, the faithful family retainer, auditioning perhaps for a remake of Jeeves and Wooster. Come to think of it, didn't his voice also have a touch of the Stephen Frys?

"Anyway, the agency woman said he's brilliant, and he is, so that's all that matters."

"And it's all right, having a man to look after, er, Tarquin, I mean?"

"Oh, Rose," Susan gave a tinkling laugh, "how old-fashioned you are. Why shouldn't it be?"

"Well, no reason, really."

"Anyway, I said it had to be a man this time – for Roddie's sake."

"Oh?" Rose looked at her encouragingly, but she had slumped back into the chair again, moodily gnawing her thumbnail.

Rose thought of something else. "What did he mean, about giving Tarquin his bottle? I thought you were dead against bottle feeding." She was beginning to wonder if she had inadvertently stepped through the looking glass on the doorstep. A quality of unreality had set in.

"I am."

Susan took the cup of coffee which Rose poured out, stirred it round and round, then looked up. Rose realised that her blue eyes were blazing with anger.

"That little whore!"

"Who?" Rose dropped half her biscuit.

"Birgitta, of course. Oh, the bloody bitch."

Rose stared at her. Vulgar curiosity had brought her here, and she was being repaid with a vengeance. She should enjoy seeing Susan become more human than she had ever known her, hearing her use words which to Rose's knowledge had never before passed her small, pink mouth. But she didn't. She felt as though something was unravelling in front of her.

"Tell me, Susan, please."

Susan swallowed her coffee in a few gulps.

"Sunday afternoon. The girls were out. I was – tired. I went up to bed for a little rest. Roddie was mowing the lawn. I was thirsty. I got up to get a little drink, of water. I heard a funny noise in the kitchen. I went down and, oh, and, oh, Rose, it was disgusting." Red blotches had broken out on her face and neck. "She'd pulled him down across the table – she was such a strong girl – she'd got his trousers off." Rose tried to imagine anyone wanting to pull Roddie's trousers off, and failed. "And she was on top of him – they were – oh, it was horrible –"

"Oh, Susan." For the first time in her life, Rose felt a surge of compassion for her sister. She knelt beside Susan's chair and put an arm round her.

"So you see, with the shock, my milk dried up. Instantly. I swear to you, Rose, I could feel it draining away." In a dramatic gesture, she cupped her breasts. "That little whore."

"But –"

"Oh, I know what you're going to say. But it wasn't his fault, not at all. Poor Roddie, he's so hot-blooded, you know."

He is? Since when did a cold fish have hot blood? But Rose stayed silent.

"And I never, well," a maidenly blush suffused Susan's scalp "want *it*, you know, when I'm pregnant. And then there were all those stitches. I tell you, Rose, what we women go through ... So you mustn't blame Roddie."

"Blame him?" Rose drew back, surveyed the dutiful wife, still dutiful after her betrayal. "Blame him?" Her voice, vibrant with the pain of Ryan's treachery, went up an octave. "I'd chop his bloody balls off. That's what I'd do, Susan."

"Oh, Rose." Susan's laugh cracked, she put her hands to her mouth, and started crying softly.

"Oh, don't." Reaching up, Rose cradled her head, rather awkwardly. "You're right, love. You must forget it. You've got three lovely girls, Susan," she could hear herself taking on her old games mistress's hearty tones, "and now a beautiful baby, so –"

"Yes, and I just hope Roddie's satisfied now he's got his son and bloody heir."

"Oh?" To Rose it was as though a kitten had just emitted a tiger's snarl.

"Honestly, Rose, since he turned forty last year – you remember the party?"

"Ye-es." In fact, she was hardly likely to have forgotten the day, with Roddie steeped in Stygian gloom which the bunch of red balloons tied to the gatepost only seemed to mock.

"Well, that was the day he calmly announced that he wanted a son and heir. Before it was too late, he said. Oh, it was dreadful, Rose. You'd all barely left before he ..." Susan picked convulsively at the arm of her chair. "He went on and on, night after night – he was like some sort of animal – until I became pregnant."

"Well, at least it was a boy."

"Yes, thank God. But since then, well, of course, the stitches and everything."

All in all then, it was no wonder that her sister had taken to drink. Rose patted her shoulder encouragingly.

"So now you've got four super kids. I mean, I haven't even got one."

"Oh well, you –"

"And a really nice home. Just look at this lovely house."

In fact, the dark furniture, tasteful prints, gilt carriage clock, were not at all to Rose's taste, and for the first time she realised that just as Susan had chosen for a husband a replica of her father – and was reproducing her mother's attitude to men and women's morality – so she had created a facsimile of her parents' house. She glanced at the clock again.

"I really must go, love. I'll just pop up and see Tarquin before I go."

"Why?" Susan sounded surprised that anyone should want to pop up and see Tarquin.

"Well, he is my godson."

"Oh, I see."

"And how are the girls?"

"All right, I suppose. Emily's upstairs."

"Oh? Is she ill?"

"No, she's finished her GCSEs."

"Yes, of course. How's she got on, do you think?"

Susan shrugged. "Who knows?"

"Well, I'd better say hello."

"I wouldn't bother. She's sulking. Roddie says Tarquin's put her nose out of joint – well, she always was Daddy's little girl." Oh, yes, Rose knew all about Daddy's little girls. "And anyway, she wanted to go off camping in Wales with some friends next week but of course we've forbidden it. Honestly, Rose, you've no idea, these days – children." A heavy sigh. "Anyway, Roddie said she couldn't possibly go. I mean, boys as well as girls –"

And he wants the monopoly on bad behaviour for himself, thought Rose.

"And now she says she won't go with us all to Southwold next month. She says she's sick of the place. We've always gone there – except that one year in the Dordogne, *and* it rained every single day – it was *awful*. Anyway, Roddie's parents left us that little cottage, and it was where he'd spent all his holidays until we got married ... So I s'pose it's natural that he wants to go there. And now Emily says it's the most boring place on earth and she's never going there again."

All at once, Rose felt bone weary. Why was it that life never *ever* ran smoothly? Up and down the country, behind green-ribboned lawns and gleaming front doors, life was churning away in a turbulent flood. And now, Susan and Roddie, who had appeared to break the mould ...

Abruptly, she set down her coffee cup. "I'll peep in on Tarquin, then have a quick word with Emily before I go."

When she knocked and hesitantly opened the door, her eldest niece was lying on the bed, staring at the ceiling.

"Hi, Emily."

"Hi." Reluctantly, the girl removed the headphones from her ears, and as she did so Rose caught the full volume of heavy metal.

"Do you think you ought to have that on so loud? I was reading the other day –"

"Don't you start."

"No, no, of course not." Rose perched on the bed, where she found herself eyeball to eyeball with the bulging crotch of a guitar-wielding Neanderthal, whose poster adorned the opposite wall. "How are you?"

"Oh, all right, I s'pose." The girl gave a bitter little laugh. "If you don't count dying of boredom, that is."

"Oh, Emily, love. Surely it's not that bad." But Rose, remembering times in her own teenage years which seemed like empty deserts, knew that it was.

"Mmm, well, it's just that everything's so awful." Of course, her aunt couldn't be expected to understand. She was so old. She didn't ever go dizzy and weak at the knees for no reason. She didn't feel as if she was melting like wax in hot sunshine. She probably didn't feel anything ... "Nobody cares about me here any more. All they care about is that loathsome baby."

Rose looked down at the small, closed face, and felt a real twinge of alarm. Emily had changed so much, so suddenly. But didn't everyone, as they reached the cusp between child and adult? She had so little experience, but she felt that Susan ought to be more aware of this eldest daughter of hers. She had a sudden conviction that Emily was not getting the attention she needed, even the love. Was her own pattern going to be repeated?

Hardly able to believe what she was hearing herself say, she went on, "Look, Emily, how about coming to stay with me for a few days? That's if your Mum and Dad agree, of course. You've never been to stay with me, have you?"

"We-ll ..."

"It's just me, of course." Rose gave her a wry smile. "I mean, Ryan won't be there."

"No, I know. Oh, Rose, why's he gone?"

"He found someone he liked more."

"Oh God, that's terrible." Emily sat bolt upright.

"Don't worry, love. I'm over it," Rose said, ignoring the painful stab that even saying the loved-hated name had given her.

"Men are all the same, aren't they?" the girl burst out fiercely. "They're all absolutely horrible."

"No, no, you mustn't think that, love." Rose was shocked to hear her own views being pushed back at her.

"Yes they are. Look at Dad, getting his leg over –"

"Emily!"

"– that ghastly Birgitta. I mean, you'd think he'd have more taste than that, wouldn't you?"

"No, Emily, it's – it's not true."

"Of course it is. We were all out, just for a couple of hours, and when we got back bloody Birgitta had gone and Mum was yelling at Dad. Course, she was half-pissed, as usual –"

"*Emily*, that's enough! Are you coming to stay with me or not?"

The girl expelled a long breath then flopped back onto the bed, her hands behind her head.

"Well, I might as well."

Rose's heart sank at the thought of all the work she had on. "Great. We'll fix a day for me to fetch you. Of course, you may be bored. I'm working quite hard at the moment."

"Bored?" Emily scowled at her pretty Laura Ashley room. "I mean, anything's got to be better than this boring dump."

CHAPTER EIGHT

Daniel tossed the fax towards his in-tray then got up, flexing his back muscles and went over to the window where he stood leaning on one elbow. The gallery was up one of the little alleys off Sheep Street so that, from up here in his tiny flat, he had a view of higgledy roofs and just a glimpse of shimmering tree tops. But he gazed out unseeing, his dark eyes brooding. He had just learned that he was one step nearer to his ambition of opening a gallery in New York. He should be happy, deliriously happy. But he wasn't. He was deeply, utterly miserable.

From the pavement came a burst of laughter. Opening the lattice window, he craned out, and just caught a glimpse of a group of young girls going past. One of them, although her hair was dark, her quick, eager way of walking, the way she tossed her curls back off her face, reminded him for an instant of Rose.

Rose. He banged his hands down on the sill and began pacing his living room. Every bloody thought he ever had in his head came back to Rose. He'd never tried to make love to her, never really kissed her even, never tried to claim her as his, because he knew he simply could not have borne her rejection, the sadness for him which would be in her eyes as she gently put him back in the place she'd picked out for him so long ago, of best, closest friend.

Get a life, Bradshaw! Before it's too late. He sometimes wondered if Rose was even the reason why he'd chosen to take a Fine Arts degree when his natural aptitude had been for the sciences. Had it been a subconscious attempt to mirror her, to stay close to her? And had he only opened this, his first gallery as a platform for her work; when she produced any, of course?

There was a rustling sound outside on the tiny landing, a knock at the door.

He called, "Come in. It's not locked."

"Um, hello, Daniel," said Rose.

He'd conjured her up. As he stared at her silently she stood in the doorway, giving him a faintly nervous smile.

"Come in, Rose." He registered that her arms were full of large plastic bags. "Put them on the sofa."

"Thanks."

She dropped the parcels and they regarded each other warily.

"Been treating yourself to a new wardrobe?"

"You mean, I could do with one?" she said wryly, gesturing towards her black dungarees and old white T-shirt.

"No, of course not." To him she always looked perfect, her reddish hair tumbling round her pale face, the powdering of gingery freckles.

"Well actually, they're all from charity shops. I've been round every one in Stratford."

"Oh Rose. I've told you, if you want –"

"No, no! Actually they're for my scarecrows," she went on apprehensively.

"Oh, right."

"I've got three to make now."

"That's good," he said neutrally.

Rose hated it when they were being super-polite to each other. She almost preferred fighting with him. Almost.

"Daniel."

She put out a hand to touch his shirt-front, then, as she saw him move back slightly, she herself took a step away from him. She stumbled against the coffee table and set the small sculpture on it rocking. She steadied it, then stayed bent over it, her fingers resting on the wood, smooth as marble.

A couple of years previously, she'd just been getting over 'flu and Daniel had taken her down to Sand Bay for the day. They'd walked the length of the scruffy beach, then out to the headland. She'd collected some bits and pieces of driftwood and made him this little unicorn. It had been a good day, the pale winter sun shining, the air like chilled champagne ...

"Well." She made a move to pick up her parcels then stopped. She'd come here to make her peace with Daniel, and was going to make it. She couldn't bear being on bad terms with him any longer.

"I'm sorry, Daniel," she said huskily.

"What for?"

"The way I went for you at Angela's party. You were quite right. It's just that ... Anyway, what I came for was to ask you to have lunch with me – my treat. And we'll go wherever you want," she added, nobly suppressing her own desire for a Chinese. "Anywhere."

"Thanks, Rose." He gave her his first natural smile. "I'd love to, but in fact I'm waiting for someone."

He glanced down at his watch, as simultaneously light footsteps came up the stairs. A young girl appeared in the doorway. She was smiling.

"Hi, Daniel. Mr. Paige said it was okay to come up."

"Come in, Lucy. You're late."

"Yes, I know. I'm sorry, but the first bus didn't turn up and the second one went all round the villages. Oh, what a super room." She glanced around and saw Rose. "Hi, Rose."

"Hi," Rose replied, rather stiffly.

She looked at the girl in astonishment, barely able to recognise her. Instead of the neat little black and white waitress, she was a sophisticated young woman. Her sleek dark hair in a knot, her skin deeply tanned, the cream mini-skirt and yellow top showing off a lovely figure. Rose felt all at once dowdy – and old. Very old.

There were strange undercurrents swirling around the room, and they all three stood, somehow aware of them and not quite sure how to break free.

Finally, it was Daniel who said, "Lucy's probably going to work for me, Rose. Just this summer, of course, until she goes off to university."

"Oh yes. What are you going to study?"

Lucy lifted a negligent shoulder. "Oh, Law and Political Science, I think."

"Good heavens."

"On the other hand," Rose saw her shoot Daniel a laughing glance, "if I switched to History of Art I could maybe do a master's in Scarecrows Through the Ages. How about that, Rose?"

Rose was taken aback. Usually, she never minded in the least being teased, but there was something about this girl, something in her own feelings towards her, that made her defensive, angry even, and, could it be, jealous?

"I tell you what," Daniel glanced at his watch again. "It's almost twelve and I'm starving, so what say I interview you over lunch, Lucy?"

"Oh, that would be great. Thanks, Daniel."

"And you're welcome to join us, Rose. Although it'll probably be a bit boring for you, us talking shop."

"Oh. No thanks," Rose replied hastily. She gathered up her

bags. "I really ought to get back. I promised Jamie I'd help with Lettie's dogs later."

"Why? What's wrong?"

"Oh, of course. You don't know. Lettie's in hospital, she's broken her ankle, and Jamie – you know, Leo's son – he's moved into her cottage and is looking after them. He's absolutely marvellous with them, actually."

"That's good. I always thought that young man had hidden depths. Well ..." They were all standing on the pavement in the hot sun and as a gaggle of Japanese tourists bore down on them he went on hastily, "Come on, Lucy. Bye, Rose." His lips brushed her cheek. "I'll be in touch."

"Bye, Rose." Over her shoulder Lucy gave her a dazzling smile as they went off towards the Dirty Duck.

"Bye."

She walked slowly, allowing herself to be overtaken by the chattering group, then stopped and turned. They were just in sight. Lucy was laughing up at Daniel, he had his hand on her arm, then they turned into Waterside and were lost to her. She hitched up the bags and started walking towards the multi-storey car park.

"Oh, I'm sorry."

"I'm so sorry."

They both spoke at once.

"No, it was my fault," Rose said. "I wasn't looking where I was – oh." She stopped.

"Hello, Rose. It is Rose, isn't it?" The tall man smiled down at her. "Yes, I know, I'm very forgettable. My mother's garden? Last Tuesday?"

Rose put all thoughts of Daniel and Lucy out of her mind. "Of course, I remember you. Hello again."

"How are you?"

"Oh fine, er, Christopher."

He pulled a face. "Please. My friends call me Christo. Look, are you in a hurry?"

"Well, I –"

"I was just going to have some lunch. Come and eat with me. Please," as she began to protest, "I promise you, you'll be doing me an immense favour. I've just spent three hours with our accountants, sorting out our tax returns for the year and there's a stack of estate business waiting for me at home, which I'm putting off the evil moment of dealing with. So, what do you say?"

Rose laughed. "Well, if you put it like that, I say, thank you very much."

"Good. How about the Dirty Duck?"

"Oh no. That is, I'd rather not."

"Of course." If he was surprised by her tone, he was too well bred to show it. "I tell you what, let's try that new one, out on the road towards Charlecote."

"But I'm not really ..." Rose looked down at her dungarees.

"Nonsense. You look perfectly charming."

The *maître d'* abstracted Rose's parcels. "I'll take care of these for you, madam."

As they sat down, Christo remarked, "Until today, I thought my mother was the world's greatest impulse shopper."

"Oh, they're not for me," replied Rose hastily. "They're outfits for my new scarecrows."

"But I thought you were a sculptress."

"Yes, I am. But I've just started developing a line in scarecrows." Why had she lowered her voice, when Daniel was safely ensconced in the Dirty Duck? "Sort of ornamental ones. You know, for people to put in their gardens."

"Ah, I see," he said politely.

As the wine waiter hovered, she studied Christo over her menu. Fair hair, wind-tanned skin, a vertical crease between his brows which gave him a faintly worried air. His clothes were almost a parody of a weekender's country-style, but worn with an air which no townie could capture. If she ever got an order for a country landowner scarecrow she'd know where to look: old tweed jacket with leather patches, check shirt, his only concession to the heat a blue silk cravat instead of a tie.

"Yes, I am rather overdressed for such a warm day, aren't I?" he smiled, and Rose had the good grace to blush at his almost feminine perception.

"Oh no – not at all."

"But you had exactly the sort of expression that my mother has when she is saying, 'Christo, you surely aren't going out in *that*?' "

"I know just what you mean," Rose replied wryly. "Do you like living with her? Your mother, I mean."

"Well, as I told you the other day, I moved out to the old gamekeeper's cottage a few years ago. We were both beginning to get on each other's nerves, so it answers very well. I do need to be around to run the estate, but this way it gives us both our freedom."

And from the little she'd seen of his mother, he would need plenty of that.

Last Tuesday afternoon ... Still stunned by her visit to Susan, she'd said very little all through lunch, and then in the garden Leo and Steve had gone off to look at the hosta collection again, leaving her to wander around on her own. She went round the back of the sprawling Hornton-stone manor house, in search of more sculptures, and saw under the window of an outbuilding, just the other side of a 'Private' sign dangling from a rope, a bed of tall white lilies.

Rose could not resist lilies. She looked about her then hopped over the rope and bent to inhale their exquisite perfume. As she straightened up she saw, through the half-closed Venetian blinds which obscured the window, a pair of eyes watching her. She turned to escape, but a man had appeared in the doorway.

"Please do come and look at them."

"No, thank you." She was hot with embarrassment. "I'm sorry. It's just that I love lilies, especially the Regale ones."

"Yes, they're striking, aren't they? But you can't admire them properly from there," as she still hesitated. "I think my mother's secret is dried blood. Dollops of the stuff, every autumn."

"Your – ?"

Rose, half-intoxicated by lily perfume, looked at him properly for the first time. Yes, there was a similarity between this man and the tall, white-haired autocrat she'd seen in the tiny chapel adjoining the house. She'd been giving hell to some minion of a flower arranger whose delphinium display had dared to fall below standard.

"I must go. I'm really looking for the other sculpture. It's in the –" she looked down at her garden plan "– in the long pool area."

"Are you particularly interested in sculpture, as well as lilies?"

He had a nice, teasing smile, which crinkled up the corners of his cornflower blue eyes. She smiled back.

"Well, actually I'm a sculptor."

"Really? Oh well, in that case you absolutely must see Madre's latest acquisition. It's in her private garden, where visitors aren't normally allowed. Hold on," he overrode her half-hearted protest.

"I'll get the key. But before I do, there is just one problem with lilies. If you'll allow me –"

From his pocket he took a pristine handkerchief, gently brushed it across her nose then held it up to her, yellow-streaked with pollen.

"Penny for them?"

Daniel, who had been absently moving his glass round and round in small tight circles, looked up to see Lucy smiling across at him.

"Sorry. It's just that I've got rather a lot on at work."

"And?" she prompted.

"And nothing." How was it that this self-possessed young girl could always make him feel so defensive? "Just a lot on at work," he repeated.

She shook her head. "It's Rose, isn't it?"

"What do you mean?"

"Oh come on, Daniel. I'm not stupid. You're crazy about her."

"Who the hell told you that?" he demanded angrily.

"No-one, I swear it. But I've got eyes. Poor Daniel." She laid a small warm hand on his bare arm. "It's horrible, isn't it?"

When he did not reply, his attention seemingly on a loaded riverboat wallowing its way upstream she went on, "When I was sixteen, I was desperately, everlastingly in love," she laid her other hand on her heart, self-mocking, "with someone in my class at college, but he never knew I existed."

"So what happened?" Almost against his will, he turned he eyes to look at her. God, the lad must have been blind.

She gave a little shrug. "Oh, I decided not to waste any more of my life on him. I suppose you could say I grew up. Daniel …"

"Do you want coffee?"

"No thanks. And thank you for a lovely meal."

As he hunted for his credit card, she said, "Well?"

"Well what?"

"Do I get it – the job, I mean? Or have I blown it, talking about Rose? You haven't exactly interviewed me yet."

In fact, they had spent lunch talking about the theatre, actors – and him, Daniel now realised. Should he give her the job? She was too pert, too knowing by half. She'd have to be well and truly kept in her place. But she was bright – and pretty. A perfect foil for

Oliver Paige who, as you'd expect in a retired Senior Lecturer in Fine Art, was at least as knowledgeable as Daniel himself, but more than a touch pedantic.

"Can you start this afternoon?" he asked, as she went down the steps ahead of him, then added, in a belated attempt to assert his authority, "You'll be on trial for a few days, then I'll make a final decision at the weekend."

"Oh, great." She turned up a smiling face, dimple in place. "Thanks, Daniel."

Christo's mobile phone rang.

"Sorry." He fished it out of his pocket. "Christopher Mallory. Oh, Mother." He grimaced at Rose. "What? Yes, of course I have ... No, it went very well ... Yes, I'm having lunch now ... Oh, by three at the latest ... All right ... Bye."

He put it back in his jacket pocket.

"I do apologise. As you'll have gathered, it was my mother. She's embraced cell phones with a vengeance – which is more than I have, I must say."

"Perhaps you could tell her that their over-use can cause brain tumours," suggested Rose innocently.

"You know, I just might do that." They exchanged smiles of mutual complicity.

"Your garden really is beautiful," Rose said, when the waiter had removed her empty plate. "One of the loveliest I've ever been in."

"You should have told Madre." Christo grinned. "She's like a cat – she's never averse to having her fur stroked."

"Er, yes."

In fact, after earwigging the one-sided conversation in the chapel, Rose had steered well clear of Mrs Mallory.

"It said in the leaflet that your mother designed it all herself."

"Yes, she did, more or less. My father died early, you see, a month off his fortieth birthday, and, well, I was at school still, so I think she flung herself into her garden. She's devoted herself to it ever since."

"And she does it all on her own." Rose had been deeply impressed.

71

"Good lord, no." Christo put back his head and laughed, showing strong white teeth. "We have two full-time gardeners, and one of the old estate workers comes in one day a week through the summer, to mow the lawns."

"I see." In fact, last Tuesday there had been no sign of any underlings, and the leaflet had subtly implied that, by unremitting toil, Mrs Mallory did the lot. "And you help, of course."

"Not really. I just run the estate."

"Well, that sounds an ideal arrangement."

"I suppose so." His long fingers were twisting his wine glass to and fro. "Actually, I wanted to be an architect. I'd been offered a place at college, but, being an only child, Mother obviously wanted me back here."

"Oh, Christo." Rose felt a surge of compassion. "What a shame."

"Well," he roused himself and gave her a rueful smile, "who knows? I might have been an appalling architect. My houses would probably have fallen down after five years."

"You mean they'd have lasted that long?" Rose's eyes twinkled at him. There was something about him that almost invited teasing.

"Probably not." He smiled back at her. "Do you want a pudding? The menu looks very inviting."

"Oh, no thank you." Rose clutched at her stomach. "I've eaten far too much already. I've been a real hog, I'm afraid, but it was all so delicious."

"Coffee, then." Christo beckoned to the waiter.

"And is the garden finished now?" asked Rose. "The overall design, I mean."

"Oh, no. Mother's latest scheme," he was spooning brown sugar into his coffee, "or rather, one of them – she never has just one project on the boil – is the arboretum."

"Yes, of course. I peeped over the fence at it, but I couldn't see it properly."

"Oh, she wouldn't include it in the garden tour. A pity, but she's a perfectionist and it's all a bit of a mess. We've still got some of the ground to clear and a lot of the trees won't be planted till the autumn. If you come again," he slid the plate of chocolate mints towards her, "and I very much hope that you do come, you'll see it then."

Rose lowered her eyes. "And what's her other project?" she asked in a neutral voice.

"Oh, that's the vegetable garden."

"Haven't you got one already?"

"No. Well, she's always had her vegetables delivered from Harrods. But Mother wants to live forever, and she's decided that the best way to do that is to grow her own organic vegetables. From the earth to the kitchen in five minutes is her aim. That way she'll get all the life force, apparently."

He was joking, but even so Rose felt a shiver of distaste for the woman, clutching on to life with greedy hands.

"Do you know what, Rose?" His features lit up in a beaming smile. "I've just had the most marvellous idea."

"Oh?"

"You said you make scarecrows. Well, Mother can have one for her new vegetable patch."

"Oh." Rose was completely taken aback. "But you haven't seen any of my work – and neither has your mother."

"I'm sure your scarecrows are wonderful. But I tell you what, why don't you come out to the house again? You can meet Mother, see the veggie area."

"Well," Rose was still doubtful, "I always do like to see the setting for my work, but –"

"Splendid. When can you make it?"

"Well, any day next week, I think." In the face of his enthusiasm, she really had no choice; and if she could tell Daniel that she was doing a scarecrow for Mrs Mallory of Fenton Curlieu, surely even he would be a tiny bit impressed.

"Can I come in?"

Lucy appeared in the doorway.

"It looks as though you're in already," he said severely, switching off the computer – not that the screen had much to show for an afternoon's work.

"Oh, sorry." She slowed her impetuous rush. "But look – I've got to show you."

Gleefully, she waved a credit card slip at him. "Here you are."

Daniel took it from her. As he looked at it, his eyes widened.

"Six hundred pounds?"

"Yes, my first sale. Isn't it wonderful? That lovely Peruvian wall hanging. Ollie –" Ollie? The prim and very proper Oliver Paige? "– said it's been sticking for months. I can't think why, it's absolutely gorgeous. Anyway, he said I could try this guy who was looking at it. He was American, from Pennsylvania, and when I said it was so beautiful that if I could afford it I'd buy it myself, he laughed and said in that case he'd better snap it up."

In her exuberance, she was like a charming Labrador puppy, he thought inconsequentially.

"Well done, Lucy."

As he put the slip down, the girl flung her arms round him. "Oh, I'm so excited."

He held her to him, in an unthinking response, and they stared into each other's eyes for a long moment. Daniel could feel her heart fluttering against him, then he pushed her away.

"What's the time?" He looked at his watch. "Good lord, it's closing time. I must go downstairs."

"Oh, don't worry. I've locked up." She held up a bunch of keys.

He frowned. "You've locked up?"

"Ollie told me about the security code, but now he's gone. His Siamese is having kittens any time and he's really worried about her. They often have problems, apparently, so I said I'd finish off. That is all right, isn't it?"

"Well, yes."

"He really loves that cat. Well, I think she's all he's got, and everyone needs someone to love them, don't they, Daniel?"

He stared at her. In one afternoon she had found out as much about the dry, unforthcoming Oliver Paige – his tutor, after all, in his Finals Year at Warwick – as he had in all the years he'd known him.

"I'd better run you home."

"There's no need, thanks. There's a bus soon." He sensed some of the excitement drain from her, and felt a twinge of guilt. "Can I just use your bathroom?"

"Of course. It's through there."

He heard the door close behind her, but stood quite still. The air in the room seemed heavy, almost stifling. The weight on him made his ears buzz, sent a dizziness coursing through him. Abruptly, he crossed to the window and flung it open to its widest extent.

He was still leaning up against the frame when he felt Lucy's arms go round him again. Her skin brushed against his, creating tiny charges of electricity. Half-stupefied, he allowed himself to be turned around, and saw that she was naked.

"Well?" she asked softly.

"Well, what?" His voice was hoarse.

"You're a connoisseur of modern sculpture." She veiled her eyes with her lashes. "So ...?"

"You are beautiful."

"In that case –" she cupped his face between her hands and, drawing it down, kissed him on the lips "– come to bed," she whispered, her mouth against his.

They made it only as far as the sofa, though, where Daniel took the young, warm, rounded, welcoming body and buried himself in it, blotting out Rose, himself, everything, so that in the end he had to run Lucy home after all, because the last bus had gone.

CHAPTER NINE

"So there you are."

Rose, who was squatting on the floor of her studio, looked up and saw Emily leaning in the doorway.

"Hello, love. Did you get yourself some breakfast?"

Her niece wrinkled her nose. "Didn't feel like any."

"Now, Emily, you know –"

"What on earth's *that*?"

Rose got to her feet and picked up the shape she had been working on.

"Meet Mr Hole-In-One, world champion golfer."

"And what are *those*?"

Rose, who had spent a great deal of time getting her scarecrow's outfit just right, felt a whiff of irritation.

"Ginger plus-fours, of course; what all the best-dressed golfers are wearing."

"God." Emily surveyed the figure with something like contempt. "They look as though they came out of the Ark."

"Out of Oxfam, actually."

"Mmm." The girl slouched over to the old red armchair, threw herself down in it and began pulling out bits of grey wadding. "I'm bored," she announced morosely.

Rose regarded her without much auntly affection. She had totally given over the last three days to Emily. In fact, she thought, she'd done pretty well by her. They'd been to the cinema, to McDonald's, with Rose swallowing down her aversion to beefburgers, and had a long session at Bicester Village, which had left Rose drained, and her purse empty. They'd been over to her parents where, fortunately, Emily had been so monosyllabic that she'd said nothing to undermine the heavily bowdlerised account that Rose had already given her mother after her visit to Susan.

Friends had rallied round. George had given her the freedom of their swimming pool. "After all, it will be nice to see it being used." For the pool had been another of Angela's short-lived enthusiasms; twenty lengths before breakfast every day; every other day; once a week; occasionally; never. And Leo had invited them to supper the previous evening. Jamie had been there as well, but as he had said barely a word and Emily had ignored his presence, it had been left to

Steve who, having exhausted the supply of English gardens, was off to Scotland in a day or so, to charm and flatter Emily into something approaching good humour.

"I told you, love," Rose said, with a touch of asperity, "I can't keep taking time off. I'm not like your mother. If I don't work, I don't eat. Simple as that."

"Yeah." Emily was tracing a pattern in the dust.

"I mean, if you want to go home, do tell me. I shan't be offended, not at all." Au contraire.

"Oh, I'm not *that* bored. It's just that I don't see why I couldn't go to Llandudno, camping. I should be there now, if *they* hadn't been so – so bloody-minded. Honestly, Rose, you've no idea. I mean –"

"Well, I think your Mum and Dad thought you were a bit young. Maybe next year. And anyway, you'll soon be going to Southwold."

"They can stuff Southwold," Emily said sullenly.

"Oh, Emily, you know your Dad loves it there – a real family holiday."

"Yeah, with a force twenty-five gale blowing sand all over us. No, I've made up my mind. I'd rather stay here than go with them. That'll be all right, won't it?"

Rose, who had been mentally ticking off every day of the ten until Emily went home, stared blankly at her.

"I'm not sure, love. I don't think your Mum and Dad – oh, good grief, look at the time. I really must go."

Pushing aside the half-completed Mr Hole-In-One, she scrambled to her feet, brushing straw off her jeans. With memories of Christo's mother, seen from a distance in the chapel, she had intended wearing one of her few really decent outfits, a turquoise linen suit, but she was late already, so ...

"Where are you going?"

"Back to that garden; you know, the one Leo and Steve were talking about last night. I may be doing a scarecrow for the owner."

"Oh, right." Emily was still slumped in the chair.

"You can come if you want. I'm sure Mrs Mallory wouldn't mind."

"God, no." Emily rolled her eyes. "Gardens are so utterly boring."

"Well then," Rose hesitated. "What will you do with yourself?"

"Oh, I'll be all right. I'll watch one of those videos you bought me yesterday."

"And you'll get yourself some lunch, won't you? There's plenty of food in the freezer."

"Yeah, sure. Can I borrow that," she gestured towards Rose's dilapidated bicycle propped in the corner, "if I decide to go for a ride?"

"Well, only round the village. Promise me you won't go miles out on your own." The burden of parental worry settled itself snugly on Rose's shoulders. "Emily, are you listening?"

"Course I am. And don't worry; we did self-defence classes at school last term. If anyone tries anything, they'll be sorry."

"Oh, *Emily*." Rose suddenly bent and hugged her niece. "See you later." She paused in the doorway. "Of course, you could always go and help Jamie with the dogs. They're a bit of a handful for him on his own."

"That shaven-headed punk? No way."

And as she hurried into the house, Rose could not but be relieved. It had been an idle thought, but Susan and Roddie would have kittens at the mere idea of Emily coming within a hundred yards of Jamie Brinkworth.

"So what do you think of my little vegetable patch, Miss Ashenby?"

"I think it will be absolutely super." Rose had no difficulty in sounding enthusiastic. Mrs Mallory's little vegetable patch was a beautifully laid out potager, which Leo would have been proud to own up to: narrow brick paths; small, symmetrically arranged beds lined with rope-edged terracotta tiling; green cast-iron obelisks at each corner; and in the centre a huge lead urn, beside which Christo's two golden Labradors lay, noses on paws, watching them.

"Of course, it isn't planted up yet, but I'm reasonably satisfied with it."

"Oh, it's great. I see where Christopher gets his love of design from," Rose blurted out, but saw the other woman frown slightly.

"And you were saying, Mother," Christo put in smoothly, "that all it needs, over there by the gate, is a scarecrow."

"Was I? Of course, the last time I went round Penelope's

garden, she had one. It was charming, utterly charming – so well dressed. I said to her, Penelope, where did you get that scarecrow from? But she wouldn't tell me." A faint frown of annoyance.

"That sounds like one of Miss Ashenby's," Christo said seriously, not looking at Rose. "And she could do an even better one for you, Mother."

"Could you?" The woman fixed Rose with her piercing blue eyes, so like her son's, yet with none of his warmth or wry humour.

"Of course." Suddenly, Rose wanted this commission very badly. But instinct told her that she would have to handle it with propriety. "But before you make up your mind, Mrs Mallory, I'll come over and show you my portfolio."

"I tell you what, Mother," exclaimed Christo. "Let's make him a Jim Fitzpatrick." He turned to Rose. "Jim was our last gamekeeper – until he was poached by an estate in Norfolk. No – not *that* estate," as Rose's eyes widened. "I don't think Mother would have minded quite so much if it had been. *Droit de seigneur*, and all that. As it is, she's never forgiven him; in fact, we've given up on pheasants entirely."

"Jim? Well, that might be an idea." Mrs Mallory pursed her lips.

"You'll love doing him, Miss Ashenby. A shock of black curls, black moustache. And, of course," he slapped his thigh, "I told you I live in the old keeper's cottage – well, I'm pretty sure there are some of Jim's old clothes in the outhouse."

"Marvellous." Rose was beginning to sense that the power was pretty evenly balanced between these two; it was just that Christo was more Machiavellian in his methods.

"I'll run you down there," he went on. "You can see what we've got."

"Great. And I've already got some things left over from my Victorian head gardener. I even managed to find two pairs of flannelette long johns."

"*Long johns*?" Mrs Mallory sounded outraged.

"Oh, yes." Rose turned to her. "All my scarecrows are correct in every detail – right down to their underwear."

"Long johns, really? What a good idea." And Rose felt certain that it was, almost, settled. "Now, Miss Ashenby, let me show you my arboretum."

"So you see," an elegantly manicured hand encompassed the slope where the three of them were standing, "my idea is to create a river of trees."

"What an absolutely brilliant idea."

"Thank you, my dear." The older woman nodded graciously. "It will begin somewhere up here and meander down to the valley. I shall just keep a mown area for people to walk through, otherwise it will be natural."

"And you'll plant woodland flowers, of course?"

"Oh yes. Christo, you did order those bluebell bulbs that I told you to?"

"Of course, Mother. Two thousand, you said? It's all in hand."

"They are coming from a legitimate source, aren't they?" Rose put in, without thinking.

"Legitimate source?" Mrs Mallory raised her eyebrows. "What *do* you mean, Miss Ashenby?"

"Well," Rose cleared her throat, "apparently a lot of English bluebell woods are being ruined, with all the bulbs being ripped out and people buying them without realising. And then in Greece and Turkey they're –"

"Oh, I'm quite sure all ours will be from a – what did you say? – legitimate source. Isn't that so, darling?"

"Yes, of course. But to put your mind at rest, Mother, I'll double-check."

Behind his mother's back, he gave Rose a wink and she hastily stifled a giggle.

"Now, Christo, how easy would it be to divert the stream down there?"

"Hmm, not sure. Let's see."

They moved off, followed by the Labradors, but Rose stayed where she was. Her eyes were dreamy, her imagination filling the still bare hillside with graceful, rustling trees; beneath them, sheets of bluebells; cowslips, orchids; all drawing the eye down, down, to where, at the very bottom, a muddy patch showed where the spring welled up. There should be a sculpture there – the Spirit of the Spring. Or of the Wood. It would be an abstract, of course; something light and airy, something that perhaps moved a little, barely tethered to the ground ...

"Coming, Rose?" Christo put a hand on her elbow.

"Oh, sorry." She shook herself free from her daydream and followed the other two.

Mrs Mallory looked at her watch. "I must go, I have a committee meeting at four. Goodbye, Miss Ashenby." She extended a hand. "I look forward to viewing your portfolio. And I'll see you later, darling. You know the Latymer-Dassets are coming for dinner. And Candida, of course."

"Am I likely to forget?" There was the faintest irony in his voice, which his mother, as she turned away, either did not hear or chose to ignore.

"Do you really have a portfolio?" He sounded genuinely curious.

"Let's just say, I'll have one by the time I next see your mother."

"Ah, I see. Come on you two."

He opened the back of the Land Rover and the two dogs, now filthy, their tongues lolling out in happy grins, leapt in.

"They're absolutely gorgeous." As Rose climbed into the front seat, one of the pink tongues slurped across her neck in a slobbery kiss.

"Have you got a dog?"

"No. I don't think Bugsy would take very kindly to a dog, somehow. My cat," as he raised an enquiring eyebrow.

"I see. Er, unusual name."

"He's named after the gangster, Bugsy Moran. He's an absolute villain. Oh –" She put a hand to her mouth.

"What's the matter?"

"Angela Smethurst, my neighbour – well, my landlady, actually," although Angela always resisted such a sordid word, "had a Japanese garden set up recently, by a friend of mine, Leo Brinkworth – she's a brilliant designer," Rose added, in the unlikely event that Mrs Mallory should ever decide that she needed professional assistance. "Anyway, I met her in the village yesterday and she's certain that some of her koi carp have gone missing."

"You mean, perhaps Bugsy ...?"

"I *know* perhaps Bugsy," Rose amended meaningfully. "He's been looking very smug; plus, just before I met Angela, I'd found a fish skeleton on the lawn. A sort of mini Jaws skeleton." She giggled then went on rather shamefacedly. "I shouldn't laugh. Those fish

81

cost a fortune – and Angela's so nice. I don't want her to be upset."

"If I were you, I'd talk vaguely of having seen a couple of herons around, and suggest that she nets her pool. Tell her all the best Japanese pools are netted."

"What a good idea. Thank you, Christo."

Rose smiled at him, then clutched at the door as the Land Rover lurched down a deeply rutted track, barely wide enough for it. Undergrowth brushed it on either side, so that they seemed to be clearing a way through virgin forest.

"Oooh."

"Sorry about that," he said, as she rubbed the top of her head. "I keep it like this in order to – well, can you guess why?"

"To discourage unwelcome visitors?" Rose winced as her elbow came in sharp contact with metal.

"Exactly." Their eyes met in unspoken amusement.

The vehicle rounded a final bend and the track opened out to a large grassy space, with a small, estate-type cottage in the centre. They passed a pile of disused pheasant coops, then drew up in front of the house. The dogs leapt out and crashed off into the undergrowth.

"Come on in." Christo unlocked the front door, under its little arched porch and gable, and led the way into a small hallway. He pushed open a door. "Make yourself at home, Rose. I'll go through and make us a pot of tea."

"Oh, great."

She perched in one of the armchairs and looked about her with frank curiosity. The room was beautifully furnished, almost incongruously so for a small cottage. She guessed that much of it must have accompanied Christo when he moved out of the manor house, that the creamy chintz suite, the lovely old silk rugs on the polished floor, the pair of Chinese vases standing on the elegant Pembroke table, had all made the tortuous journey down that same rutted track. There was a quiet harmony about this room which somehow mirrored its owner. Daniel would like it. He'd love those vases; and that gorgeous jade lion on the mantelpiece. Daniel ... As the door opened, she pushed him out of her mind.

"I've made Indian tea, but if you prefer China?" He set down the tray.

"No, thanks, I don't like China. Leo – that's the designer –" in case he hadn't got the name the first time, "always says it tastes of Bugsy's pee."

"I'm inclined to agree with her. Not that I have an intimate knowledge of Bugsy's pee, of course," he added gravely. "Mother drinks nothing but China tea since she read an article saying that it contains – what is it? – oh, yes, anti-oxidants, which apparently slow the ageing process."

"Really?" Rose laughed.

"I promise you. Milk? Sugar?"

"Milk, please. No sugar." He handed her a cup. "This is a lovely room, Christo."

"Thank you."

"And so tidy."

Rose thought of her own hovel. Even Emily had sufficiently roused herself one day to remark that she wondered how anyone could possibly live like *this*.

"I'm afraid I can't claim the credit for that."

"You have a cleaning lady?"

"Not exactly. A contract firm come out from Banbury once a week to go through the place."

"How nice." Maybe if her scarecrows really took off, she'd have contract cleaners.

"Who's Candida?" she asked suddenly.

"Candida Latymer-Dasset." He pulled a face. "The daughter of friends of ours; or perhaps I should say of Mother's. I dislike them immensely, Candida most of all. Mother's been trying to matchmake us for years." He sighed. "She's quite indefatigable, I'm afraid."

"What's she like?" Rose could not contain her curiosity.

"Oh, stupid, dull, utterly bland. Can only talk about shooting, and hunting. Do you approve of fox hunting?"

"No," Rose said repressively. She had some time ago decided that life was too short for arguments on politics, religion and fox hunting.

"Neither do I, actually. Oh, I was made to hunt when I was small; the fox's brush smeared all over my face, all that revolting ritual, but as soon as I could I just refused to go any more."

"What did your mother say?"

"Pretty much what you'd expect her to say." He grimaced. "My father was MFH, of course, and Madre still hunts. Which is why she considers Candida to be an ideal wife for me."

"And who do you consider to be an ideal wife for Christopher Mallory? Oh, I'm sorry," her cheeks burned, "I shouldn't have asked that." But this man was so easy to get on with, she could all too readily forget that she had known him barely a week. "I'm sorry," she repeated.

"Oh, it's all right." He set down his cup and leaned back on the sofa, his arms linked behind his head. "My ideal wife? Well, she would be tallish, slender, rather angular, even, but with a quick, lively way of moving, talking; a sense of humour, of course; eyes, grey; hair, oh, reddish, I think, and I must admit I do find freckles rather endearing. Oh, and absolutely not in favour of fox hunting. Is that enough?"

For the first time he looked straight at her, and Rose, staring back at him, felt the warm colour flood back into her face. His blue eyes were laughing at her, but behind the laughter there was an expression which she could not read.

"Goodness," she said breathlessly, after a silence. "You certainly know what you want. Poor Candida."

"Oh, don't waste your sympathy on her."

There was a message in his eyes, she was sure of it, but she simply could not translate it. To break the tension, she glanced up at the marble clock on the mantelpiece.

"Is that the time? Emily will be wondering where I am."

"Your niece? Of course, you must go. But let me get those clothes for you; and I've an idea there's even an old shotgun out there somewhere. Oh, the breach is rusted through, so it's quite safe, but you must have a gun for your Jim. He was never seen without his. Rumour had it that his wife slept in the spare room so he could sleep with it across his pillow."

Your Jim ... must have a gun ... sleep across his pillow.
Rose was humming a little song as she turned into her small yard. Narrowly avoiding her bicycle, which lay sprawled on the cobbles, she switched off and got out. When she kicked one of the tyres it was hard – so Emily had been out on it. Perhaps the fresh air had put her in a better mood; maybe this evening at least there would be no more sulks, no more, 'I'm boreds'.

There were sounds coming from the kitchen and when she went

through, Emily was there. She was laying the table; a cloth, nearly clean; plates, a wine glass by one of them; and the room –
"Emily? Did you do this?"
"Clean up? Yeah, well, I told you it was a tip."
"Are you all right?" Perhaps she was sickening for something.
"Never better. Oh, I've got something out for supper."
"You've –"
"It doesn't have a label, but it looks like lasagne."
"Great." Rose spoke automatically. "So you had a nice ride, did you?"
"Yeah, super. Do sit down, Rose. You look tired."
"Well, I am a bit." Her aunt was deeply touched. "And thank you for doing all this."
"Oh, no problem. I've been back a couple of hours and I was getting a bit –" her eyes met Rose's and she grinned "– bored."
"Yes, well," Rose was still grappling with this sudden metamorphosis, "you didn't go out of the village, did you?"
"No, course not. But I've made a friend – Sophie. She's a really nice girl."
"Sophie. Do I know her?"
"Don't think so. She's invited me round to her house tonight to listen to some tapes her Dad brought back from the States. She says they're really great, and if I like them, she'll make a copy for me. I can go, can't I?"
"Well, I'm not sure. I mean, I really ought to meet her first." The loco parentis weight slid across Rose's shoulders again. "I don't think your Mum and Dad would like you going to someone I didn't know."
"Oh, Mum and Dad." Emily waved a dismissive hand. "And anyway, she knows you, Rose. Or at least, her sister does."
"Oh?"
"She's called – what is it? Lucy."
"Lucy? Not the girl who's working for Daniel?"
"Well," she shot Rose a sidelong glance, "that's one way of putting it, I suppose."
"Of putting what?"
Emily gave a salacious smirk. "Just wait till I tell Dad that his precious Tarquin's godfather is having it off with an eighteen year-old."

Rose stared at her. "You mean …?"
"Daniel and Lucy – they're having an affair."

CHAPTER TEN

"So, how are the dogs?"

"Oh, fine." Jamie set down his mug.

"And you're managing all right on your own?"

"Sure, Mum. Anyway, people call in most days. And I've got nothing else to do. I'm enjoying it."

And Leo, looking at her son, saw that he actually looked happy. She smiled at him, the usual mix of pain and love warring in her.

"Good. Oh, I nearly forgot. I got a couple of pounds of strawberries at that pick-your-own place yesterday. Would you like some?"

"Great. Thanks."

As his mother tipped a mound of scarlet berries into a dish, he said suddenly, "Do you remember that time – I think it was just after we left – just after we came here – I had a little garden, with some strawberry plants in it?"

"I remember." Leo was pouring cream with a liberal hand. It was not often that she had the chance to feed him up. "It was at the end of the garden, near the shed."

"Well, I used to go down every morning to see if there was a strawberry yet, but there never was. So in the end you sneaked down before I got up and tied some ripe ones to the plants. Then you said, Jamie, I've got a feeling there'll be strawberries today, so we went down and a blackbird was sitting there, eating the lot. And you ran at it, shouting, Fuck off, you bloody bird. I'll wring your sodding neck."

Leo, who had been gazing at him, the cream carton in her hand forgotten, gave an unsteady laugh.

"Did I? God, what a dreadful mother I was."

She turned away to replace the carton in the fridge then, unwilling for him to see her face, moved to the sink.

"No, you weren't." Jamie was shovelling down strawberries. "We had some good times together. I remember –"

But Leo, whose heart was already full almost to bursting, did not want any more. Over her shoulder, she said, "How's Lettie? I meant to ring the hospital yesterday, but I forgot."

"Much better. She's out of bed and hobbling round the ward on crutches. Rose said she'd have been home by now, but she's caught an infection and will have to stay in a few more days."

"When did you see Rose?"

"Oh, yesterday teatime. She'd been somewhere, a garden, I think. She was looking very pleased with herself."

"Good. So," she went on carefully, "when Lettie comes out, what will you do?"

"Well, she'll still need a bit of help at first."

"And after that?"

Leo was trying not to press him too hard, but their fences were being mended so fast, and seemingly so effortlessly, after the years of alienation that she now had an almost superstitious dread that he would disappear before – and until this moment she had not even formulated the thought to herself – before she could show him how much she loved him.

"Well, I haven't really got any plans. I thought I might stay on here – with you – for a bit. If that's all right?" He spoke tentatively. "You wouldn't mind?"

"Mind? I'd be delighted."

Before she could stop herself, she went round the table, her heart lifting, and put her arms round her son. He wound his arm round her waist and they stood for a few moments, before both simultaneously moved back a little from the embrace.

"Someone's coming," Jamie said, as a car stopped.

Leo peered out. "Good grief, it's Steve." She opened the door. "Hi, Steve. I thought you'd be halfway to Scotland by now."

"Just on my way." The big man came in. "Hi, Jamie. How you doing?"

"All right, thanks. Well," he got to his feet, "I'd better go, Mum. Look," he hesitated, "I really came round to see if I can borrow the car. I need to go into the market for food – for the dogs, not me," as he saw her face.

"Well, if you promise to be very careful." Leo unhooked the car keys. "The brakes need relining – it's going into the garage next week."

"Sure. Thanks, Mum – you're a star. And …" He stood, keys in hand. "Lettie left some money for food but I've run through it."

"Oh, right." But as Leo reached for her purse, Steve put a large hand on her arm.

"Please, let me."

"No, I couldn't possibly."

"Yes, you can." He turned to Jamie. "Your mother's very kindly doing some garden plans for me. She won't hear of me paying her, so –" he took out a chunky wallet "– how much do you need?"

"Well, twenty pounds would be fine."

Steve extracted three twenty-pound notes and handed them to him, ignoring Leo's protests. "Here you are – my contribution for the dogs."

"Thanks, Steve. Bye. Bye, Mum."

When he had gone, Leo said, rather stiffly, "He'll spend every penny of it on the dogs, you know."

"Sure he will. He's a great kid – a credit to you, Leo."

"Oh, well, thank you."

"Well, I guess I'd better be on my way, too."

But as they went down the path, a blue van drew up alongside his car.

"Morning, love," called Leo, as Rose leapt out and came towards them. "Steve's just on his way."

"Oh, yes, of course. Scotland next, isn't it?" She gave him her hand. "Goodbye, Steve; safe journey."

"Sure." He held her hand for a moment, looking down into her face, then released it. "Goodbye, Rose. It's been great knowing you – and good luck with those scarecrows."

"Take care," Leo shouted, as he drove off.

"You were right about him, you know," said Rose, as they turned away.

"Hmm?" Leo sounded preoccupied. "Right about what?"

"Steve. He is a nice man."

"Yes." She roused herself. "Come on in." She led the way into the kitchen. "Coffee?"

"Please."

As Leo prepared it, Rose took up from the dresser several sketches of a garden design.

"These look good. New commission?"

"Not exactly. Steve's mother's been having problems with one area of this garden they're doing, so I said I'd rough out a few ideas. Nothing fancy, but I'll get them done in time for him to pick up on his way back to Heathrow. I thought it might help."

"I'm sure it will." Rose dropped the papers. "Leo."

"What?"

"Daniel's having an affair."

Leo hesitated just for a second. "Good for Daniel. Who's the lucky girl?"

"Lucy Smith. Honestly, Leo, it's dreadful, isn't it? I mean, do you know her?"

"Vaguely. She was waitressing at Angela's do, wasn't she?"

"That's right."

"Pretty girl. Her older sister – what's she called, Jane? – she's a looker, too, from what I remember."

"But – it's horrible."

Leo gazed down at Rose, who had flung herself down in the pine rocking chair. At that moment, all her affection for her friend was submerged in total exasperation. How could anyone be such a fool as Rose was? Vague, zany, loving, loveable – but a complete and utter fool.

"Just why is it so horrible?"

Rose looked up, startled. "Well, it just is. For one thing, she's so young."

"And Daniel's so old, I suppose."

"Well –"

"He's exactly the same age as you. Remember?"

She longed to get hold of Rose's shoulders and give her a good shaking. She longed, also, to tell her to wake up. But over the years, silence over the relationship of her two friends had been so ingrained that she was not about to break it, even now.

"Anyway," she went on, "how do you know about it?"

"Emily's made friends with her other sister, Sophie, and she told her."

"Yes, well, I suppose things like that do get around."

"And she's an employee of his. It's – it's unprofessional." Rose sounded as sulky as her niece. In fact, looking at her downturned eyes, her mouth, Leo was faintly reminded of Emily.

"Oh, Rose, don't be so childish. Anyone would think you were eighteen."

"Well, I still think he's taking advantage of her."

"For goodness sake!" Leo burst out laughing. "From what I've seen of Miss Lucy Smith, nobody, but nobody takes advantage of that young woman. She's got more street-cred in her toenails than you've got in your whole body."

Rose stood up abruptly. "Thanks for the coffee. I must get back to work."

"Rose."

"What?"

"You aren't going to say anything to Daniel, I hope?"

"Why not?"

"Listen to me, love." Leo gripped her friend's wrist, shaking it in emphasis. "It's nothing to do with you, what Daniel does – or with whom. Nothing at all," she repeated. "Just let this thing run its course. Believe me, Rose, you'll be sorry if you interfere. Keep out of it."

CHAPTER ELEVEN

"What a remarkable, er, animal." Mrs Mallory adjusted her glasses and peered at Rose's portfolio, open on the polished table. "It's not a fox, is it?"

"Good gracious, no. That's Wolfie."

"A wolf? Oh yes, I see that now."

"He's the mascot of Wolves – Wolverhampton Wanderers Football Club. I did him as a birthday present for someone who's been a fan all his life."

"What a very good idea."

Mrs Mallory scrutinised Wolfie, who leered back at her through his ball-bearing eyes. Rose was quite proud of that photograph. She'd taken it a couple of evenings ago, late, so that with the darkening sky behind him and his long, angular shadow cast across the rows of vegetables, he looked extremely sinister.

In fact, she was proud of the entire scarecrow portfolio. Out of nothing very much, she'd whipped up a substantial, professional-looking product. Rather like making a soufflé without eggs, she thought now, with a touch of self-cynicism. It wouldn't have fooled Daniel, of course, but as she wasn't allowing herself even to think of Daniel, ever, that didn't matter. It certainly seemed to be fooling Mrs Mallory.

"And my son thinks that Jim Fitzpatrick will be a good idea."

"Yes. I've done a mock-up of him." Rose riffled through the pages. "Here he is."

She opened the book at a watercolour sketch of a keeper, complete with flat cap, Barbour, broken gun slung from his hip. "Of course, you don't have to decide now, Mrs Mallory. In any case," she added, with a touch of cunning, "I am rather busy. I have quite a backlog of orders at the moment."

"Oh, but if I do decide to have one, I would want it by next week – before the Gardening Club come for their annual evening."

"I think I could manage that," Rose replied smoothly. Nothing so mercenary as a fee had been mentioned yet, but if she was going to dance to the woman's tune, she'd at least make her pay for it. She just hoped that the old autocrat did not hold to the traditional view of 'pay the tradesmen last, if ever.'

She dug in her bag. "I'll leave you my card."

Another stroke of genius, that card had been. She had designed it herself, had six dozen run off; think big, she'd told herself. Cream, brown-edged, with the name ScarecRose Ashenby in black, a tiny scarecrow dancing above the 's' in 'Rose'.

"ScarecRose." Mrs Mallory took the card and read it aloud. "Most amusing. Thank you."

"This is a super room."

Rose sat back in her chair, looking around her. They were in the library, a smallish room, the tall white shelves crammed with leather-bound books. Above the ornate fireplace was a mirror, in three parts, its glass silvered with age. French doors opened out onto a paved terrace.

"Yes." Mrs Mallory sighed faintly. "This was always my husband's favourite room. He used to say he could escape from the world in here."

She looked around the room with a faint air of puzzlement, as though asking herself what Mr Mallory could possibly have been escaping from.

Just then, the inner door opened and Christo came in, Simba and Jasper at his heels. They slurped wet kisses over every part of Rose's bare skin that they could get at then collapsed on the hearth rug.

"Good afternoon, Mother. Miss Ashenby." He smiled at her and came over to the table. "All fixed up?"

"Your mother is going to think about it."

"Think about it?" Christo raised his fair brows. "What nonsense, Madre. You know you've already decided you're having one. In fact," he took from his pocket a crumpled piece of newspaper, laid it in front of Rose and smoothed it out, "I thought you'd like this. It's the only photo of Jim I could find."

Yes, there were the black moustache, the thick hair, the big, burly shoulders she'd imagined. Beside him, the policemen looked quite small. She looked up enquiringly.

"It was taken the day he was arrested for peppering the backsides of a couple of poachers. They took exception to it and sued him."

"Disgraceful." Mrs Mallory's face had gone quite red.

"Oh, come on, Mother. Poaching's always gone on, always will."

"Well, at least they did not get much satisfaction," his mother replied grimly.

"Yes." Christo gave Rose the barest wink. "It just so happened, Miss Ashenby, that the magistrate was at school with my father."

"I see," Rose said politely. "You mean, the old school tie network."

"Precisely."

"Shades of Squire Weston, in fact."

He wrinkled his brow. "Mmm? *Tom Jones*, you mean? Well, not exactly, but I get your drift."

He was a strange man, thought Rose, watching him as he flipped through her portfolio. Wry, self-deprecating, a fine sense of irony – and yet, happily accepting all these anomalies.

"That's settled then, Miss Ashenby." He closed it and handed it to her.

"Thank you." She took it and scooped up her shoulder bag, then smiled down at Mrs Mallory. "Thank you for the tea. I'll get on with Jim right away."

"Yes, of course. Goodbye, Miss Ashenby." Mrs Mallory graciously shook hands but then, as they were turning away, she shot a piercing glance at the two of them. "By the way, darling, did I tell you I've invited Candida to come and ride Major tomorrow morning?"

Rose saw his lips compress slightly, but he only said, "No, Mother, you didn't."

"Well, you never ride him now, so the poor beast gets no exercise."

He shrugged. "Richard will have to see to her. I told you yesterday, I'm going into Banbury for the morning." He turned back to Rose. "We can go out through the French door."

At the far end of the terrace was the large armillary sphere which Rose had admired on her first visit to the garden. She stopped beside it now, running her fingers up its wrought-iron struts.

"This is lovely, isn't it?"

"Yes. My father bought it for their tenth wedding anniversary, I think." As they moved on, he said, "Do you ride?"

"Good heavens, no." Rose was thoroughly alarmed. "When I was five, I fell off a donkey on Weston beach, and I've never ventured into a saddle since."

He laughed. "And the tea Mother gave you – was it China?"

"Of course." She gave him a straight-faced look.
"Bravery beyond the call of duty."
"Well –" she brandished her portfolio "– I've got my order."
"Tell you what. Come into my office and I'll make you a proper cup."
"Oh, I'd love to, but I really must get back."
"The niece?"
"Yes, Emily." She shook her head. "Honestly, Christo, how anyone ever survives twenty years of this. I mean, I've got her for less than two weeks and I'm a nervous wreck."
"Oh dear, is she still sulking?"
"No, not at all. In fact, it's –" She shook her head again, this time in perplexity. "It's all a bit unnerving. She's behaving brilliantly; she insists on doing the washing up, has tidied the house all through. Thank God for Sophie – that's her new friend. She's such a sensible girl."

In fact, Sophie was a very quiet girl, with almost nothing to say to Rose when she had invited her round the other evening. Not a bit like her older sister, she had thought, before thrusting Lucy out of her mind.

"But even so," she went on, "I still fret about her constantly."
"Oh, you'd be more laid back if she was your own."
"I doubt it." But he was probably right. It was because Emily wasn't hers that she felt so responsible for her.

They had reached her van, but just as he opened the door for her a tractor drove into the cobbled yard. The driver, a middle-aged man in dungarees, leapt down.

"Want me, Dave?"

Rose watched as Christo went across to him. They seemed on easy terms, man and master, Christo listening intently; nodding, gesturing up the hill behind the house, then finally clapping the man on the back, as he touched his cap then clambered back into his cab. When Christo came back over to her though, he was frowning.

"Problems?"
"Not really. Well, yes. Some of the young bullocks have trampled down a fence and got into the second cut of hay. Dave and his son have got them out and secured it temporarily, but I'd better take a look."
"Can I help?"

"No, thanks, you must get back. Oh, tell you what though, could you give me a lift to the top of the drive? I'll see what's been going on, then walk back down. I've had no exercise today – I'll be running to fat." He patted his lean stomach.

Rose opened the passenger door and he tucked himself in beside her, a tight fit. As she took off the brake, her palm brushed across his hand, and she felt a little tingle in her skin. Neither of them said anything as they drove up the hill.

"This'll do nicely. I can walk across from here."

She pulled onto a grassy patch, not switching off, but he did not hurry to get out.

"This is one of my favourite spots," he said. "If you look down there you can see the house – just there – almost hidden by the trees."

"Oh, yes, there it is."

It was below them, a tiny child's toy of gingerbread stone. Among the trees which surged around it she glimpsed water, while beyond, fields of wheat stood, almost ripe for harvest. She shot a glance at Christo, but he seemed absorbed by the view. What must it be like to run this place, to own it; to know that, however many bushels of green tea she consumed, one day Mrs Mallory would trot off to that little churchyard, hand-in-hand with the grim reaper, and it would be his? All the joys and, she saw that faint vertical crease between his brows, all the cares and responsibilities. Her worries over Emily were nothing, a drop in the ocean. Would he marry, to share the burden? Had he been serious when he'd talked of his ideal woman? What would it be like to be married to Christo? Imagine her parents' reaction if ... With one mighty bound, she would overtake Susan. 'My son-in-law ... Curlieu ... our daughter's house, you know...'

"You're very quiet, Rose."

"So are you."

She turned to him, smiling, and found that their faces were very close. His blue eyes held hers, she felt his soft breath on her cheek, smelled the sweetness of hay meadows, of the open air, on his tanned skin. Then, as she held her breath, he leaned forward and gently kissed her on the lips. He drew back and looked at her, his eyes dark and rather sombre.

"Oh, Christo." Rose gave a shaken laugh.

"Oh, Rose." He brushed the back of his hand across her cheek, then got out. "Can I see you again?" He bent to look in at her.

"If you want to."

He seemed on the point of saying something, then straightened up. "I'll give you a ring – tomorrow."

"Bye, Christo."

But he was plunging down off the path through a thicket of young trees, and was already lost to sight.

Daniel's route took him through the village where he and Rose had grown up. He passed the two semi-detached cottages, prettified – and pricefied – beyond all recognition from when their parents had bought them nearly forty years before. After his father's death ten years ago, his mother had moved back to her native Cumbria, but within a year she too had died. Of a broken heart, his aunt said, but she'd always been sentimental.

He slowed down as he approached the house which had once been the village school. The builders had kept the big school window where their classroom had been. The playground was now a thriving vegetable patch. A little girl, barefoot, in a white sun hat, was wielding a miniature watering can.

His mind leapt back suddenly to – had it been their very first day in school? He rather thought so. He had been a very timid, retiring child in those days, and when two older boys began taunting him, telling him to scrub himself in the bath every night so he'd be white, he'd done nothing, just stood there burning up inside in an agony of shame and misery.

It had been Rose who, from the far side of the playground, had somehow heard, and launched herself at them. She'd hit the bigger boy so hard that one of his front teeth was knocked out and he fled, and she was sitting astride the other one, pummelling him, when, almost beside herself with fury, she was dragged off him by one of the teachers. When she'd refused to stand at the front and repeat to the whole class: "I am a very naughty girl and must learn to control my temper," explaining with sweet reasonableness that what she'd done had been wholly necessary, Mrs Ashenby had been summoned post-haste from the garage.

The little girl emptied her can. She raised her eyes, saw Daniel and smiled at him, a gappy smile. He waved back, then grimaced at the sharp needle jab of unwanted memory. He slammed the car into gear and drove off.

Watched over by Bugsy, Rose was in her studio. Emily was out when she got back and she'd gone straight through to her studio where, to stop any other thoughts intruding, she had thrown herself into her work. She was giving a final adjustment to her Head Gardener's gaiters and did not at first see Daniel as he stood, looking down at her.

He was not at all sure why he'd come. If she answered her bloody phone just once in a while, there would have been no need. What he did know was that, just now, he did not much care for Daniel Bradshaw – and cared even less for Rose Ashenby.

She wiped her arm across her brow, reached up for a ball of twine, and saw him. If there was a flash of welcome in her eyes, it was gone before it was there.

To forestall her, he said, "Don't you ever answer your phone?"

"What do you mean?"

He went across and stood over her as she knelt on the dirty floor.

"What I mean is, I have rung you, and rung you, and rung you." His voice throbbed with suppressed anger. "Emily answered yesterday. She told me you were out but promised you'd call me back. I gather she didn't tell you?"

"Oh." Rose, who was straightening up, looked guilty. "Well, she did, actually, but I've been busy."

"Too busy to ring an old friend?"

"Let's just say I've been too busy. What do you want, Daniel? I'm –"

"Busy," he finished.

"As you see." She waved her hand at the row of sagging forms slung on hooks. The scene was not unreminiscent of an old-fashioned butcher's shop, minus the blood and entrails.

"So these things are doing well?" He flicked at the nearest shape with his finger and it swayed to and fro.

"My scarecrows are taking off, yes," she replied stiffly.

Reaching a small card from a pile on the table behind her, she handed it to him.

"ScarecRose Ashenby. Very neat." His voice was expressionless.

When he went to hand it back to her, she said, "Keep it. You never know, one of your clients might be interested."

"I doubt it." He laid the card back down on the table. "But it's one of my clients that I'm here about. He's a potential buyer for your fish – in fact, I'm pretty sure I'll be able to clinch the deal for you."

"My fish?" Rose looked vague for a moment. "Oh, it's over there."

It lay in the corner, behind coils of iron chains, themselves a modern sculpture, and half-hidden by piles of hessian and bales of straw, where she had flung it the morning after Angela's party. Daniel dragged it out into the centre of the studio, wiped some of the dust off with his handkerchief, then stood back. It was the first time he had seen it completed. The creature was poised, arching as it leapt joyously from the waves. Life rippled through every fin. A simple design, yet she had imbued it with some element of herself, he thought – that elusive something that was Rose.

"It's beautiful," he murmured. "He'll take it, I promise you. And I'm almost certain I can get you another commission from him."

"Oh, but I'm only doing scarecrows now," Rose said quickly. "Sorry, Daniel, but there it is."

She met his eyes for the first time, hers defiant and, he realised now, hostile. He shrugged.

"If that's the way you feel. But I'll send the van out from Stratford tomorrow. Will you be here?"

"Yes." And she did have the grace to feel grateful. "Thank you, Daniel. But leave it for a few days, if you don't mind. I think I'll have another look at the fins."

Here we go again, he thought. JMW Turner at the Royal Academy finishing day all over again.

"The fish is perfect, Rose," he said sharply. "Leave it alone, please."

"All right." She was still very angry with him, but at least she could remember her manners. "Would you like a cup of tea? Or a soft drink? You must be thirsty after driving up the motorway."

"Thanks, but I won't stop. And actually, I haven't come up from London. Just for once, I've been in Stratford all week. In fact," he glanced at his watch, "I must be getting back."

"Ah yes, of *course*."

"And what's that supposed to mean?"

"Nothing. Nothing at all."

He eyed her narrowly. "Something bugging you?"

"No, of course not. Should there be?" Mindful of Leo's exhortation, she closed her mouth. Keep out of it, Rose. It's nothing to do with you.

"Yes there is. Come on, out with it."

"Well, if you must know – it's that girl. Daniel, how could you?"

"I presume you mean my relationship with Lucy Smith?"

His voice was so frigid, that even now she should have backed off. But her anger, and what else? – she did not stop to answer herself – was driving her on now.

"Why? Are there any more eighteen year-olds that you're having affairs with?"

"For your information, no there are not. But if there were, it would be bloody-well nothing to do with you."

"But it's just not right."

"What do you mean – not right?"

"Well, she's working for you."

"Oh, Lucy and I –" he used the phrase deliberately, she was sure of that "– Lucy and I are quite mature enough to separate business and – pleasure."

"I suppose she's given up her university place because of you."

"Oh, what rubbish." He laughed but there was no humour in his eyes. "She's far too sensible a girl for that."

"So this is just one of those oh-so-romantic summer affairs, then."

He regarded her sombrely. "I don't know what it is – yet. And I've already told you, it's none of your business what it might be."

"But," Rose felt the need to justify herself and, with Emily never far from her thoughts these days, she went on, "you're as good as in loco parentis to the girl."

"Meaning, I suppose," Daniel's olive-brown cheeks had taken on a tinge of red, "that I'm old enough to be her father."

"No. Well, yes, you are, actually."

"And that's what you object to, is it?"

"No."

Too late, Rose was wishing desperately that she had obeyed Leo's stern injunction. She and Daniel were separated by just a few feet of dusty floorboards, but she could almost hear the chasm, dark and bottomless, opening up between them.

"I just don't think it's right, that's all," she repeated weakly.

"Have I ever said one word to you about your string of no-hopers?"

"You haven't needed to," she retorted. "Your feelings have always been quite plain enough."

"I mean, for heaven's sake. Darren. And then there was that trashy – what was he called? Oh, yes, Dougie." She tried to interrupt him but he swept on. "He was the one who nearly got you banged up, wasn't he, because he was growing cannabis in that rundown greenhouse of yours. And of course, Ryan. We mustn't forget Ryan, must we?"

"Shut up about Ryan, damn you. Just shut up."

The colour flared in Rose's face now and as she stared at him, grey eyes blazing, he saw again the fierce little five year-old. But the image only gave his voice an even harsher tone.

"You're on shaky ground, moralising at me, Rose. If I were you, I'd –"

"Don't talk to me about morals." Rose was beyond all reason now. "Lucy Smith, she – she's nothing but a little whore!"

For a moment, as she saw Daniel's hands bunch into fists, she thought she had gone too far. But then he thrust them into his pockets, and went on more quietly, "Rose Ashenby, you are a dog in the manger."

"A what?"

"You heard. You don't want me, but you don't want anyone else to have me, either."

"Want you?" She was gazing at him, her eyes blank. "But, Daniel, we're friends. You're my very best friend. At least," she faltered, "you always have been."

His mouth twisted. "So you always say."

"It's just that I want you to be happy."

He gazed at her, his dark eyes unreadable. "Do you, Rose?"

"Of course I do. And I couldn't bear for you to be hurt."

"Nothing's going to be hurt by this affair – except possibly your pride."

For what seemed a very long time, they stared at one another across that chasm. Then at last he said curtly, "The van will be out in the morning. Ten o'clock suit you?"

"I'll be here."

He nodded. "Goodbye, Rose."

She stayed where she was until his car had gone and Bugsy came rubbing round her legs. She picked him up and he nuzzled at her, butting her chin with his dark head.

"Oh, Bugsy."

She buried her face in his black fur. As usual with Rose, all her anger had instantly evaporated. But it was too late. She shouldn't have said that about Lucy – even if it was true. But he shouldn't have gone on about Ryan, either. Your string of no-hopers. She should have told him about Christo and how he'd kissed her. That would have proved something, though she was not sure what. But in any case, it was too late.

CHAPTER TWELVE

Rose pulled a face at the phone.

"Yes, Roddie, I will ... Yes, of course ... Yes, I'll make sure she is ... Love to Susan – and the children, of course. Bye."

As she replaced the receiver, the kitchen door opened and Emily came in.

"Was that Dad?"

"Yes. How did you guess?"

"Oh, you've got that expression you always have when you're talking to him."

"Of course I don't." But Rose felt the guilty blush. "Don't be silly."

"OK, you don't. What did he want, anyway?"

"Oh, just to say that he'll be here about nine tomorrow. Emily," as her niece scowled, "you will get packed up this evening, won't you?"

"Oh, Rose, can't I stay with you? *Please.*"

Rose's heart sank. "You know it's not possible, love. And you may even have a good time, if you just give it a chance. You're sixteen, remember – you won't have many more family holidays together."

"Thank God."

"And Southwold can't be that bad, surely."

"Want a bet? But it's not really the holiday. It's just – oh, Rose, everything's so horrible at home these days."

Rose looked at her, perplexed, as the girl stood, her slim shoulders sagging, her mouth turned down at the corners.

"Please, Rose," she said again, with something like desperation in her voice, "let me stay. Or perhaps you don't want me, either."

"Oh, Emily." Rose put her arms round her. "Of course I do. It's been lovely having you – and the house is tidier than it's been for months." But Emily did not respond. Maybe, Rose thought suddenly, this was what all the girl's efforts had been leading up to. "I hope you'll come again – I'd really like you to. How about half-term?"

"But that's *months* away."

In other circumstances, Rose would have smiled at the desolation in her voice.

"I'd love you to stay, honestly, but it's just not possible. Your Dad won't let you; and anyway, I'm going away myself for a few days."

"Oh? Where?" Emily's muffled voice sounded suspicious.

"Well, it's funny, really. You know, the Head Gardener I made?"

"Mr McGregor."

"That's him. Well, just before your Dad rang I had a call from a man on holiday up here who'd seen him in the antique shop. He's putting on a – wait for it –" though Emily did not look exactly overexcited "– a Scarecrow Festival. Yes, really – and he's asked me if I'll go down and do a sort of master class each day – showing people how to make scarecrows, and so on. So, I'm off down there in a few days."

"Oh, well, that's it then." Emily released herself from Rose's arms. She stood for a moment, drooping, then seemed to brace herself. "Don't worry about it." She gave her aunt a pale smile. "I'll be all right. And you never know, maybe I'll even enjoy it once I get there."

"That's my girl. And you must let me give you some spending money. No –" as Emily tried to protest "– you've kept this place spick and span. And anyway, the way things are going, I'll be the first scarecrow millionaire in ten years' time." And what would the family think of that? "So I insist. You can treat Cordelia and Abigail sometimes."

"Thanks, Rose. You're great." The girl smiled at her.

"What are you going to do for the rest of the day?"

Emily shrugged. "Don't know."

"I've got to go out later, I'm afraid. I've promised to deliver that gamekeeper scarecrow this afternoon."

"Is that the one you've been working on all the time?"

"Yes. Jim Fitzpatrick."

In fact, she had worked on Jim almost non-stop the last few days. He had served the twin purposes she so badly needed: fully occupying her mind, and keeping her away from other people. So, apart from taking Mr McGregor to the shop in Moreton, and dragging a deeply reluctant Emily on a second visit to her parents, with the girl only brightening up when her grandmother slipped her a ten-pound note as they were leaving, she had kept her head down.

Not that she had any fear that Daniel might come back. He wouldn't, she knew that – and was glad. But she didn't want to meet Leo, whose advice she had so stupidly ignored. She didn't even want to see Christo, and when he had rung, as he'd said he would, she'd told him that she was very busy.

"Of course, you could always come with me," she went on tentatively. "I'm sure Christo – Mr Mallory – would show you the Jersey calves at Home Farm if he's around. Honestly, love, they really are gorgeous. Cream fudge, with eyelashes a foot long."

"Thanks, Rose, but it's really too hot to bother with anything." And the girl did look very pale, with beads of sweat on her brow.

"So what will you do with yourself?"

"Oh, go round to Sophie's, I suppose."

"Yes, of course. She's a really nice girl, isn't she?"

"Yes."

Rose, with her own preoccupations, had been intensely grateful for the way the girl had taken Emily off her back. The two of them had spent nearly every day together, and a few nights ago Rose had even, after a lot of soul-searching and a reassuring phone call to Susan, who didn't sound particularly bothered, let her join with a group of Sophie's friends in a sleep-over.

"Maybe we'll go and see the dogs," Emily said.

"Dogs?"

"The greyhounds. Miss Johnson's back."

"Back home? I didn't know. Who told you?"

"Oh, somebody. Can't remember." Emily lifted her heavy blonde hair from her neck then let it flop again. "Sophie's Mum, I think."

"Are you sure? The last time I rang the hospital, they said she'd be in for a few more days."

"Yeah, but she told the doctor that she only lived for her dogs, and if she didn't soon see them she might as well pop her clogs anyway and be done with it."

Rose laughed. "Well, that certainly sounds like Lettie Johnson. Oh hell, I ought to go round. I feel awful, not knowing – that she's home, I mean."

"There's no need. When – if I go, I'll tell her you're busy and you'll come in a couple of days. OK?"

"Thanks, love. And I shouldn't be late back. I'll help you with your packing, shall I?"

"No." Emily wrinkled her nose. "I'll do it before I go out. I shan't be able to face it tonight."

"All right. And I'll give you your money now, in case I forget later."

"Thanks, Rose." The girl hesitated. "Rose –"

"What?"

"Oh – nothing."

Abruptly, she put her arms around her aunt and hugged her tightly until Rose was breathless. Then just as suddenly she released her and went off upstairs.

Rose stood listening to the footsteps going to and fro overhead. Things would work out all right, wouldn't they? They always did, somehow, turn out for the best. Didn't they?

Emily was right about one thing, at any rate. The heat, which had been steadily building for days, was almost unbearable today. Even though her kitchen door stood open and the blind was down at the window, there was not a whisper of coolness. Outside, even though she had watered them earlier, she could almost hear the tub of petunias panting, while inside, Bugsy lay stretched out, a half moon of black fur against the kitchen tiles. When she bent and stroked him, he did not open his eyes, only gave an irritable little growl in his throat and flexed his claws.

She was just getting into her van when he appeared in the yard, followed, of course, by Jasper and Simba. She fended them off ineffectually and waited for him.

"Afternoon, Christo. You look hot."

"And you look smug." He smiled down at her, drawing the back of his arm across his forehead, which was sheened with sweat. His blue shirt clung to him, dark and sticky. "My excuse is that I've been helping with the baling. What's yours?"

"Oh, just that your mother likes her new acquisition." Plus the fat cheque that lay snuggled safely in her bag.

"Jim? I'm relieved to hear it."

"Why? You didn't doubt my scarecrow-making ability, did you?"

"Oh, I never doubt you, Rose." His look sent little shimmers up and down her spine. "But Mother is, to say the least, unpredictable. I was afraid she might link her deep attachment to Candida to a sudden and equally deep aversion to your scarecrow."

"Oh." She nodded, though she did not quite grasp his meaning.

"Do me a favour, will you, Rose? Come for a walk." As she hesitated, he grimaced. "Don't tell me – the niece."

"No, no, she's out for the rest of the day. Making the most of her last day of happiness, was how she put it to me." Really, it was because, having pushed all thoughts of Christo out of her head for several days, coming suddenly face to face with him again made her feel uncertain, nervous even. But she couldn't tell him this.

"In that case, come on."

He closed her van door and she found that she was walking by his side across the yard, the dogs at their heels. They went out through the rear gate and onto a wide track.

"Let's go down to the lake," he said. "You haven't seen that yet, and we might even get a breath of air down there."

"Yes, it's scorching, isn't it?"

Taking out her cream sunhat, she jammed it low over her eyes, whilst beside her Christo exuded an almost animal heat.

"I don't imagine it'll go on," he remarked. "The forecast was for storms in the south west this evening, maybe moving up country overnight."

"I suppose you listen to the farming forecast every morning."

"Well, if we're waiting for harvest or anything, I ring a special line. Mind you, I sometimes think I'd be better off with a piece of seaweed outside the office door."

Round the next bend the track opened out and Rose saw ahead a small lake, hardly more than a large pool, its banks fringed with willow and ash trees and tall bullrushes.

"Last time I was down here I saw a kingfisher."

"Oh, how lovely, I've never seen one. I know all about them though – just ask me." She rolled her eyes. "I did a small sculpture a year or so back. This couple had just got married and wanted a weather vane that was different for their new house, and as the house was called Kingfishers I suggested having one instead of a cockerel."

"You mean Simon and Milly's place?"

"The Fairfaxes? Yes, that's right. Do you know them?"

"They're very old friends. I was at school with Simon, and

Milly was another of Mother's, er, candidates, when it was beginning to look as if Candida might be a non-runner."

"They seemed very happy," Rose said tentatively. In fact, they'd been just the sort of laughing, teasing couple of which she had once dreamed of being one half.

"Oh, yes, they're ideally suited. Milly's far happier than she'd have been with me, I'm sure. That kingfisher of yours is really striking, though." He gave her a slanting look. "Perhaps we can persuade Mother that the roofline of Curlieus just isn't complete without one. Or maybe you could do one for me."

"Oh," she felt that *frisson* of uncertainty again, "but my scarecrows are taking up all my time just now."

"Ah well, in the future perhaps." He sat down on the bank, his back against a willow, and patted the ground beside him. "This is where I saw the kingfisher, on that low branch over there."

Rose sat beside him, risking a glance from beneath the brim of her sunhat. He looked tired, rather abstracted, a little sad even. She put a hand on his arm.

"What's wrong, Christo?"

He looked down at her hand then took it in his, running a calloused thumb across the palm.

"Sorry. Is it so obvious?"

"Well –"

"It's just – it's the farming. One of our tenants came to me this morning. He told me they're giving up, going to Canada to try their luck there." He heaved a great sigh. "Robert's father and his grandfather had the farm from my father and grandfather. It's breaking his heart to go; and he says it'll all but kill his father. But they can't do any more. They work all hours, his wife drives the minibus that takes the local children to school, she bakes stuff for the WI market – and still they should be on Income Support, but Robert's too proud. Oh, God." He released her and ran his hand through his fair hair. "What a bloody mess."

"And they won't let you help them – to stay, I mean?"

"I've frozen all the rents for the last three years. I've done what else I can, but it's no use."

They were both silent, watching the reeds quiver as a moorhen pushed between them.

It was Rose who finally broke the silence. "I went to a folk festival once with Ryan." She realised that she could actually say the name and not feel anything. "My boyfriend," as he looked at her, "my *ex*-boyfriend. He's a sort of pop poet – he performs with jazz groups and things like that. There was an old chap there, a lovely man, a Buddhist, I think. Anyway, when Ryan left me – we'd been together for four years and I was just beginning to think it was really working out for us – anyway, Donald rang me one day, said he'd heard, how sorry he was, and how no door ever closes in our face, unless another much better one is going to open for us. I just thought that might help with your farmer," she added, rather lamely, when he did not reply. "Maybe it will be for the best."

"Oh, Rose." He gave her an odd little smile and, lifting his hand, gently tapped the end of her nose with his forefinger. "I'm sure it will."

Their faces were flecked by the shifting pattern of willow leaves and sunlight. Their eyes met, lingered, then by mutual consent turned away to look across the lake.

They sat for a long time. The pool shimmered in the sunshine, the willow rustled softly, the moorhen appeared again, this time towing two fluffy chicks in her wake.

"Look," exclaimed Rose. "Aren't they sweet."

"Oh dear." Christo pulled a face. "There were four last time. Rats, I expect."

"Oh, no. How horrible."

"There's always a serpent in Eden, Rose." His tone was light enough, but when she looked at him she saw with surprise how sombre his eyes were.

She looked at her watch. "It's lovely here. I could sit here forever, but I really must go."

"Emily?"

She laughed. "Well, yes and no. I don't *think* she'll be back early – she's out with her friend – but, just in case, as it's her last evening, I ought to be around. Sorry."

"That's all right. I'd better get back to work myself." He got up, pulling her to her feet with him. "We'll take a short cut if you like."

The end of the pool narrowed to where the feeder stream came into it and three old railway sleepers had been laid down as a rough bridge. Rose was halfway across when something flickered across the corner of her eye – a flash of intense blue.

"The kingfisher – look!"

She turned, pointed, lost her balance and fell into the stream. Christo leapt down and, taking hold of her hands, pulled her out. With the heat wave, the level was low, more mud and trampled cow prints than water, and Rose erupted from it with a horrible sucking noise, then stood on the bank, oozing mud.

"Oh, *no*."

She looked down at her legs and arms, at what had been a smart navy dress, put on in deference to Mrs Mallory and Jim Fitzpatrick. She moved tentatively and squelched.

"Ugh." Her dress was clinging to her, every little step she took she felt mud, or worse, ooze between her toes. She picked a long strand of pondweed off her arm and looked up at Christo.

"Don't you dare laugh," she said crossly, as she saw his lips twitch. "And you two can take those stupid grins off your faces, too," as the dogs lolled on the bank, watching her. Then: "Oh, what a fool I am," and she burst out laughing herself.

"But at least you saw the kingfisher."

"Well, I didn't really."

"Come on, let's get you cleaned up."

"But you have to go back to work."

"No, I don't. I'm the boss, remember? If we cut through that new plantation up there, we'll be at my place in ten minutes."

The bath water was cooling. Rose tugged at the plug with her big toe and got out. She dried herself, put on the white towelling robe which Christo had given her and went out onto the landing. She heard footsteps and he appeared at the top of the stairs.

"Good. I thought I heard the water running out. I've made tea."

He had changed too. He had obviously showered, his hair was still dark, and he was wearing a black T-shirt and shorts. Rose stood quite still, looking at him. He came slowly towards her and gazed down at her.

"You know, with your hair piled up on top of your head like that, you look about fifteen years old."

"But I'm thirty-five, Christo." Thirty-five, and if I listen hard I can hear my sands of time running through the hourglass.

Between his brows there was still that faint crease, which she longed to stroke away. Instead, she laid her hand across his cheek, and he caught it and pressed his lips to her palm. Then, very slowly, he untied the scrap of ribbon and let her long curly hair tumble onto her shoulders. He lifted a strand between his fingers, so that the light caught it, turning each individual hair to auburn gold.

"Rose?" he said softly, a question in his eyes.

In response, she put her arms around his neck. They kissed then drew apart, their breath on each other's cheek. Christo lifted her up, nudged open the bedroom door with his knee and laid her on the bed.

There was a gentleness, a tenderness, even a kind of sweet restraint about his lovemaking, which seemed almost like inexperience – although the condom he had used belied this – so that afterwards, when Rose lay in the crook of his arm, their bare thighs touching, she felt a peacefulness she had never experienced before. She twisted round, so that she could look at him.

He was lying, his other arm crooked behind his head, staring at the ceiling. When he felt her move, he turned his head slightly towards her.

"Hi." She smiled at him shyly.

"Hi."

In this light, his eyes were very dark blue. That frown line was still there, and now she did gently smooth it with her finger, then on down his nose, his mouth, his chin.

"Oh, Christo, you've such an aristocratic profile."

"Have I?"

"Yes, you have." She lay back luxuriously. "You know something?"

"What?"

"I could murder a cup of tea."

"No sooner the word." He rolled off the bed and put on the bathrobe. "I'll make another pot – and I just might have a chocolate cake."

"I prefer ginger biscuits with tea – that's if you have any."

"Could do."

Rose sat up, hugging her knees, her chin on her hands. She could hear him downstairs in the kitchen, running water, moving to and fro. He must have mown what passed for a lawn earlier; she could smell the sweet aroma of cut grass. Christo ... She smiled faintly to herself, her eyes dreamy.

How gentle his lovemaking had been; so utterly different from the other men whom, through the years, she had been involved with. So different from Ryan; sweeping her with him or leaving her stranded, he hadn't much cared which, while Christo had been – tentative, almost. No, more than that; it was as if he was afraid of frightening her off. He must have been badly hurt by a woman; that would account for the hint of sadness she glimpsed in his eyes sometimes. The thought made her long to hold him, comfort him.

Oh dear. Rose smiled wryly at herself. How long ago was it that she had assured Leo that she was giving up on men forever and a day? Well, she'd been high on gooseberry wine at the time – and she hadn't met Christo.

He was out in the yard now. She could hear his voice, talking to Jasper and Simba, presumably. She got out of bed and went through to his dressing room where, from the window, she could look down on him, squatting on his haunches, petting the dogs. As if sensing a pair of eyes on him, she saw him stiffen and half turn and, suddenly shy, she stepped back.

Her elbow jarred against the wardrobe and the door swung open. She went to close it, then stopped. She went very still. Unable to believe what she was seeing, she lifted out the first hanger.

CHAPTER THIRTEEN

It was a dress, an evening dress, she saw when she half unzipped the plastic cover. Black chiffon, with a beaded bodice. Rose slowly rezipped it, replaced the hanger. Beside it was another, and she swung it slowly to and fro. It was in midnight blue silk, with shoestring straps, a lattice back, across the bust a glittering spray of sequins. When she replaced it, she could see several others, each hanging in its anonymous bag.

There were shelves down one side, stacked with smaller plastic bags. She opened one. It contained a pale lemon sweater, soft as down when she laid her cheek against it. Cashmere. She sniffed and caught a whiff of perfume, rich and sensual. In the bottom of the wardrobe there were shoes, all in plastic bags. She glimpsed a pair of strappy gold high-heeled sandals. When she opened the two small pull-out drawers, she saw but did not touch silk underwear, stockings.

She closed the door and stood for a moment, motionless, feeling the despair – and the anger – well up in her. Yet again, she'd been wrong. Yet again, when she'd begun to think that Mr Right just might be there, waiting for her, the joy had turned to bitter ashes in her mouth. Who was the woman? Not Candida, surely, not from everything he'd said about her; unless that was all one gigantic smokescreen. No, not local, presumably. Married, probably; that was why she had to keep a complete wardrobe of exquisite clothes at her lover's house, ready for when she could slip away. And did his mother, happily plotting wedding bells for Candida, know? No, of course not. 'I keep it this way – to discourage unwelcome visitors.' Conscious all at once that she could still smell that perfume on her cheek, she went through to the bathroom and violently splashed cold water over her face and hands.

Wrapping herself in a towel, she went downstairs. Christo was still outside. On the kitchen table stood a tray and a plate of ginger biscuits, neatly arranged. She stared at the plate, feeling something tight squeeze her ribs. The dryer was just slowing down and snatching out her clothes, still warm, she scrambled into them. He had cleaned the mud off her sandals, and she was putting them on when he came in through the door, the dogs at his heels. While they greeted her as if they had not seen her for months, he stopped, his eyes on her dress.

"I was going to bring you the tea in bed." His gaze went to and lingered on her face.

"I – I must go. I'm sorry."

"Emily?"

"No. No, I told you, she's out. I just have to go. I'm sorry."

"So you said." He came across to her. "It was too soon, wasn't it?"

"Too soon?" she echoed, not meeting his eyes.

"To make love. It's just that – I thought you wanted me to. And I wanted to."

"Oh – oh, no. I did, honestly."

His mouth twisted. "I know I'm not the world's greatest lover. No doubt, in comparison with – what was his name? – Ryan ..."

"No, that's not true. Ryan was –"

"Well, then –"

Reaching forward, he went to tuck a stray strand of hair behind her ear but she jerked back sharply and his hand dropped to his side.

"No, don't touch me, Christo." She drew a deep breath. "I've seen the clothes – in the wardrobe."

"Ah, I see." His face took on that closed look, which she had glimpsed once or twice when his mother was around. "So it wasn't locked?"

"No. And I didn't pick the lock, if that's what you're thinking. It just came open."

"And it makes a difference, does it?"

"Make a difference?" She stared at him. "Of course it does. What do you take me for? I'm sorry, Christo." Her voice trembled. "You must lead your life the way you want, but don't expect me to be any part of it."

"But if I can just tell you about my –"

My lover? My mistress? "*No*. No, I don't want to know." She picked up her bag, where it lay on the table, bent to pat the dogs. "Goodbye, Christo."

He nodded slowly, accepting her decision.

"Your car's up at the house. I'll run you up there."

"I'd rather you didn't, thank you. I'll be glad of the walk."

She heard the dogs go to follow her, heard him call them back. The scent of the mown grass was bitter in her nostrils. Something forced her to turn her head and she saw Christo, still where she had left him, shoulders hunched, staring into space.

Rose was dreaming. She was running along an endless corridor, the only windows high up in the wall. She was flinging open door after door, and behind each one was Christo, smiling, beckoning her inside. She could hear her own heartbeats, and behind them an insistent ringing.

She rolled out of bed and staggered downstairs.

"Hello?"

"Rose. It's me, Roddie."

"Roddie?" She pushed her hair, tangled by a restless, wretched night, out of her eyes and squinted at the kitchen clock. "What time is it?"

"I don't know – oh, about quarter past nine."

Quarter past nine! "So you're on your way, are you?"

"Of course I'm not. I wouldn't be ringing you if I was, would I?"

"No, I suppose not. Sorry, Roddie, I've had a bad night." She'd heard the dawn chorus before finally dropping off. "But – did you say you're not coming?"

"That's right."

For the first time, she registered that behind his customary irritation with her there was something else.

"Is anything wrong?" she asked sharply.

"Anything wrong?" He gave an odd little laugh. "You could say that, I suppose. It's Susan. She's left me."

"Left you?" Rose sat down on the nearest chair. Bugsy came rubbing round her, miaowing, and automatically she pushed him away.

"I don't believe it. Susan wouldn't leave you – she just wouldn't."

"Yes, it is rather out of character for her, although I must say, Rose, that nothing your sister has done over the past few weeks has been in character. For one thing – I don't suppose you've noticed – but she's been drinking quite heavily. Much more like –" He broke off, perhaps recollecting who he was speaking to.

Rose let it go. "But are you sure?"

There was a minor explosion. "Of course I'm bloody sure. I've told you, why would I be ringing you otherwise? Really, Rose, you sound positively half-witted."

"I'm sorry. I just can't take it in." She shook her head slowly to and fro. "Er, when did she go? This morning?"

"I've no idea," Roddie said stiffly. "When Emily came to stay with you, Susan announced that she needed to catch up on her sleep, and moved into her room."

"Ah."

"So the first I knew of it was when I went in there this morning to see why she hadn't been into Tarquin, who was screaming his head off. The bed hadn't been slept in."

"Oh, Roddie, I'm so sorry." And Rose did feel a prick of sympathy for her pompous, stuffy brother-in-law. "Look, would you like me to come? I'll bring Emily, then stay and help. Oh, but you've got that superb au pair, haven't you? What's he called? Josh."

There was a little silence, then Roddie said, "Actually, he's gone as well."

"You mean they've run away? Together?" Had the world gone mad? Susan? Her prim and proper sister?

"Yes. And I can tell you, Rose, it wasn't a spur of the moment decision. Her passport's gone, all her summer clothes, plus," his voice vibrated with anger, "the entire contents of our joint bank account. By happy coincidence, the statement arrived this morning."

"I still think there may be a rational explanation."

"Oh no. She left me a note. Said she couldn't face another holiday in Southwold. She was sick of the place, and she was sick of –" He stopped, cleared his throat.

Poor Roddie. He sounded bewildered, dazed. Another of those utterly selfish, utterly self-absorbed men, totally lacking in sensitivity and imagination who, if Life throws a vicious little spanner onto the track, tumble off their rails.

"I'm so sorry," she repeated soberly. "I really am. So, would you like me to come?"

"That won't be necessary, thank you, Rose. I rang the agency first thing, they were so apologetic, assured me nothing like it had ever happened before with any of their staff, and they've sent round their top employee."

"A woman, I hope?" Rose felt a nervous giggle welling up in her.

"What?" Roddie's voice crackled. "Oh, yes. Excellent woman, by the look of her; middle-aged, what you might call matronly; not one of those flighty flibbertigibbets." Like Birgitta, you mean? Rose could not suppress the thought. "And in view of the inconvenience, she's come at a reduced fee, of course."

"Oh, good." Another thought struck her. "Have you told Mum and Dad?"

"No. I'm going to ring them now."

"Well, leave it a bit, if you will, Roddie. You never know, Susan may think better of it, then they need never know."

"Hmmm, perhaps."

"Look, Roddie. Women, people sometimes do really weird things, if they're a bit down; quite out of character ... What I mean is, what will you do if – when she comes back?"

"Have her back, of course."

Poor, dear, stupid Roddie. Tears came to Rose's eyes and, for the first time ever, she wanted to put her arms round him, hug him.

"I'm sure it will turn out right in the end. Susan just is not the sort to do anything like this." Though she was beginning to wonder if she'd ever really known her sister.

"Well, let's hope so." Rose heard a woman's voice. "Yes, I shan't be a moment, Miss Lathbury. Anyway, Rose, what I'm really ringing for is, can you please keep Emily for a few more days?"

"Yes, of course." Those scarecrow master classes would just have to swing in the wind. "And what do you want me to tell her?"

"The truth, of course."

"Oh, right. Well, we'll keep in touch." She hesitated. "Take care of yourself, Roddie."

Outside Emily's bedroom door, Rose hesitated. She really was not looking forward to the next few minutes ... She'd take her out for the day. Bicester Village seemed to be the girl's idea of Nirvana.

She took a deep breath and knocked. There was no answer. Sulking? She couldn't still be asleep. Her bedroom curtains were already drawn when she arrived home – much to Rose's relief, for she was in no mood for conversation – and she'd kept her word about packing. The tapes, the videos, all of Emily's possessions had been cleared away.

Maybe she'd barricaded herself in. It was the sort of thing she herself might have done – and she sometimes thought that Emily had more of her aunt about her than her mother. Although after this, no-one would ever call Susan predictable again.

The door opened easily.

"Come on, lazybones."

She pulled back the curtains, flooding the room with light, set down the cup of tea she was carrying – and saw, first, that the bed was empty, second, that the room was empty of any sign of Emily.

CHAPTER FOURTEEN

Rose sat down on the bed. Almost without noticing, she drank the tea. Emily ... Susan ... Josh ... Had they run off together, all of them fleeing Southwold? A crazy laugh bubbled up inside her. Perhaps Miss – what was her name? – Lathbury had been calling Roddie to tell him that Tarquin's cot was empty, that he too had fled at the thought of his first family holiday in Southwold!

No. Think, think. Where could she be? She'd be at Sophie's. Yes, of course. She was still more than half a child. Maybe she'd thought she could escape simply by hiding away. Taking the empty cup and saucer, she went back downstairs. She'd ring Sophie now, and Roddie need never know. No, she'd go round and fetch her.

As she went up the brick-paved drive of the neo-Georgian house, the door opened and Lucy, in a crisp little navy suit, came out. Rose had forgotten, temporarily, all about Lucy.

"Hi, Rose." She stood there, swinging her shoulder bag, her dark hair glossy in the sunlight. "Want me? I'm late –" a smile in which there seemed to Rose to be more than a touch of malicious humour "– not that Daniel will mind, of course."

"No, I don't. I want to see your sister."

"Sure." She pushed the door wide open. "Soph – a visitor."

As she went to walk past Rose, she paused then put a neat little hand on her arm.

"Don't worry, Rose. You can have him back – when I've finished with him."

Rose stared at her blankly, then shook her arm free.

"You silly little cow," she snapped and stepped onto the doorstep.

There were raised voices from what was presumably the kitchen, from the whine of the dishwasher, then Sophie appeared in the hall. Rose's immediate thought was that suddenly she looked far more like her older sister than the demure young girl she had got used to seeing with Emily the last couple of weeks. It also seemed to Rose, not so very far from her teens herself, that there was a shifty air about the girl.

"Oh, hello, Rose."

"Hello, Sophie. Can I have a word with you, please?"

"But I was just going out." Even though she was wearing what looked suspiciously like an oversized nightshirt, with Snoopy leering out of it.

"It won't take long."

Sophie looked over her shoulder, then mutely stood aside for her to come in.

"Who's that, Sophie?"

A moment later, a woman in scarlet lycra shorts and top which showed off her tanned limbs, her dark hair caught in a scarlet headband, appeared. As she looked her up and down Rose had the surreal impression that here was the older version of Lucy to put alongside the younger one.

"Mum," said Sophie. "It's Emily's aunt."

"Oh?"

"Hello, Mrs Smith. I'm sorry to burst in on you, but I need to talk to Sophie."

"Oh?" The woman jingled her car keys. "Well, I'm just off to the gym. But, well, you'd better come in, I suppose."

She led the way into the sitting room, which opened onto a patio. It was a pleasant room, but to Rose it felt pretentious, with its heavily swagged curtains, pale blue sculptured carpet, brocade suite. On one wall was a set of mahogany shelves, which held rows of miniature, exquisitely made women's hats.

"God, what a tip." Mrs Smith snatched up the only thing which to Rose's eyes seemed out of place, a magazine, and threw it into the waste paper basket. She began plumping up the cushions along the sofa, but did not invite Rose to sit down. Sophie stood in the doorway, watching her.

Rose's nerves could stand no more.

"Is Emily here, Sophie?" Then, as the girl seemed to hesitate. "Please. I shan't be angry – though she might have told me. But it's very important."

"Oh no!" Sophie was staring at her now, wide-eyed. "Oh, God – she hasn't? I mean, I never thought she'd really do it."

"Do what?" Rose was beginning to feel sick. "What has she done?"

"Oh, nothing, really." Sophie's fingers were pleating Snoopy's nose into a snub.

"Tell me. What has she done?" Rose's lips were tight with apprehension, almost terror.

"Well –" the girl shot a glance across at her mother. "She's ... gone off. With Jamie."

"*Jamie?*" Rose gaped at her. "You mean – Jamie Brinkworth?"

"Yes."

"*Emily* has gone off with *Jamie?*"

"I told you." Sullenly.

"But – *where?*"

The girl shrugged. "No idea. They wouldn't tell me, because they said you'd be round."

Rose stood for a few moments, holding onto the back of the sofa. She was completely unable to speak.

Finally. "Are you absolutely sure?"

"I hope you're not doubting my daughter's word, Miss er –"

"Ashenby," snapped Rose, all her attention on Sophie. "You're quite certain?"

"Well, she said she was going to. Anyway," a flash of defiance, "it's all her Dad's fault – not letting her go with her friends, dragging her off to some boring dump."

"But Jamie. She didn't even like him," Rose said at last, with something like appeal in her voice. "Tell me it's not true."

Sophie's laugh jangled against her overstretched nerves. "She's crazy about him. She spent all her time with him, while Lettie Johnson was in hospital, looking after those scabby dogs."

"But I thought she was with you. She always told me she was going to see you."

Rose's mind, almost numb with terror, could only creep forward an inch at a time.

"That was her Dad's fault, too. She knew he'd go spare if he found out she was going round with an ex-con. Anyway, she was with me, some of the time. And I sometimes went round to them as well."

"Not those appalling dogs." Her mother's face tightened. "Sophie, how could you? You could have picked up *anything.*"

"Oh, I didn't touch them. Honestly, Mum."

Honestly. Rose did not think, somehow, that honesty and this young girl had ever had much to do with each other.

"So when she said she was going for bike rides with you she wasn't?"

"Well, we did go a couple of times – and we used to ride out to

Lettie's place."

Another thought popped up, black as burnt toast, into Rose's mind.

"She told me you were having a sleep-over here. That you'd invited her."

"Oh, no." Mrs Smith bridled visibly. "There's been no sleep-over here, I assure you, Miss er. Whatever your niece has been up to, she has not been doing it under my roof."

Rose ignored her. "Where was she then? Come on," she took a couple of steps towards the girl, "you must tell me. I have to find her. What?" as Sophie muttered something.

"I said, they – Emily and Jamie – they went clubbing in Birmingham. And don't look at me like that. It's nothing to do with me." A glance at her mother. "Emily made me lie – cover up for her. I didn't want to."

"If you've got any idea where they've gone – any idea at all – please tell me, Sophie."

"I've already told you. I haven't." The girl had moved closer to her mother.

Rose was struggling to think. She clutched, drowning, at a straw.

"Do you know the name of the club they went to?"

"Oh." The girl wrinkled her brow. "Oh, yeah, the Gemini. Jamie said they have the best music in town. And anyway, they were going there because it was near a squat," a stifled exclamation from Mrs Smith, "where some of his friends were living. I know they went on there after the club."

"So she didn't even come back here afterwards?"

"Oh, no." Sophie's eyes – Lucy's eyes – began to fill with tears. "Oh, Mum, please. I don't want to talk any more."

"Of course not, darling." Mrs Smith put her arm around the girl. "I'm sorry, Miss er, but you must see that Sophie can be of no further help to you. I'm upset, of course, at what has happened, but it does occur to me that if you had kept a closer eye on your niece –" Rose winced inwardly as the barb struck home. "Sophie told me that you make scarecrows."

"Yes, I do."

"Well –" The woman caught Rose's eye and did not finish the sentence. "I'll see you out."

Without another glance at Sophie, Rose followed her mother into the hall.

As she opened the door, Mrs Smith said, in an undertone, "Of course, Miss er, I didn't say so in front of Sophie – she's such a sensitive child – but there was *something* about your niece that did make me wonder –"

"Oh?"

"Oh, yes. You haven't got children, of course. When you have, you become so much more attuned to their – natures. A sort of radar, if you like."

"Really?" Rose raised her brows slightly. "I'm afraid, Mrs Smith, your radar doesn't seem to have been working lately as regards your middle daughter. Goodbye."

She was halfway down the path before the door was slammed.

When she reached Leo's house, she sat in her van for a few minutes, trying to compose herself. In the short drive from Cedar Grove, her imagination had leapt in a hundred directions. Emily ... Jamie ... a squat ... sleeping together, because that was what Sophie Smith had been implying. Oh God. She buried her face in her hands. How would she ever face Roddie, tell him that his cherished, cocooned Emily, whose chastity he had guarded like a priceless diamond ... Roddie ... Susan ... What a mess.

But maybe Sophie was wrong – and if she really was like her sister, she was a malicious little trouble-maker. Maybe Emily, in an act of teenage rebellion, had gone to join her camping friends in Wales. Maybe her 'relationship' with Jamie had been all a pretence – a double-bluff. Maybe Jamie had even helped her; he was an amiable, good-natured boy, if you looked beyond the hairstyle and the tattoos.

Leo was bent over a sheet of drawings spread out on the kitchen table, a feather of smoke rising from a cigarette in the ashtray beside her. She looked up.

"Oh, hi, Rose. I thought I heard your van just now."

"Hello, Leo."

She came in and stood, irresolute.

"Well, sit down. I haven't seen you for days. Busy, I hear." She grinned. "When you're riding around in your Ferrari, kindly remember old Leo, who started you off on this scarecrow lark."

Rose perched on the chair which Leo had pulled out for her, then immediately got up again.

"Leo, is Jamie here?"

"Jamie? No, he isn't."

"Is he looking after the dogs?"

"No. Well, Lettie's back, of course, and she seems to be coping. In fact, I got the feeling that she rather wanted him gone now. Oh, don't get me wrong. She was touchingly grateful – tried to pay him – but I think she wants those dogs of hers all to herself for a while now."

"So where is he, then?" Rose sat down again.

Leo's brows went up fractionally at her tone, but she only said, "Birmingham. He's gone to see some friends – he referred to them as ex-colleagues." She gave her a rueful smile which Rose, watching her own fingers tap dance on the table, missed. "They're in Edgbaston somewhere, in a squat."

"A squat!" Rose's fingers leapt together convulsively.

"Oh, I know – leafy Edgbaston. But even squatters have gone up-market these days, apparently. Why? Did you want to see him? He'll be back soon, he's just gone for the one night. He's borrowed my car, and he knows I need it this afternoon. I'm going to see that client in Worcester."

"He's borrowed your car to go to a squat?" Rose sounded incredulous.

"Oh, you're so behind the times, my dear." Leo gave a mock-sympathetic grin. "Eco-warriors don't walk – or hitch these days. Anyway, how's Emily? Oh, Roddie's been for her, I suppose, poor kid."

"No, he hasn't." Rose's hands clenched into tight fists of tension. "I think he's – Oh, Leo, what am I going to do?"

"Do about what? Whatever's wrong, love?"

"It's Emily. She's disappeared!"

"Disappeared? Oh, what nonsense. That imagination of yours gets worse, I swear it."

"I wish to God it was my imagination. And – and you don't know the half of it. No –" Her voice rose, as Leo tried to interrupt. "Her bed hasn't been slept in, and all her gear has gone. I went round to see that friend of hers, Sophie Smith – and she says – she says she's run off – with your Jamie."

"*What?*" Leo stared at her, open-mouthed. "Oh, what rubbish."

"Well, that's what she said."

"Sophie Smith – you surely don't believe anything that comes out of that stable?"

"No. I know, but –"

"Jamie doesn't like her. He says she's sly."

"So Jamie knows her?"

"Yes. I've been round to Lettie's a couple of times and they've both been there – she and Emily."

"Yes, that's what she said."

"And you didn't know?"

"No. She just told me she was seeing Sophie. She never mentioned Jamie – in fact, the only time she has, after we came round here that evening, she said she didn't like him."

"Hmmm." Leo took a long pull on her cigarette. "Well, I suppose she knew that you – or rather, dear Daddy – would not approve of such a delicately reared child mingling with the *hoi polloi*."

"No. Sophie said that, too." Rose's mind was moving on, very fast now. "Last Thursday night, was Jamie away then, as well?"

"Thursday? Let's think. Yes, yes, he was. That was the other time he borrowed the car to see those friends in Brum. He was back next morning though, because he was still looking after the dogs. Why?"

"Because last Thursday I thought Emily was on a sleep-over at the Smiths, but Sophie told me this morning that she wasn't, that she'd gone to a club with Jamie and stayed on with friends of his. In a squat."

"Ah." Leo expelled a slow burst of smoke. Their eyes met.

"It's all beginning to add up, isn't it?" Rose spoke quietly.

"Well –" Leo reached across the table, took one of Rose's hands, cold in spite of the heat, in hers "– just supposing it is true, then at least she'll be back," she glanced up at the pansy-faced clock, "in an hour or so, and – and I'm not saying this because Jamie is my son – she will be well looked after. Oh, I know he's weak," her mouth twisted, "he's like Kevin in that. And easily led. That's what always gets him into trouble. But he's a good lad at heart and he's very protective, chivalrous even, in an almost old-fashioned way, towards women – which, I promise you, is one trait he did not inherit from his father."

Rose looked up sharply and at the expression in Leo's eyes, squeezed her hand.

"I know he's a nice boy, Leo. It's just – oh, I wish I knew where she was."

"Well, you will soon, I promise you." Leo briskly pushed back her chair and stood up. "Now, have you had any breakfast?"

"No, I didn't feel like any. Now, I feel sick."

"Low blood sugar." She lifted a cottage loaf out of the bread bin, got butter from the fridge and a jar of heather honey, then put the kettle on. "What you need is something to eat, and by the time you've finished, they'll be here." She began vigorously sawing slices of bread. "Seen Daniel lately?"

"No." She saw Rose's face close up. "Why?"

"Just wondered. Busy time of year for him, of course, with all the tourists."

"Yes."

Leo watched her, as she took a large bite of bread and honey, then licked her fingers. Just for a moment, she almost broke her vow of silence, told Rose that, barely a week since, Daniel had sat where she was sitting. He had almost been at breaking point over his feelings for Rose, disgusted with himself over his affair with Lucy. 'I'm using her, Leo,' he'd said, his eyes almost black with pain. 'It's not fair to the girl. But, when I'm with her, she blots out everything else.' And Leo, much as she might have done with Jamie, had put her arms around him, hugged him to her. 'Don't, Daniel. You're burning yourself up inside. No woman's worth it, not even Rosemary Jane Ashenby.'

She passed a mug of tea across the table. "You haven't told Roddie, I presume?"

"About Emily? Oh, no."

"Well, he need never know, then. He'll be collecting her any day now though, won't he?"

"He should have come this morning, but –" She broke off.

"But what?"

"He rang instead, to ask if I could hang on to Emily for a bit longer."

"Oh, well, it's your lucky day then."

"Not really. You see –" she hesitated again "Susan's left him."
"Susan has what?" Leo coughed then choked on her tea.
"Susan has left him. She's run off with the au pair, nanny or whatever he is – that young man I told you about. Josh."
Leo put her head back and gave a shout of laughter. "I don't believe it. Good for Susan. Whoever would have thought she had it in her?"
Rose, who herself had had to suppress a hysterical giggle when Roddie rang, discovered that it was quite another thing to have an outsider find the situation hilarious.
"It's not funny," she said coldly.
"Oh, but it is. Your sister –" Leo caught her eye and stopped laughing. "No, I suppose it isn't, not really. It's a bugger, though, isn't it? Two of them doing a runner on the same day. You don't suppose? No, Susan and Josh wouldn't want Emily tagging along to spoil their fun, would they? Do your parents know she's gone?"
"No, not yet. But when they do – and if they find out about Emily – Oh, Leo, I can't take much more." She laid her head down on her arms.
Leo studied her friend's rumpled hair with compassion. If adversity was good for the soul, then Rose's little soul must be expanding rapidly.

"You can tell them, Al, that if they try upping the price at this stage the deal's off. Not a dime more."
A pair of arms slid round Daniel's neck. He jerked himself free.
"Yes ... yes, of course. And I appreciate the early call. You're ringing from home, I take it? Oh, sorry," he chuckled, "no worms are safe from you New Yorkers ... OK, fine, I'll leave it with you, then. You know my position. Call me as soon as they come back to you. Bye now."
"A phone call – all the way from New York." Lucy ran her fingers down his arm and brushed them across his palm.
"That's right."
Daniel pushed back his chair and began sifting through the pile of papers on his desk.
"Mmmm. The Big Apple – I've always wanted to go there."
"I'm sure you have."
"Oh, Daniel, darling, don't be like that." She gave a delicious

pout, which he did not see. "Ollie says you wanted to see me as soon as I got in."

"Yes, I did ask Oliver to send you up – when you eventually arrived." He looked at his watch. "Eleven-thirty."

"Oh, I know. That bus – honestly, it gets worse every day. I swear the driver had his foot on the brake the whole way this morning." She paused. "Of course, if I had a little car, I'd always be on time."

"I rather doubt that." He still did not look at her.

"Oh, don't be such a crosspatch."

She sat on the leather sofa, stretching out her long legs. For a moment, she turned them slightly, looking with satisfaction at their sleek, tanned lines.

"Aren't you going to take me out to lunch today? I've put my new suit on." She jumped up again, twirling in front of him. "Do you like it?"

Daniel dropped the last sheet of paper onto the pile, turned and, folding his arms, leaned against the desk.

"It's very nice."

And she did look lovely, he thought. Glossy, gleaming, the skimpy navy suit showing off every line of that body which he had come to know so well over the last few weeks. His money, of course. He'd given her what was a ridiculous amount for a student on a summer job. Reward for services over and above the call of duty? He had deliberately refrained from examining his motives. Now, he realised that he had been squaring himself with himself. He'd paid Lucy as he might a mistress – or a whore.

"So, if I look so nice take me out to lunch. Or maybe we can –"

Her dark eyes held his. She came closer to him, put her hand on his chest, palm spread against the fine cotton of his shirt, her thumb gently massaging his nipple. In spite of himself, he felt his loins quicken.

He moved away. "I heard you arrive twenty minutes ago."

"Oh, but I've had a phone call, too. Mine was just from Sophie, though."

"I told you yesterday you are not to take personal calls at work. And put that down," as she went to pick up the driftwood unicorn.

"My, my, we did get out of bed the wrong side this morning, didn't we? OK, I'll tell her tonight. She won't do it again, promise."

"Oliver came up to see me before you arrived."

"Oh yes." She spoke carelessly. "What did *he* want?"

"He wanted to give in his notice." Daniel's tone was grim. "He says he can't work with you any more. Actually, he was almost in tears."

"Stupid old fart." Lucy scowled. "I suppose that was about Sophie, too, coming in yesterday. She didn't break anything. She was just –"

"She was just fooling around with every item in the gallery. More by luck than anything, she didn't do any damage."

"Well, all right, I'll tell her that as well, not to come in again. If that's all –"

"It's not. You've been putting him down in front of customers. Oh, he didn't want to tell me –" as her eyes sparked with temper. "I forced it out of him, when he still tried to hand in his resignation. You corrected him in front of some French people."

"Well, they couldn't understand his accent – and he was wrong, anyway. He said that Steve McQueen won last year's Turner prize. I mean –"

"Which he did, actually. Anyway, that's beside the point. We lost the sale as a result."

"Well, don't worry. I'll –"

"And apparently you got other customers laughing at him the other day."

"But it was only a joke. And he was being so stuffy – and old. Honestly, Daniel, the punters, especially the Americans, they don't like it. They prefer someone unstuffy, and young."

"Like Lucy Smith, in fact."

"That's right." She smiled up at him from beneath her lashes. "I've been thinking, Daniel. I don't know whether I want to go to uni after all. Three years – God, what a bore. I could take over here. Oh, I know you'll say I'm too young," though he had said nothing, "but with a superb teacher like you," she smiled a complicit smile, "I'll soon learn. I'm a very quick learner, aren't I?"

Daniel looked at her. "Oliver Paige has forgotten more about fine art than you will ever know, Lucy."

She shrugged. "OK."

"You will apologise to him."

"What for? I told you, it was a joke. Honestly, Daniel, you're getting as stuffy as he is."

"Well, it makes no difference, I suppose."

He took up his jacket, which lay across the sofa, and took out his wallet. Flipping it open, he began counting twenty-pound notes, then folded them over and held them out to her.

"Here you are."

He saw the avarice flare in her eyes for a second, before she looked from his outstretched hand to his face.

"A pressie?" she asked, a shade uncertainly.

"A week's wages in lieu of notice."

"You mean I'm sacked?" She gaped at him in disbelief.

"That's right."

"But you can't do that." Fury and chagrin warred equally in her face.

"Oh, I can, Lucy. I'm sorry – but you see I can't risk losing Oliver. He's much too valuable to me. Please – take it." Daniel just wanted the scene to be over. "No, wait. I'll put it in an envelope for you."

"You needn't bother."

Snatching the money out of his hand, she thrust it into the expensive hessian and gilt bag which he had bought her the previous week. She stood facing him, her pretty face ugly with temper, so that he wondered wearily what he had ever seen in her. Nothing beyond her corrupt sensuality, he thought, and in that moment hated himself.

"I'm sorry, Lucy," he said again. "But just go. Please."

"Oh, don't worry. I'm going." She flounced over to the door. "Good riddance – and if you're listening downstairs, you old fool," she yanked open the door, "good riddance to you, too."

In the doorway, she turned. "Oh, by the way – that phone call from Sophie. Don't you want to know what it was about?"

"Not really, no."

"It was to tell me that Rose Ashenby's precious little niece has run off with Jamie Brinkworth."

As Daniel stared at her, blank-eyed, she tossed over her shoulder, just before she banged the door, "So whoever she's thinking about just now, it's not you, Daniel darling."

CHAPTER FIFTEEN

Leo stubbed out yet another cigarette. She tried to make her glance at the clock unobtrusive, but caught Rose's eye.

"For heaven's sake, stop biting your nails," she said irritably.

"Sorry." Rose began tapping the table again.

"I'll get us some lunch. Oh, all right," as she saw Rose's expression, "I can't face food either." She was resting her elbow on the drawings she had been working on earlier. "You haven't seen these."

"Oh yes, very nice." Rose surveyed the sheet apathetically.

"They're for Steve."

"Steve? Oh, yes."

"I said I'd give him some for his mother. He'll be back in a few days, so I thought I'd better get on with them."

"Yes."

"I suppose he'll be off to Virginia then."

"Yes."

"Oh, God." Her voice cracking, Leo leapt to her feet. "I can't stand this waiting about. Where the hell *are* they? And where the hell's my car?"

"Look, borrow my van to go to that client." Rose began digging in her pockets for her keys.

"No – no, thanks, love. I do appreciate it, but I just can't think about work." She looked across at Rose, whose pale face was taut with strain and worry. "And I'm not leaving you. We'll sweat it out together. I'll give him a ring, put it off till tomorrow."

She went through to the tiny former scullery which acted as her office.

"Can you bring my glasses? I may as well at least check my e-mails while I'm here."

Rose leaned over her shoulder as the screen came to life.

"Yes, you've got some," she said. "Three messages unread."

Leo brought up the first. "Oh, well, that's saved me a phone call. He doesn't want to proceed with the job, anyway." She clicked 'delete'. "Oh, great," as the second message appeared. "That book idea I had – remember?" Rose nodded mutely. "Garden Design in Winter. They like the outline I sent them, look. Brilliant – it'll keep poor old Leo off the streets for a bit longer."

The third message was very brief. Both women peered at it then turned to each other, their faces rigid with shock. Leo clicked 'print' and snatched up the sheet almost before it emerged from the printer. She skimmed through it then, without a word, handed it to Rose, who read it through twice; once fast, once very slowly.

"Dear Mum, Your car is in the multi-storey near New Street Station. You'll need your spare keys. Don't worry about us. I'm sorry. Thanks for everything. Love, Jamie. P.S. Emily says don't worry, Rose. Love xxxxxxxxx"

She handed it back. "Don't worry, Rose." Her voice shook with equal fear and anger. "What the hell am I going to do?" She sank down into the nearest chair and raised a distraught face to Leo. "I'll have to tell Roddie. Oh, God."

"All that Roddie will do is have kittens all over the place, and that won't help anybody. He thinks Emily's here with you, so that gives us a few days, at least."

"But should I go to the police? I mean, I know Jamie's your son, but –"

"The police? Of course not," Leo said sharply. "She's sixteen – they just wouldn't want to know. No, you – *we* have got to do something for ourselves."

She held up the e-mail, scrutinising it closely.

Rose gave a bitter laugh. "You won't find any clues there, Sherlock Holmes."

"Well, actually, I have." Leo tapped the page with her finger. "The sender's address, look – fivewaysintercaf. That'll be a cyber café – and Five Ways is just round the corner from Edgbaston, where that squat is. And it was sent," she peered more closely. "Oh, hell, I don't believe it. It was sent at eleven forty-two this morning – while we were sitting around here, doing nothing. God, what a fool I've been – though I could hardly have dragged him down the phone wire, I suppose."

"No, but they'll be back at that squat now." Rose was heading for the door. "Come on."

"Maybe – maybe not. They know we'll be after them as soon as I read the e-mail – and my car's at New Street Station, remember."

"Oh, of course." Rose slumped back into despair. "They could be on their way to anywhere by now – London, Cornwall, Scotland.

"Oh, Leo, you don't think they're heading for Gretna Green, do you?"

"Oh, for Christ's sake, Rose! Sorry, sorry, love, but we've got to keep calm – and *think*."

"Can we go to the squat?"

"I don't have the address, and Edgbaston's a big place. But at least we can make a start at that cyber café. Maybe they can tell us something."

"Yes, perhaps." Rose brightened slightly. "Will they remember them, though?"

"Well, it's only – what? – three hours ago. And I've got these." She picked up a sheaf of photographs. "I took a roll of film last week in that garden near Cheltenham that I did a couple of years ago. It's maturing very nicely now. Anyway, I came back past Lettie's place, and Jamie was there, and Emily. Sorry," as she saw Rose's face, "but I honestly thought you knew. I had a couple of shots left and suddenly thought, I haven't got a photo of Jamie since his last school one, and that was pretty dire. So," she was riffling through the pile, "here they are."

She handed two photographs to Rose. She studied them. In both, there was Jamie, leaning against the tree from which Lettie had fallen, dogs all round him, one licking his face; he was half-fending it off, laughing. Emily was in the background, looking not at the dogs, but at Jamie.

Rose caught her breath. How could she have failed to spot it? Sheer naked adoration showed in the girl's face, a kind of yearning. She was almost physically leaning towards him. Feeling very old suddenly – and very disturbed – she handed them back.

"We'll take these with us." Leo looked down at them. "Hmm, they're good of Jamie, the little sod." She shook her head. "Just wait till I catch up with him."

But by then the damage will be done, thought Rose. Roddie would know ... her parents ... Feeling sick, she followed Leo out of the room.

"Mustn't forget my car keys."

As Leo lifted them down, the phone rang. She turned and snatched it up.

"Hello. Oh, it's you, Daniel." Rose jumped. "No, you wouldn't have. She's been here since morning. Well, keep it brief – we're just

off." She held out the receiver. "He wants to speak to you."
Rose took it reluctantly. "Hello, Daniel."
"Rose." He spoke rather stiffly. In fact, there was a wariness in both their voices, a remembrance of their last parting. "Have you found her?"
"How did you know?"
"Bad news travels fast, I'm afraid."
But of course, it would have been Sophie, wetting her knickers to let her big sister know.
"No, she hasn't turned up," she said, even more coolly. "Leo and I are going into Birmingham. They sent a message from an internet café this morning. Not that they'll still be there, of course, but it's better than just sitting around here."
"Is there anything I can do?"
"Well, thank you, Daniel. It's very kind of you, of course –"
"Kind?" The anger came down the line. "Oh, for God's sake, Rose –"
"– but I don't think there is. I'm not sure there's anything anyone can do."
"Well – I won't hold you up. Goodbye. Oh, Rose," as she went to put down the phone.
"What?"
"Drive carefully."

Rose, following Leo's car, saw her brake. She pulled in behind her, got out and they each fed their meters.
"It should be just round the corner."
Leo led the way back along the side street and out into the roar of early rush hour in Broad Street. A dull headache had settled round Rose's forehead and she winced at the noise.
The café, though, when they went in, was quiet. Nearly all the terminals were occupied – Rose saw an elderly woman at one, half-eaten sandwich in her hand, scrolling through lists of names, and at another a young man with a mongrel dog asleep at his feet – but all the tables were empty. A girl with lank mousy hair was wiping down the counter in a half-hearted manner. When she gave them their coffees, Leo held out the photographs to her.
"Do you remember these two people?"
The girl barely glanced at them. "No."

"Please," said Rose. "It's very urgent. They were in here this morning, sending an e-mail."

"Surprise, surprise." Surly now.

"The lad was tall, thin – probably wearing a dark coat. The girl – what would Emily have been wearing, Rose?"

"I've no idea. Jeans, probably – yes, I'm almost certain – and a T-shirt."

"Like all those, you mean?"

The girl jerked a scornful thumb at the row of jeans and T-shirts crouched over the VDU's. Leo opened her wallet, took out a five pound note, folded it ostentatiously and slid it across the counter.

"Service charge," she said brightly. "Now can you remember?"

"Sorry, I wasn't here this morning. But, hold on –" as Leo went to withdraw the note, "Winston was, and I think he's still out the back."

She disappeared through the swing door then returned a few moments later, a young black man in a yellow sweatshirt at her heels. He nodded to them, took the photographs, peered at them.

"Yeah, they was in today."

We know that. Rose wanted to bang the counter, but a glance from Leo kept her silent.

"About half eleven. Wasn't here long – just bought half an hour's worth on the terminals."

"And they only sent the one e-mail?"

"Right." He looked up sharply, his dark eyes suspicious. "You aren't police, are you?"

"Good grief, no." Leo laughed. "But we do need to get in touch with them."

"Yeah, well, I definitely remember them. The girl, she looked – well, she was only a kid. Very polite, though; asked me for tea, said she hated coffee. Then they left together. Sorry, that's all I can tell you."

"That's fine." The note slid once more across the counter. "Thanks for your help."

Outside, they looked at each other.

"Well, that didn't achieve much," said Rose.

"On the contrary, at least we know it *was* them, not someone else on their behalf."

"Yes, that's true. Emily won't touch coffee, I know that."

"But where now?"

They began walking slowly back in the direction of their vehicles. Rose, whose spirits had lifted slightly as long as she thought she was *doing* something, felt a weight of depression settled on her. It was like a nightmare: all these people, hurrying past on their way home from work, their faces intent; unknowing, uncaring of Emily; a nightmare, but she was already awake.

"Hang about."

They turned and saw a young man, with a dog on a long piece of rough string. They both tightened their grips on their bags, but he only said, "I was in there – in the café."

"Oh, yes, I remember your dog."

Rose put out her hand, but the dog curled back its top lip at her.

"Don't touch him. He doesn't like people."

"Oh."

"When he was a pup, he was set alight by some skinheads – just for a laugh."

"Oh, no. The poor thing."

Both women regarded the dog, which ignored them.

"He's lovely now," Rose said, for though the young man looked thin and gaunt, the dog was glossy and well-groomed.

"Yeah, well – he's my friend. Ain't you, Butch?" He bent to pat the shining head, and the animal gave him a look of pure love. Exactly the way Emily was looking at Jamie in the photographs, Rose realised suddenly. "He keeps people away. Anyway, I heard you back there. I'm a mate of Jamie's."

"Then you know where they've gone?" They spoke simultaneously.

"No. Only that they were off to New Street Station. They said it was better if we didn't know – and I wouldn't tell you, if we did. I don't split on my mates."

He said this with a proud lift of his head. Rose looked at him: his tattered clothes; his pinched, rather stupid face; the eyes which, like Jamie's, had already seen far more of life than she had. Poor lad, he had precious little to be proud about. The previous winter, in an effort at self-improvement, she had taken up with Charles Dickens. All at once, she thought, Dickens would have recognised this boy; his brothers moved like furtive shadows through his novels.

"Well, will you take us to the squat?" Leo asked, as they

reached the vehicles.

He laughed, without humour. "No point. When I came away, the bailiffs were just breaking down the door. We're moving on. I've been letting some mates know we're coming."

"And you're quite sure Jamie and Emily aren't with you?"

He scowled. "I told you, didn't I?"

"Can we give you a lift back there, then?"

"No." He seemed to shrink from the idea. "Well, I'll be getting back, then. Cheers."

"Wait a moment." Rose fumbled in her bag then took out a ten-pound note. "Let me give you this – for the dog," she added, as he looked at it warily.

"Well – OK."

He slipped the note into his pocket and went off down the pavement, the dog trotting beside him.

"You really shouldn't have done that, you know," Leo said, shaking her head. "He'll only spend it on drugs."

"What?"

"Didn't you see the marks on his arm?"

"No."

"Well, too bad." She was unlocking her car door. "And we didn't even find out his name. I could have told Jamie," she grimaced, "*when* I catch up with him, that he didn't split on his mate."

"Do you think he was telling the truth – about them not being at the squat, I mean?"

"Yes, I think so. My car was at New Street, as Jamie said, and if they'd got wind of the bailiffs moving in, he wouldn't have wanted Emily to be involved."

"Oh, of course. I was forgetting just how chivalrous he is."

Leo gave her a level look. "There's no point in fighting with me, Rose. We're in this together."

"Yes, of course we are." Rose clasped one of Leo's hands in both of hers. "I'm sorry, really I am. It's just – it's just getting to me so I can't think straight."

"Me too." Leo squeezed her hands then released them. "Well, what now?"

"New Street?" said Rose, hopelessly.

"Nobody's going to remember them there, and anyway they'll

be miles away by now."

"But what are they doing for money?"

"Well, Jamie gets his giro every week – and he's been living virtually for free lately."

"Of course." And Emily had barely touched the spending money she'd arrived with, plus her grandmother's tenner, and what she'd given her – to treat her sisters at Southwold! "So they'll be able to keep going; for a while, at least."

"Afraid so." Leo was silent for a moment. "Well, nothing for it but to go back home, I suppose."

But Rose didn't want to go home. She didn't want to go home ever again.

"Unless – Leo," she clutched her arm, "do you remember the name of the club they went to?"

Leo wrinkled her brow. "Um – you said the Gemini, didn't you?"

"That's it. Well, what say we go on there? You never know; someone might remember something."

"Oh, Rose." Leo shook her head. "You're chasing shadows, love."

"You go home." Rose spoke with sudden energy. "I just must try it, Leo. I – I have this funny feeling that someone – a doorman, or a barman or somebody – will have overheard something."

"And you're going dressed like that?"

Rose looked down at her jeans and crumpled shirt, the things she had climbed into aeons ago – was it only that morning? – to go round to Sophie's house. She glanced at her watch.

"Perhaps I can still buy a dress." Her gaze wandered to the shop front beside them, with its display of brilliant butterfly-like saris.

"No, I don't think so." Leo stood for a moment. "You may be right, though. Maybe we ought to try absolutely everything before we give up. Wait a sec."

She reached into the car for her mobile, checked in her little book and punched out a number.

"Hi, Cassie. It's Leo here." There was a minor torrent of squawks from the other end. "Yes – well, sort of. You all right? ... Good. The thing is, a friend and I are just round the corner from you, and we badly need help. Thanks, Cassie – you're a star."

She rang off. "Come on."

"But where are we going?" Rose stood irresolute.

"You, my child, are about to see how the other half lives. Cassie's an interior designer. I met her a couple of years ago when she was making over a house in Solihull and I was doing the garden, and we've kept in touch ever since. She doesn't actually *need* to work – her husband has to be one of the wealthiest men in the Midlands – but she says it keeps her little grey cells active. Like growing vegetable marrows," she added but Rose did not take the allusion. "She's got a wardrobe full of clothes – she'll lend us something. Oh, just one thing. Don't ask her where she comes from in the States – she's Canadian, and a teeny bit sensitive to questions like that."

Rose drove behind Leo, struggling to keep her mind on the swirling traffic. Surely, this was all a waste of time. Wasn't Leo really right, that they should be on their way home now, she bracing herself to ring Roddie? Leo was only doing this to humour her. Probably she felt a twinge of guilt. After all, Jamie was her son. Why had she ever invited Emily?

She was vaguely aware that they had turned off the main road and were driving down a tree-lined side street. They passed a church, turned again; then Leo braked and slowed to a crawl. Rose could see that she was looking at something; looking at a group of people on the pavement in front of an imposing red brick house, its security gates wide open. A tattered banner was hanging from one of the upstairs rooms. She couldn't read it, and in any case, at that moment it was snatched inside by a pair of hands. Two police vans were drawn up near several beaten-up trucks. There were several dogs with the huddled group, all growling, hackles up.

And there was the young man from the café. He saw her at the same instant, but there was not a flicker of recognition in his eyes. Another man followed his gaze, caught her eye, made an obscene gesture in her direction then turned away. A girl, fair hair to the shoulders, a pale blue T-shirt – just like one of Emily's. Rose's heart leapt, but then the girl, as if sensing her stare, turned and Rose saw the baby that she was clutching.

This was where Jamie had brought Emily. She closed her eyes for an instant. If Roddie ever found out, he wouldn't have kittens, he'd have full-blown cats.

Leo accelerated away, and Rose followed.

CHAPTER SIXTEEN

"And I'm coming into Birmingham again next week, so I'll drop our outfits off then."

"No sweat, Leo."

Cassie opened the front door. She was a slim, blonde woman, covered in that unmistakable trans-Atlantic gloss which, in some intangible way, set her apart from them, even though, Rose thought, it was her clothes they were wearing.

From behind a half-closed door at the far end of the huge, tiled hall came a shout of laughter, raised voices.

"God, I wish I was coming with you guys. Bloody dinner parties. Oh, Gareth, Arabella, hi there." A couple loomed on the doorstep. "Great to see you again. Arabella, you look stunning," as the woman bent to kiss her. "What an absolutely gorgeous dress. Go on through."

Rose felt herself and Leo subjected to a swift appraisal, then dismissed, and with a nod and a half-smile the pair went off down the hall.

"Utter assholes, the pair of them," Cassie remarked, only slightly *sotto voce*. "He's fucking his secretary like there's no tomorrow, and she's got the hots for her ice-skating instructor. I tell you, guys, she spends most of her time on her back these days. Well," she grinned at them, blue eyes sparkling with wickedness, "that ice just gets slippier and slippier."

Leo laughed. "Thanks, Cassie – for everything."

"Forget it. And mind how you go, you babes in the wood, you – all on your own in the wicked city."

"We will." Rose managed a smile. "Thank you, Cassie. I'm really grateful."

"Sure. And look, Rose, try not to worry too much. Kids these days – well, they're just a different breed. I mean, my step-daughters – I kid you not –"

A door banged open. "Cass, Josie wants to know where the hell the black olives are."

"In the big fridge, Eddie, *darling*. Like I told you." She winked at the two women, then patted Rose's arm. "Well, good luck. Let me know how it goes."

As they walked across the drive, another car swept in with a flurry of gravel and another couple got out.

"Babs, Malcolm, lovely to see you both. Come on in." Then, as Rose unlocked her van door, "Don't forget, I can't wait for that scarecrow. I'll ring you next week."

Rose heard the woman say, "A *scarecrow*? Darling, what do you mean? Don't tell me you're going into veggies in a big way. I mean, this *is* Edg –" and the door closed.

"Well." In the sudden silence, Leo looked at Rose. "Time to go, I'm afraid. Once more unto the breach, as the Bard said – or was it Longfellow?"

"Mmm." Rose, who had once been an ardent clubber, wished now that they were setting off for home.

"God," Leo grimaced. "From where I'm standing, we look like a couple of fellers in drag."

She was resplendent in a black velvet top and crêpe pants which, as Cassie was several inches shorter than her, hugged her crotch like clingfilm, whilst Rose wore a pink silk dress which ended several inches above the knees and did nothing for her gingery curls. The illusion of glamour was also rather spoilt by their both being in leather mules, as Cassie's feet were a couple of sizes smaller then theirs. But as she'd said, they weren't aiming to spend long on the dance floor.

"Well," Leo yanked at her trousers again. "let's go."

The noise was deafening. It seemed to be not only all round her, but inside her, so that Rose was not sure whether it was the beat throbbing, or her temples. She leaned her head back against the wall and glanced at Leo, who was nursing her glass, palm down on it as Cassie had instructed. "You don't want anyone slipping anything in it when you're not looking, do you?" Sensing Rose's eyes on her she grimaced, shrugged, then seemed to go back into her gloomy thoughts.

There was almost no light, except for the wandering strobe beams, which picked out dancers, occasional faces, and wreathing mists of cigarette smoke, so that the whole room had taken on a quality of unreality.

She reached into her bag for a tissue to mop her brow and her fingers encountered the crinkled edge of one of the photographs. It was a waste of time, of course. The two young men at the entrance, where they had had to pay a membership fee and sign in, had barely looked at it – in the dim light they could hardly have seen anyway – and disclaimed all knowledge.

They'd also refused to let her look back through the book, not that that would have been the least bit of use; except that it would have been just one tiny concrete thing. She could have run her finger over their signatures and somehow felt for a comforting moment that they brought Emily closer. But that was nonsense, of course. And the waitress, with a pretty, plump face, who'd brought them their obligatory drinks, had made a pretence of looking, but shaken her head.

There were two women sitting at the next table. Just maybe. She took out the photographs and tapped the one sitting with her back to Leo.

"Excuse me." She had to raise her voice to make herself heard. "I wonder if you –" Her voice tailed away as the woman turned and revealed, in spite of the heavy make-up, an unmistakably masculine face. "– if you've seen this girl in here," she finished in her normal voice.

The man did not look at the photograph, only shook his head and turned away, frowning. Rose caught Leo's eye. They exchanged a glance, then Leo bent forward.

"I think we may as well go," she shouted in her ear.

Rose nodded. "Let's just listen to this one. I quite like it – if it wasn't so loud. What is it, do you know?"

"It's Abba, I think." Leo spoke into her ear again. "They always have the best music, gay clubs."

Rose sat back, her toe tapping to the beat. In the clear centre of the room, couples were dancing and she watched them idly. Arms, legs, moving against the swirling, insubstantial background, they seemed like creatures in an underwater ballet. The coloured lights struck here a profile, there a hand, a gleaming shoulder. A white T-shirt took on a red tinge, a black sweater was etched with gold, a swirl of midnight sequins glittered and turned to fire

She looked with closer attention. The dress was of dark blue silk, which gleamed in a thousand little points of light. The woman was dancing with a tall, thin man in a dark shirt and jeans. Her blonde hair caught the light, glittered, was lost once more. When the strobe circled onto the dance floor again, the woman had turned, was facing her. She swung back her heavy mane of hair, laughing, looked directly at Rose, herself now caught momentarily in the light, past her, then back at her.

She might not even then have recognised him beneath the mask of make-up, if it had not been for the horror in his eyes. They stared at one another, the shock which each felt mirrored in the other's face. The light left them but when, half a minute later, it caught them again, they were still staring at one another.

Rose sat, stunned, her mind blank of everything except this one thing. Only when the track ended and the dancing stopped, did she rouse herself. Snatching up her bag and mumbling something about, "Must get out," she pushed her way to the exit.

When Leo caught up with her, she was leaning against the wall, taking in gulps of warm, dirty city air as though it were a life-saving elixir. She felt dizzy, as if she was going to faint.

"Rose, what's wrong?" Leo's face was puckered with concern. "That bloody drink – it tasted like pigshit."

Rose put a hand to her mouth. "No."

Two people – men? women? – passed them with curious glances, on their way into the club.

"It must be that – on top of an empty stomach. You should have let Cassie –"

"*No,* it's not the drink."

Rose spoke through clenched teeth. She retched, clutched her mouth again. But she couldn't tell Leo. In the depths of her misery, she could not spew out another's secret. Oh, God – *Christo.*

Just in time, Leo dragged her into a narrow alleyway beside the club, and Rose threw up, voiding everything in her insides, back to the breakfast at Leo's. Finally, her throat and mouth burning with acid, her eyes smarting, she leaned her clammy forehead against the brick wall. In silence, she took the wad of tissues which Leo handed her, wiped her face and mouth.

"Sorry." She straightened up, gave Leo a pale smile. "You're right – must have been that drink."

Leo scrutinised her. She looked terrible, her face deathly white, so that even in the pale summer twilight her freckles stood out. There was a sheen over her face. Poor Rose. God, when she got a hold of Jamie. She dug in her bag and brought out a miniature brandy bottle. Breaking the seal, she held it out.

"Get a swig of this down you."

"No, it won't –"

"Yes. It'll settle whatever's wrong, I promise you." She raised the bottle to Rose's lips.

"That better?"

"Yes." Rose wearily straightened up.

"Come on, then." Leo put a hand on her arm. "Let's get you home. Sure you can drive?"

"Yes."

"You'd better follow me out to the motorway."

"Thanks. And then you go on. No, I'll be all right, honestly. I don't like travelling in convoy, you know that."

"Well, if you're sure."

"Yes – quite sure."

Quite sure that she did not even want Leo to be in the car in front of her, sure that she needed to be totally alone.

CHAPTER SEVENTEEN

Rose pushed away her plate, the second round of toast untouched, and went slowly back upstairs. In her bedroom, Cassie's pink dress lay where she had flung it last night, across the back of a chair. She lifted it, sniffed and pulled a face. Turning it inside out, she looked at the label. She could have it dry-cleaned, thank God. Beyond this simple thought, her mind, as if bludgeoned, was blank.

Slipping off her dressing gown, she showered, standing under the jet until it ran cold, then dried herself and pulled on her jeans. She reached out a shirt from the wardrobe, saw that it was buttoned up and, without bothering to undo it, dragged it over her head. As she tugged her hair free, the sound of a car pulling into the yard reached her.

She groaned aloud. Leo, come to see how she was. How was she? Good question. Crossing to the window, she looked down and saw her father locking the doors of the blue Volvo, her mother advancing purposefully down the path.

"Oh, *no*. I don't believe it."

Of all the days. Her parents never came just on the off chance of finding her in. But surely they didn't know about Susan – or Emily? Just that morning, Roddie had again assured her that he wouldn't tell them.

Her mother was just knocking for a second time when she opened the door.

"Hello, Mum."

"Hello, Rosemary." A perfunctory peck.

"Morning, Dad." He inclined his cheek for her kiss. "Go on through. I'll be with you in a sec."

In the kitchen, she cleared away her breakfast things, swilled the dish and plate at the sink, giving herself a few moments to compose herself. When she went into the sitting room, her parents were in the two armchairs. They were both, unusually silent, her father lost in contemplation of his clasped hands, her mother flipping through her scarecrow portfolio, which had been lying on the sofa. When Rose came in, she closed it and put it on the side table, making no comment.

"Would you like a cup of tea?"

"No thank you."

"Dad?"

"What? Oh not for me."

"Well," Rose perched on the arm of the sofa, "this is a pleasant surprise."

"A surprise?" retorted her mother. "What's so surprising about us wanting to know what's been going on?"

"What do you mean?" Rose asked cautiously.

"Roddie rang us earlier."

"Oh, for heaven's sake!" All her sympathy for her benighted brother-in-law vanished like snow in the sunshine. Trust bloody Roddie, insensitive as ever, not to spare them –and drop her in it at the same time. "He shouldn't have."

"Of course he should," her mother said sharply. "And what we want to know – don't we, dear? – is what on earth you've been doing with Emily?"

Rose stared at her. "What have I been doing with Emily? What have *I* been doing?" she repeated, her voice rising.

"I knew it would end badly, her staying with you. I told your father so at the time. The girl was thrown too much on her own devices. You neglected her."

Rose, who had been hourly castigating herself with the self-same reproach, heard her temper begin to sizzle quietly.

"I thought when she came to see us that she was very quiet – not at all her usual happy self. I know teenagers can have their off times – goodness knows, we had enough worries with you – but Emily's never been any trouble, till now. And this young man she's gone off with – Roddie said he's Leonora Brinkworth's son."

"That's right."

"Well, I've always thought that was a very undesirable household."

The sizzling boiled over. "Leo, as you know full well, mother, is my closest friend."

"Yes, well –" She caught her daughter's eye and stopped.

After all the traumas of yesterday, and a second sleepless night, Rose quite suddenly could not take any more petty point-scoring. She took a deep breath.

"Let's get one thing straight, can we? However much I might have *neglected* her, Emily did not run away from *me*. She's run away because she couldn't face going back home, to that bloody family you're so besotted with."

"*Rosemary!*"

"I mean, you can't really blame Emily, can you, when her mother obviously hated it so much?"

She saw a strange expression flit across her mother's face and realised that two astonishing things had been happening simultaneously. First, her mother had been dominating the conversation, with her father saying barely a word, and second, they had been talking for over ten minutes and Susan had not been mentioned once. Roddie, yes ... Emily, yes ... but Susan? Did they know? Had Roddie, out of pride, of course, managed to spare them that much, at least?

"Um – have you been down there recently?" she asked. "To see them, I mean?"

"Not since we called on our way back from Bournemouth," her mother replied, more hesitantly. "We've been so busy lately."

"Yes, of course."

"Why didn't you tell us?"

"Tell you what?"

"About poor Susan, of course. I asked you to go because I was worried about her, and you said everything was fine."

There was just enough truth in that for Rose to bite her tongue on an angry retort.

Instead, she said, "I told you, if you remember, that she was depressed, but I tried to spare you the rest. I didn't want to upset you."

"But I'm her mother. I could have gone across, talked to her, found out what was wrong."

"And everything would have been all right, I suppose? No," Rose shook her head, "it's not as simple as that, I'm afraid. But you mustn't blame yourself, Mum."

"Blame myself? Of course I'm not blaming myself. I told you – you shouldn't have kept it from me."

Something snapped inside Rose. That something was all the years that she had tried to please her parents, all the years that she had encountered only criticism, when everything she had ever done had been slapped down. And now, by some sleight of hand, far too subtle for her to detect, 'poor' Susan's defection was also to be put down to her. All these things twined themselves up inside her, and snapped.

She leapt up, her arms folded across her chest, and glowered at her mother.

"All right then, it's my fault that Emily's gone, my fault that Susan's gone. I suppose you're going to say next that it's my fault that darling Roddie's been stuffing that dear, sweet little Birgitta you were so fond of."

"Don't be ridiculous, Rosemary." Her mother's face flushed. "And don't be so – so *crude*, either."

"Didn't it cross your mind to wonder why she left so suddenly if she was so wonderful? Well, the truth is she was booted out by Susan, who caught them at it on the kitchen table." She rode over her mother's gasp of outrage. "The truth is that that family, which in your eyes can never do any wrong, is riven clean down the middle. All the children know. Do you want to know what Emily said to me?"

"No, please."

Her mother held up her hands and Rose, seeing the expression on her face, relented. Half-ashamed of herself, she went on more gently, "I'm sorry, but you shouldn't have blamed me. If there's any blame, it lies with that darling son-in-law of yours. The only wonder is that Susan has put up with him for so long."

"Have you any idea where she's gone?" Her father's voice, so thin and hollow, jolted Rose and, for the first time, she really looked at him. He was very pale, and when she glanced across at her mother, she too was pale – or maybe it was simply that, for just about the only time that Rose could remember, she had no make-up on, while her hair looked as if it had, for once in its life, escaped the heated rollers. They both looked utterly shell-shocked – and also, quite suddenly, old. Bloody Roddie, she thought grimly. But of course she was being unreasonable. How could something like this have been kept from them?

"No, Dad," she said quietly, "I'm sorry, but I don't know. Look, are you sure you don't want a cup of tea, either of you?"

"No, thank you." Her mother was getting to her feet. "Come along, John."

Rose nobly suppressed the thought of all the work she wanted to bury herself in. "But you don't have to hurry away, surely. I will make a drink, and there's a cake in the fridge." She'd bought it for Emily's last day, but it hadn't been touched.

"No, we must go. We're going on to Roddie, to see if there is anything at all we can do."

Which, if you had any family feelings at all, was the clear implication, you would have done already.

"Well, if you're sure you can't stop," said Rose. "I am rather busy, in fact."

"Busy?" her mother said sharply. "How can you work at a time like this?"

"I spent all of yesterday searching for Emily and got nowhere. If there was anything else I could do, I would do it. And I do have my living to earn."

"But surely you'll be able to get down in a day or so." Mrs Ashenby had taken up her handbag.

"Whatever for? He has an excellent new nanny, Miss Somebody or other, and there's the home help, of course. I presume she's still coming in five days a week, so he certainly doesn't need me. And I'm sure you wouldn't want me to have Abigail and Cordelia staying here. In any case, I'm going away at the weekend. I've been invited to hold master classes at a Scarecrow Convention down in Devon."

Ignoring their astonished expressions, she escorted them to the front door. But just as she opened it, another vehicle drew up alongside the Volvo. Rose felt the blood drain from her face as Christo got out and stood watching them come down the path towards him.

CHAPTER EIGHTEEN

For a split second, seeing him dressed in his slightly old-fashioned corduroy trousers and short-sleeved shirt, his familiar face which, only in this instant did Rose finally realise had become very dear to her, for just that second the memory of how he had looked the previous night faded to a shadow in her mind.

She saw her mother's eyes skim Christo, his clothes, his car, then saw her smile at him.

"Well, Rosemary, aren't you going to introduce us?"

"Oh, yes. Christo, my mother and father." She turned to them. "This is Christopher Mallory, a friend of mine."

"Delighted to meet you, Mr Mallory." Mrs Ashenby shook hands warmly. "Do you live locally?"

"No. Over the border in Oxfordshire, actually."

"And what do you do?" She gave a light laugh. "Nothing to do with scarecrows, I hope?"

"Well," he glanced at Rose, "I suppose I do, in a manner of speaking. I farm."

"Ah, I see." And it was clear that she did. As Rose's toes began to curl with embarrassment, she gave him an even more effusive smile. "You really must talk to my husband some time. He has very strong views on the state of farming and the what is it? Oh yes, the Common Agricultural Policy. Don't you, John?"

"What? Oh yes, certainly."

"You must get Rosemary to bring you to lunch. She's very remiss, I'm afraid, over introducing us to her friends." Rose, remembering the ice-chamber that had been her parents' sitting room when she had first taken Ryan to meet them, could barely repress a hysterical shriek. "Yes, what about next Sunday?"

Christo looked at Rose for a long moment, as though reading her eyes, then, still watching her, said, "I'm sorry, Mrs Ashenby, but I'm going to be very busy for the next few weeks. Harvest, you know."

"But of course. How silly of me."

Her husband cleared his throat. "Well, we must be on our way. Nice to have met you, Mr, er, Mallory."

Rose stood at the gate, waving till they were out of sight, then turned slowly back.

"Christo," she said abruptly. "Why have you come?"

"Can we talk inside?" He gave her a wry half-smile.

Without another word, she led the way into the kitchen, hesitated, then went on into the sitting room.

"Please – sit down." She gestured to an armchair.

"Thank you."

"Would you like a drink? Coffee? Tea? Or I've got some beer."

"Nothing for me, thank you. It's green tea, I hope."

"What?"

"Green tea – what you were offering me. Sorry," as she stared at him blankly, "I've always gone in for gallows humour, I'm afraid."

Bugsy, who as usual had made himself scarce when her parents arrived, was now ensconced in the chair facing Christo. Rose picked him up and, ignoring his protests, knelt on the window seat and gently deposited him in the flower bed outside. She sat down on the cushion warmed by his furry body.

"The famous Bugsy, I presume."

"Yes."

"But no more koi carp?"

"What? Oh, no." She gave him the ghost of a smile. "Um, how are the dogs?"

"Oh, fine. Yes, fine."

In the howling silence between them, Rose's sharp hearing could pick out tiny sounds. Sparrows in the ancient branches of the pear tree which grew against the wall, the faint tick-tock of the clock – a small, beautiful clock of blue glass which Daniel had brought back from Venice years ago, a fly buzzing softly. On the table beside her, one of the flowers fell from the bunch of white foxgloves which she had picked a couple of days before. She took it up. Creamy-white outside, with exquisite greenish-gold freckles inside. If she were a painter ...

"Rose."

She looked up sharply. "Sorry, I – oh, Christo, why did you come?"

"Not sure – except that I wanted to try to set things right with you."

"But it doesn't matter."

"Of course it does," he said roughly. "It matters more than anything. Please, Rose."

When she spread her hands in acquiescence, he hesitated, then,

"When you found – the clothes, and came down, I thought you'd guessed, you see. It was only after you'd gone that I realised you'd jumped to the wrong conclusion. You were angry because you thought I'd got a mistress. Ironic really, isn't it?" His sensitive mouth twisted. "I could hardly ring you, could I, and say, Rose, you've totally misunderstood. I haven't got a mistress, so everything's all right. Those are *my* clothes, my very own – for when I feel like wearing them."

"Please, Christo." Rose leapt out of her chair and went to lean against the mantelpiece, her hand shielding her face. "Don't do this. I don't want to know – and I'm sure you don't want to tell me."

"Not really, no. But I have to."

"But – why?"

"Why does one part of me want to wear them? God knows. The buzz of adrenaline I get in an otherwise predictable life? The risk of being found out? Perhaps – although in other ways Birmingham's ideal, of course. Way off my – usual patch."

"I see."

"But it's not," another rueful smile, "quite far enough."

"No," she said quietly.

"Tell me, Rose, what on earth were you doing there last night? I somehow didn't think clubs were your scene."

"No, they're not; not these days, anyway. I was there looking for my niece."

"Emily?"

"Yes. Two days ago, when I –" she looked down into the empty grate "– wasn't here, she ran away."

"Oh, no! But why?"

"Oh, it's a long story. But we knew that she and the boy she's gone with were at that club last week and – and that's why I was there." Their eyes met then looked away, as each shied from the recollection. "It was no use, of course. No-one remembered them. Oh, Christo, it's such a mess. I wanted to keep it from Roddie – her father – but he rang this morning, asking to speak to her, so I had to tell him." She put her hand to her mouth. "He was terribly upset, of course, but he was furious, too – with me – he said it was all my fault. Which it is, I know. And now my parents have found out. Oh God, I can't bear it."

"Oh, my poor girl." Christo half got up out of his chair but then,

152

seeing her flinch, dropped back into it. "Do you have any other leads, anywhere else to look for her?"

"Not really. All we can do is hope she comes back soon. She's supposed to be starting at Sixth Form College next month, but – Anyway, that's my problem." She dashed away a tear which had trickled onto her cheek. "I'm sorry, I interrupted you."

"No, I must go." He stood up. "If I can't be of any help, I won't intrude any further."

"No, sit down, Christo. Tell me – please."

"Well, if you're quite sure?" When she nodded, "I wanted you to try and understand." That wry half-smile again. "Somehow, it's very important for me that you of all people try to understand, Rose. It began when I was at school. I wasn't brilliant at anything else, but I was a surprisingly good actor." He was flicking his thumbnail against the upholstery. "Any parts, really, I enjoyed, but I realised quite soon that I particularly liked women's roles – Titania in the *Dream* – and the local paper said my Beatrice had definite echoes of Maggie Smith. Later, I wasn't very happy about what I was doing, although it's never been that often – you must believe that, Rose. I struggled to break the habit, but eventually – well, I learnt to live with my secret." His mouth twisted. "I suppose you could say, I'm still a good actor. For years, I resisted all the females my mother put in my way for me to trip over, told myself I was happy as I was. And then –" He got up and went over to sit on the windowsill, looking out over the garden.

"And then, one afternoon, I was in the office, feeling jaded, sick to the heart with Life, with myself – I was staring out through the blinds, when a young woman came into view. I watched her pick up one of the little fallen apples, smoothing it over and over with her thumb. Then, just when I thought she was moving away, she noticed the bed of lilies under the office window. She looked around, guiltily –" the faint smile in his voice tore Rose's heart "– then hopped over the rope and went all along the row, smelling every single lily, solemnly, like a child. I could hear her sniffing, even a tiny sigh of rapture. When she finally straightened up, I saw that her nose was covered in pollen dust – and in that moment, Rose, I fell totally, hopelessly in love with her. I wanted her, and I felt that there was nothing in my life before that I had ever wanted a quarter as much."

"Please, don't." Rose's voice broke on the word.
"So now you know. Oh, don't look like that, my darling – please – and I swear I would try to give it up, if you would only – couldn't you possibly –?"

"Oh, Christo." Rose, choking with emotion, could barely speak. "I'm so sorry, so very sorry. You don't know how –"

"That's all right. Don't worry." But when she looked at him, his eyes were filled with tears.

"Oh, Christo, don't." She crossed the room and, pulling him to her, cradled him against her breast, rocking him, as he broke down and wept. "Hush, hush," she whispered.

She saw that endearing little curl at the nape of his neck, which always went the wrong way, and the sight of it broke something inside her, so sharply that she almost heard it twang, and tears began cascading down her face.

"I'm sorry, I'm sorry," she said over and over again.

They drew apart at last. Rose blotted her face on her shirt, moving away to give Christo space to compose himself. She turned back when she heard him stand up.

"I must go."

"Do stay and have a drink."

"No, I won't. Thank you, but work – or, rather, harvest – calls."

She followed him out to the hall. They faced each other.

"We will stay friends, won't we, Rose?"

"Of course." But she knew that he also knew that they would almost certainly never meet after today. "Christo," she said, with sudden force, "you're one of the nicest men I've ever met. I do love you – very much."

"But it's not enough. It's all right, Rose, I understand."

She held his face between her hands and, drawing it down, kissed his brow, then his lips. He took her hands, turned them palm up and stood looking down at them for a few moments, holding them so tightly that she could feel his pulse beating. Then he raised them and pressed his lips to each in turn. Next moment, he was gone.

From the shadow of the porch, she watched as he reversed out of the yard and drove down the lane, and she thought, he will never come back. I have sent this lovely, warm, kind, gentle man out of my life forever.

CHAPTER NINETEEN

A small table in the corner was still free. Rose threaded her way through the crowded hall, set down her tray and laid out her cheese ploughman's, roll and butter and pot of tea. *Green tea, I hope ...*
"Can I take your tray, please?" A small girl was hovering at her elbow.
"Here you are."
Rose gave it to her but the girl – about eight, she judged, although she was never very good at children's ages – held it to her like a breastplate, regarding Rose over its rim with solemn eyes.
"I was at your Master Class this morning."
"Were you? Oh, right." Rose sat down.
"It was *very* good," the girl said, earnestly.
"Well – thank you." She smiled at her, faces on a level.
"I'm coming to the Make Your Own Scarecrow comp this afternoon, as well."
"Are you? Oh, great."
"I shan't win, though." The brown eyes suddenly brimmed with tears. "My Dad says I'm stupid, I've got two left feet and I'm no good at football, like Darren."
Rose's heart swelled. She put her hand on the child's thin arm.
"Now you listen to me. What's your name?"
"Amelia."
"Well, Amelia, you tell your Dad that you don't make scarecrows with your feet – at least, I don't. And I'm sure you'll make a brilliant one."
The girl still looked doubtful though. "I'm only going in for it 'cos Mum says I must, but Marianne Westmacott is making one and she says she's going to win 'cos her mother's the Chairperson" she enunciated carefully, "of the Scarefest Organising Committee."
"Does she now?"
Rose had met Melissa Westmacott when she arrived in the village the previous evening, a forceful lady – quite unlike her mildly spoken husband, who had first approached her about the festival – with decided views on everything from the maximum number of bales of straw she would require for her demonstrations to the precise siting of the portable lavatories.
"Well, you just remember that I'm the judge, not Marianne's

mother, so *I* decide whose scarecrow's the best."

Amelia went off, wreathed in smiles, and Rose, her small appetite rapidly vanishing, looked around her. The hall itself, huge for such a small village, with its massive walls of Dartmoor granite and soaring roof of grey cruck-beams, must once have been a barn – probably the tithe barn, for out of the window beside her she could see the squat church next door, its tower like the fo'c's'le of a grey ship in a green sea, the billows the graves of long-ago villagers. Maybe they'd made scarecrows, real, working ones, to guard their crops.

"Mind if I join you?"

A tall, thin man was standing over her, tray in hand.

Rose did mind. After the stressful morning, she did not want to make polite conversation to a stranger. Good manners, though, prevailed. She smiled, gestured to the chair opposite.

"Help yourself."

"Thanks."

He unloaded a plate of pasty and chips, the pasty about the size of a small dustbin lid, and apple pie and a dish of clotted cream. Rose's eyes widened, and he caught her stare.

"I know, I know." He grinned.

"What do you know?" Rose laughed in spite of herself.

"You've got that 'Oh, my God, look at all that cholesterol' expression that my ex-wife used to have."

"Sorry." Rose picked up her fork.

"You ought to try one, instead of that rabbit food. Seriously, they're great. The farmer's wife where they've put me up this year makes them, so I can vouch for them. I saw her making a batch last night."

She looked at him. "You mean, you're one of the –"

"Performing seals? Yeah. I've been here every year since it started. Wouldn't miss it."

"Are you one of the Morris men?"

In a brief coffee interval that morning, she had watched the dancers perform on the village green, and had been transfixed by the intricate patterns they wove, the twirling ribbons, clashing ankle bells, that insistent rhythm which slithered its way into her bloodstream.

"Good grief, no. I'm Adam Harding."

"Oh. Oh, wow – the children's author."

"The very same. And you're Rose Ashenby, scarecrow maker extraordinary. Delighted to meet you."

They shook hands and he sat down.

"I wouldn't exactly say extraordinary," Rose said, through a mouthful of lettuce. "I mean, have you had time to walk round the village yet?"

"And seen all the scarecrows?" He dug into the pasty, releasing a little spurt of fragrant steam. "Yes, they get more every year. Practically every house has made one this time."

"I was amazed. Some of them are really clever, aren't they?"

"Yes, very imaginative. Did you see that one like Mrs Thatcher – complete with handbag, of course – working away on that cottage roof?"

"Yes." Rose laughed. "And then there was that SAS guy abseiling up to the bedroom window."

"All because the lady loves –? Yes, a very good idea, that one."

"But it all makes me feel hopelessly inadequate."

"Nonsense. I caught part of your master class this morning – it was brilliant."

"No, it wasn't. To be honest, it's the first time I've ever done anything like this. I was terrified." So terrified, in fact, that she had visited one of Melissa Westmacott's portaloos three times before she started.

"Well, it didn't show, I promise you. Only sorry I couldn't see more, but I was doing a story session."

"You read your own stories, do you?"

"Tell them, yes; and others that I make up as I go along."

"I gave Cordelia, my little niece, two of your books a few years ago. She loved them."

"Good. What were they?"

She pulled a face. "Sorry. I can't remember."

"That's all right. *Sic transit* and all that." His plain, rather bony features were lit up by a smile, making him seem younger than the mid-forties or so she guessed him to be.

"Have you always been a writer?"

"Well, I've always *wanted* to be a writer, yes. I wrote the obligatory adult novel when I was at Cambridge."

"Good gracious."

"My dear girl, you don't have to look so impressed. I'm tempted to tell you that it ran to six editions in three months, was snatched up by Hollywood and made into a record-breaking movie starring Robert Redford."

"Like *The Horse Whisperer*, you mean?"

"Precisely. The only problem is, it's still in a drawer somewhere at home. Once in a while I get it out, dust it, read a few pages, think 'God, what a genius I was when I wrote this', and put it back again."

"So you went over to children's books?"

"Not straight away. Livings have to be earned, don't they?"

Rose gave him a rueful smile. "They certainly do."

"I was a teacher for ten years, before it dawned on me that the only lessons I really enjoyed – and therefore my kids, as well – were story time. I used to make up endless stories, when I should have been teaching them long division and all that, actually. I handed in my notice and started writing full-time, lived on baked beans for five years."

He scooped up a large chunk of pasty with his fork, as Rose nodded sympathetically. She knew all about baked beans times.

"Then one of my books was taken, it got a mention on a telly book programme, and overnight –" he shook his head. "You know, Rose, I still can't get over it. One day I'm hunting for money for the gas fire, the next I'm in bookshops alongside all those *Harry Potters*, wondering when the bubble will burst."

"You're too modest, Adam." This was a man whose sales were legendary. "Aren't some of your books in a Channel 4 series at the moment?"

"Yes. They've done them quite well, I think."

"So –" she looked at him curiously "– what are you doing down here?"

"You mean, aren't I too grand for a tinpot little affair like this?"

"Well, I wouldn't put it quite like that."

"Neither would I. As I said, I've been coming every year since it started, and I wouldn't miss it. Writing can be a very lonely business, you know, and this sort of thing keeps me in touch with my readers. For one thing, I can try out new ideas – and kids are the most honest audience in the world. If they don't go for something, boy, do they show it. So, if a new story or character gets the thumbs down, I bin it and think of something else."

"I see." Rose poured herself a cup of tea.

"Anyway, that's enough about me," he went on. "Talking of scarecrows –"

"We weren't." she said firmly. "I am not looking forward to this afternoon at *all* – and tomorrow morning even less."

"Why even less?"

"Well, the kids take home their half-finished efforts, complete them at home and bring them back tomorrow, for *me* to judge."

"Ah, yes. I see your problem."

"I just hate the thought of all the losers," Amelia's doleful brown eyes swam into view, "who aren't really very good."

"Oh, I wouldn't worry. There're a lot of incomers in this village and from what I know of them, it won't be the kids who sit up all night finishing their 'crows. It'll be their pushy parents. Oh yes," as she raised astonished eyebrows. "And everyone knows that everybody else does it, so in a way they're all winners and losers at the same time – not that they see it that way, of course. Want some?" He gestured with his spoon to his apple pie, over which he had spooned a mound of yellow cream. "It's delicious."

"Oh, no thanks." Rose was nibbling daintily at an apple. "I'm not very hungry."

"Are you coming to the dance tonight? They've got a great group up from Plymouth, apparently."

"I don't think so. An early night for me, I'm afraid."

"Where are you staying?"

"With Mr and Mrs Luscombe. They're in the last house before the open moor."

"Yes, it's just across the hillside from me. They'll do you very well."

"Mmm, they're a lovely couple."

"Tell you what, I'm not in the mood for dancing, either. What say we go out for a meal this evening, instead? There's a great pub in Bovey, tables by the river, they do a superb grilled salmon."

Rose, who had intended a solitary evening, decided that this sounded much more inviting. "Fine – on condition that I pay my share."

"Well, all right." He picked up the book which lay on the chair alongside them. "Mind if I take a look?"

"My portfolio?" She gave a self-deprecating smile. "I only

brought it because, oh, I don't know, I feel a bit of a sham, somehow. I mean, a top writer like you is one thing, but –"

He looked up from the pages he was riffling through and regarded her seriously. "Don't put yourself down, Rose. Have you been doing this for long?"

"No, just a few weeks, actually. I came into it by chance – I used to be a sculptor."

Used to be a sculptor! If Daniel could have heard how lightly that 'used to be' tripped off her tongue.

The thought of Daniel made her sad. Once, they'd been so close, knowing what the other was thinking before they spoke. Now, she hadn't even told him she was coming down here. Probably, although she could barely admit it, because she'd been afraid that if she rang, it would be Lucy Smith who answered, her smug, cat-like smile creeping down the phone.

"Well, it looks as though you've found your true vocation. Not that I've seen any of your sculptures, of course, but these are brilliant – they really leap off the page at you. I mean, look at this one," he jabbed a finger at the page, "this gamekeeper," he read underneath, "Jim Fitzpatrick. And surely that's a real gun he's carrying?"

You must have a gun for your Jim ... must have a gun ... must have a gun ...

"Hey, Rose, are you all right?"

"Yes. Sorry." Keeping her face averted, she turned over the page. "I just felt a bit dizzy for a moment."

He put a hand on hers. "You really mustn't worry about this afternoon, you know. But – I tell you what. I always bring a pile of my old paperbacks, hand them out to the kids if they want them. Anything to get the little buggers reading in this age of computers. Well, I'll give you a load, then you've got runner-up prizes for everybody."

"Oh, thank you, Adam." Rose smiled gratefully at him. "That's brilliant." She looked down at the portfolio again. "This one's my Victorian Head Gardener. He's the reason I'm here, actually."

"Mmm." It was Adam's turn to go into an abstraction. "You know, Rose, I've just had an idea. Sky have been on at me to write another series for them. I was thinking of doing something built round a leprechaun called Donovan Doolally, but I tried out a couple of stories this morning and poor old Donovan went down like a lead balloon. But I'm sure I can dream up some stories built round these," he gestured at the portfolio. "They've all got such distinct personalities – set them in a real place – down here, perhaps – the Teletubbies are based on a farm in Warwickshire, aren't they? – and you can make the scarecrows. What do you say?"

"I'll see you all back here with your scarecrows tomorrow morning, then." Rose smiled round at the group of twenty or so youngsters. "Ten o'clock sharp. And remember what I told you – no sitting up all night to finish them. Scarecrows need their beauty sleep, just like you."

A few moments of excited chatter, a stampede for the door, and then, blessedly, silence. Rose stayed where she was, propped against a table, recovering slowly. How the hell did teachers do it? Not two hours, but two days ... weeks ... months ... two years ... twenty years. There was, she supposed, a knack.

"Ah, good, Miss Ashenby, you've cleared up." Melissa Westmacott appeared in the doorway, no doubt come to check.

"The children did most of it." Rose gave the woman a cool smile.

"Good, good. Oh, some straw seems to have spilt out of that bag over there."

"Yes, I had noticed." She brandished a dustpan and brush. "I was about to see to it."

"Splendid, splendid. I'll leave you to it, then. I just want a word with Colonel Trebithick – our main sponsor, you know," when Rose looked blank. "He always takes a great interest in all the village activities."

"How nice," Rose said politely.

"Yes. Such a lovely family. They'll be at the dance this evening, so you'll no doubt meet them then."

Rose, thinking of grilled salmon in that garden by the river, merely smiled, hoping that her silence would be taken for joyful anticipation.

She moved across to the little pile of straw and began gathering it up. It felt quite new, not dry and brittle as it often was. She took a handful and sniffed it. Was it her imagination or could she smell the growing crop, the sunshine in it? Christo – he was probably out in one of his harvest fields at that very moment ...

"Tut, tut, Miss Ashenby, you've missed a bit."

As she went rigid, a hand reached over her shoulder, picked up a piece of straw and dropped it in the bag. Very slowly, she straightened up and turned to face Ryan.

"Well?" He gave her his old, lazy smile, a smile which once, long ago, would have knotted her up inside. "Don't look so shocked. And keep still."

Leaning forward, he plucked one, two wisps of straw from her hair, held them flat in his palm then blew them away.

"What on earth are you doing here?" It was the only thing Rose could get out through frozen lips.

"I could ask the same of you. Well?" He raised his brows in ironic mockery. "What are you up to in this godforsaken neck of the woods? I mean, I saw the posters," he jerked a thumb at one on the wall beside them which, among the Morris dancers, brass band, fireworks and Adam Harding, featured Scarecrow Master Class, "but I never dreamed it could be you."

"But it is, you see." Rose was recovering her poise, though only slowly.

"Yes, but – scarecrows, for heaven's sake?"

"They're what I do now, actually." And I've got a really good one hanging in the studio, which I still punch occasionally, when I'm in the mood.

"But you're a sculptor – and a bloody good one."

"Pity you never said that once in all the years we were together."

"Didn't I?" He gave her a slanting smile. "How very remiss of me."

"Well, anyway, I'm turning myself into a bloody good scarecrow-maker now."

A burst of adrenaline was surging through Rose. Just for an instant, when she heard his voice, she had felt a sharp, physical pain. Just for an instant. Now, the knowledge that he meant nothing, less than a handful of that straw at their feet, gave her an exhilarating sense of freedom.

"What *are* you doing here, anyway?" she demanded. "You're too late for my master class, if that's what you wanted."

"Good God, no. Not my line at all."

He really did look very like his scarecrow, even if he was more handsome in the flesh than in the straw. She had to admit that. Even though she was now totally immune to the disease which was Ryan-worship, she could still see what the attraction had been for her.

"No. I'm performing with a jazz group at the Tinner's Arms tomorrow lunch-time."

"Good grief! At a tinpot little affair like this? A bit of a come-down, surely?"

He looked at her sharply, uncertain whether she was serious or trying to needle him. Responding to something in her eyes, he snapped, "Actually, I'm doing it as a favour for Gerald – Colonel Trebithick."

"Oh, I see." Although from what she had heard of Colonel Trebithick, it was certainly not Gerald to his face.

"Julia's father. Remember Julia?" Ryan added casually.

Of course. Trebithick – Julia Trebithick. For a moment, she felt the pain of his betrayal all over again. But, knowing him as she did now – far better than in the four years they had been together – she knew instinctively that he was hoping for a display of weeping and jealousy, waiting for her to break down in front of him, as she had that morning in the studio. Well, she would disappoint him. It was not merely that she felt nothing for him, not the least flicker of affection or desire, it was more that, after the deep sadness of Christo, weak, shallow Ryan, with no backbone, no principles, and no more fibre than one of her scarecrows – in fact, probably less – *was* nothing.

"Julia? Yes, of course I remember her." She gave a light laugh. "How could I have forgotten?"

"Hmmm." He was still studying her closely. "You know, Rose, you're looking very fetching."

"Surely not." She gestured to her dungarees and navy ScarecRose T-shirt.

"No, it's more," his eyes narrowed in concentration, "there's something different about you."

"If you say so, Ryan." She shrugged. "Now, if there's nothing else, I must finish clearing up this place."

"Well, see you at the dance, then."

"No, sorry." All at once she was very glad indeed of that grilled salmon. "I've got a date elsewhere."

"Oh. Oh, well." But he still did not go. "Rose –"

"So *here* you are, darling. Whatever are you doing?"

They both swung round, to see a tall young woman framed, as if for effect, in the doorway. As she came towards them, Rose took in pale linen trousers, a lemon shirt, a fall of hair the colour of the clotted cream Adam had been spooning onto his apple pie. Julia Trebithick, she could hear an echo in her mind of Ryan's voice. She's younger than you, she's prettier than you and – what she had not been able to bring herself to say even to Leo – she's better than you in the sack.

"Darling, what are you doing?" Julia said again. Sliding a proprietorial arm round Ryan's waist, she regarded Rose with a pair of ice-blue eyes.

"I'm sorry, sweetie." Ryan, keeping his eyes on Rose, brushed the smooth, tanned cheek. "Julia – this is Rose Ashenby. You know," his eyes were full of malice now, "I told you about her."

"But of course." Julia smiled at him, obviously sharing some complicit joke. Once, the thought would have hurt Rose deeply. Now, she did not care.

"Actually, we have met," she said, keeping her voice neutral. "Newquay, last summer, if you remember."

"Really?" the girl replied indifferently. Dismissing Rose, she turned to Ryan again. "Darling, we're all waiting for you, across in the Tinner's Arms. I want to go through those lyrics again. I don't think I'm quite perfect in them yet."

"Of course. Sorry, darling." Ryan nuzzled her neck. "And I need another go at that new piece of mine. Oh – give me the keys to the car, will you? I've left the script in it."

"All right. But don't be long."

She went without another glance at Rose, who turned away and lifted up the bag of straw.

"Well," Ryan was still watching her, "I'm so glad you two have met up again."

"Yes, so am I," Rose agreed warmly. In fact, she was glad. Many times in the past weeks, Julia Trebithick had haunted her dreams, and it was quite pleasing to discover that, in the unforgiving light of a Dartmoor afternoon, behind the gloss which only money and social position could give, Julia was a bottle blonde, already running a bit to podge, and with eyes just a shade too close together.

"Well – I suppose I'd better go." He sounded almost sullen.
"Yes, don't keep them waiting."
"Rose."
"What?" She scooped the last remnants of straw into the bag.
"Look," he lowered his voice, gave a half-fearful glance over his shoulder, "I'm coming up your way next weekend to a gig. Julia can't make it, it's her bloody mother's birthday. How say we get together, make a night of it – just for old times' sake?"

Rose looked at him thoughtfully. Daniel, Leo – they'd both been right. Ryan was a little shit. In fact, little was the apposite word, for under the strong influence of Julia Trebithick, he really did seem to have shrunk slightly. He'd always been little inside, of course. A little, a mean little man.

"Come on, Rose." He gave her a wheedling smile. "We had some good times, didn't we, you and I?" He lifted his hand and twined his finger through one of her curls. "Remember that night I set out to kiss every one of your freckles?"

His voice had taken on a sensual tone, but behind that she sensed anxiety, and thought with sudden clarity, Of course, Ryan can't take rejection; *he* has to be the one to walk away.

"Don't." She wrenched away, hurting herself, but glad of the pain. "I'm sorry, Ryan, but I'm busy next weekend." She patted his arm in a motherly way. "Now, run along to Julia, before she comes looking for you again."

She was just stooping, rather wearily, to pick up the bag of straw again when Adam appeared at her elbow.

"Here, give me that. You look all in." He shook her hand free of the bag. "Was that our Poet Laureate I saw leaving?"

"Yes. Do you know him?"

"Slightly. And believe me, I have no wish to deepen the acquaintance. Ryan doesn't know it, but I put him in my last book. He was devoured on page ten by a giant alien caterpillar."

Rose put back her head and laughed. So poor Ryan would achieve some sort of immortality.

"That's better." Adam smiled back at her, although he did not quite know what the joke was. "Hungry?"

"Ravenous." And she was. "Just lead me to that grilled salmon."

"Well, back to our digs, then. And I'll pick you up about half-

six. OK?"
"Sounds great."
They headed for the door together.

CHAPTER TWENTY

The lane had cut itself deep into the red earth, so that the hedge tops were way above the roof of her van. It was impossible to drive fast, and in any case Rose was glad of the excuse to go slowly, her window open, ferns and ragged robin brushing against her bare arm where it rested on the sill.

A mud-spattered tractor was coming towards her, taking up the whole of the lane, and she edged into a passing place to let it through. As she acknowledged the driver's wave, she saw the two collie dogs sitting bolt upright in the trailer and was reminded, in an instant, of Jamie and Emily.

Jamie ... Emily ... Roddie ... Susan ... Christo ... Daniel ... Lucy Smith ... They all occupied their separate areas in her mind, sandpapering each bit to rawness. This weekend, apart from phone calls each evening to Leo and a duty one to Roddie, when thankfully there had been no answer, had been a kind of ointment to spread over all the sore spots. Boosted by Adam's encouragement, she'd actually enjoyed the second of her master classes. Mrs Westmacott, despite the fact that Marianne's astoundingly sophisticated scarecrow had come nowhere, while a glowing Amelia had won second prize, had invited – commanded? – her to come back next year, and had given her the dates. She'd had a great evening with Adam, chatting like old friends while the little river gurgled beside them. He'd had to leave straight away yesterday evening but was going to ring her in a couple of weeks to report progress on the TV series, when he'd be glad to have any input from her. And the ghost of Ryan had been well and truly laid to rest, so that it had no more substance than his straw image, slung from a butcher's hook in her studio. Yes, the weekend had been a great success. Now though, she was heading for home.

A mile or so further on, she rounded a blind corner, then braked hard. Ahead of her, the lane was blocked by several cars, their drivers standing in a group, talking to a yellow-jacketed policeman. Beyond them, she could hear engines revving, voices shouting, and when she got out she could see, a hundred yards or so away, the entrance to a farmyard. A police car was parked in it and a lorry was edging its way out into the lane, where a crowd of people had gathered.

"Is it an accident?" Rose came up to the little huddle of drivers.

"Animal Rights yobbos." One of the men, a farmer by the look of him, spat forcibly.

"What are they here for?"

He jerked a thumb towards the crowd, some of whom had climbed onto a bank facing the farm gateway. Several were brandishing rocks and hefty branches torn from the hedgerow, whilst others held up placards: STOP LIVE EXPORTS ... BAN THE TRADE OF SHAME.

"Perfectly legal business," another man put in. "Stupid buggers. I know what I'd like to do to them." And Rose could easily guess.

"Morning, miss." The policeman, his boyish face puckered with worry, turned to her. "Where are you heading for?"

"The M5 – the Midlands."

"Why don't you turn, then? You can get back to Moretonhamstead, then through to Exeter that way."

But just then two more cars came to a halt behind her, completely closing her in.

"Look, Dick," the men seemed to be on first name terms with the policeman, "why the hell don't you do something?"

"I've called for reinforcements. But we had no warning of this little lot, and I can't tackle them on my own. Maybe you'd fancy lending a hand, Dennis?"

The burly man spat again, the other man said again what he would like to do to them, but no-one showed any inclination to move.

Another car joined the queue behind them, its horn blasting, and the policeman squared his shoulders.

"Right, I'll see if I can make a way through. And wind your windows up – they're none too fussy who they're aiming at with those rocks."

He went off down the lane and as the men got back into their vehicles, Rose did the same. A couple of minutes later the car in front inched forward and she followed, at a snail's pace. The shouting became louder and, mingled with the shouts, as she drew level with the lorry, she could hear the cries of terrified animals, see through the slatted sides woolly faces, frightened faces, eyes rolling, pressed to the gaps as the rocks and branches thudded against them.

The car in front squeezed past. The policeman beckoned

frantically to her to follow. Among the group up on the hedge bank someone was banging a drum, and when she glanced up, a face among all the others floated out at her and it was Emily's.

In a reflex action, she slammed on her brakes, just as Emily saw her. From that instant on, it seemed to Rose as if everything was happening in slow motion, as though she was struggling through wet concrete. As she flung open the van door the girl, still keeping her eyes fixed on her, turned, obviously bent on escape.

"Now then, miss." The policeman, red-faced, bore down on Rose.

"Emily!" She shouted the name above the din.

The lorry driver saw the gap her van had made, snatched at the chance to break free.

"*Emily!*"

Rose screamed this time as the girl half-scrambled, half-fell down into the lane, just as the lorry lurched forward.

Ever after, reliving those terrible moments, it would seem to Rose that in that split second everything fell silent. It was like an old movie, no sound, but jerky, frame-by-frame movements. As she stood, frozen, a tall figure, arms outstretched in front, leapt down from the group on the bank and was lost to view.

A squeal of brakes, more shouts, which dimly seemed to Rose to be surging to an angry crescendo, the wailing siren of a police van which came nosing its way down past the cars. The noise beat in on her ears until she flung up her hands to cover them and, as waves of dizziness washed over her, for the first time in her life, she fainted.

"You all right?"

Someone hauled her up into a sitting position. The farmer and another of the drivers were standing over her. They advanced and retreated alarmingly, until the farmer pushed her head down to her knees. He had a surprisingly tender touch for such a huge pair of callused paws, Rose thought incoherently. Used to dealing with new-born lambs, lambs which then were loaded onto the lorry ...

He kept his hand on her head, all the time talking in a low voice to the other man.

"Come on, my lover." The other man uncorked a silver hip flask. "Get some of this down you."

Rose swallowed obediently, her teeth clattering against the cold metal. She coughed, then swallowed again.

"Thank you." She gave a wan smile as they regarded her, their weather-beaten faces concerned, but then, as an ambulance, blue light flashing, edged past them, she went to get up. "Emily! Oh God."

The young policeman appeared. "You OK, miss?"

"Emily." Rose clutched his hand. "Where is she?"

"Is that the young woman's name?"

"Yes – *yes*. Is she all right?"

"You know her, do you?"

"She's my niece – Emily. Whatever shall I do if –"

"Don't you fret, miss. They're putting them in the ambulance now."

Them. For the first time, Rose remembered that tall, rather gangling figure.

"And Jamie? How is he?"

"Is the young man a relation of yours, too?"

"No – no. He's the son of my best friend, Leo Brinkworth. He's called Jamie Brinkworth." She stood up. "I must see them."

"I told you," he barred her way, "they're in the ambulance."

Looking past him, she saw the ambulance doors closing.

"I must go with them," she babbled. "Where are they going?"

"Derriford. That's the nearest A and E department."

Another policeman came up to them. There was a brief, muttered conversation, she saw them both look at her, then the first one said, "I'll take you in my car. Dennis, park the young lady's vehicle in the yard, will you?"

"Will do." The farmer reached a brawny arm into Rose's van, took out her bag and put it into her leaden hands. "Here you are, my lover. And don't you worry – everything will be all right, you'll see."

As in a dream, Rose went across to the police car. The lorry itself was parked up against the stone wall of the farmyard, the driver, white-faced, leaning against the wing. Most of the protestors seemed to have vanished; only a few broken branches and stones lay in the lane where they had been flung. She got in, then, as they pulled out behind it, the ambulance moved slowly away and its wailing siren began, drowning the crying of the lambs.

Rose sipped the tea, then, realising that it was stone cold, set the cup down again. It clattered against the saucer. Outside in the corridor, more feet went hurrying past, but in this small side room, the only sound the faint tick of the wall clock, she felt wholly insulated from the rest of the hospital.

Unable to sit still any longer, she leapt up. There was a small window, but it only looked onto an inner courtyard. On the far side were rooms, figures pacing to and fro. Behind one frosted glass window, she could see intense activity. Accident and emergency ... Life and death ...

Footsteps came down the corridor again, and this time the door behind her opened. It was an older, more senior nurse, not the young woman who had deposited her in here and fetched her a cup of tea what seemed now like days ago.

"Miss Ashenby? I'm Staff Nurse Rogers."

"Is there any news?" Rose asked abruptly. "How's Emily?"

"Your niece is going to be all right. I promise you," as Rose gazed at her. "We were a little concerned at first – she had quite a knock on the head, as you know – but the x-rays have shown up nothing, beyond concussion."

"Oh, thank God." Rose sank into the chair. "Thank God." She put her hand to her mouth, biting on the knuckle to stop the tears of sheer relief. "Can I see her – just for a moment?"

"I'd rather you didn't. She's sedated, and I don't want her reminded of everything that's happened. There'll be time enough for that." She paused. "But you can look in through the window at her – just to reassure yourself."

"Oh, thank you." Rose picked up her bag. "And can I see Jamie as well?"

"Jamie? You mean the young man, James Brinkworth?"

"Yes. Surely –" she frowned, struggling to recall those dream-like events "– the policeman said they were *both* going in the ambulance."

"You know him?"

"He's the son of my best friend."

"I'm very sorry."

Very sorry? What did she mean? Why was she looking at her like that?

"There was nothing we could do. Ruptured intestines, spleen.

He was DOA. Dead on arrival," as Rose stared blankly at her. "I'm so very sorry. The police are waiting outside. They'd like a word with you."

She opened the door and a policeman – not *her* policeman, an older, grey-haired man – and woman came in.

"Miss Ashenby." As they sat down beside her, the man took out a notebook. "We shall need a statement from you, I'm afraid."

"Yes, of course."

"And I understand you are a friend of James Brinkworth's mother."

"Jamie," she said, her voice on automatic pilot. "Jamie Brinkworth. He hates being called James. He saved Emily."

"Yes, we know. Could you give us her address and phone number, please?"

"She's in Warwickshire."

"Ah. Is there a relative or close friend of the family down here in the south-west, do you know?"

"I don't think so. Leo doesn't have any relatives, really. But – I'm a close friend –" Her voice tailed away.

"You see, there needs to be formal identification of the – of the young man."

They were both looking at her, waiting for an answer.

"And if I don't do it –"

"We shall have to ask her. Yes."

"Very well."

Somehow, she got up and they walked, one on either side of her, along endless corridors. They stopped outside an unmarked door.

"Is – is he – ?"

"No, it's all right." The young policewoman, a pretty girl, took her hand. "Hold on to me if you like."

Jamie lay on the narrow bed. Apart from a faint bruise over his left temple, his face was unmarked. More than that, the last fifteen years had been wiped away, so that he looked like the gentle, shy little boy he had been when Rose and his mother first met.

"Well?"

"Yes." Rose's voice was dead. "That's Jamie."

CHAPTER TWENTY-ONE

Rose risked a sidelong glance at Emily. When she had tucked her into her seat back at the hospital – it was only later, much later, that she asked herself how her van had got there – the girl immediately turned her head away and closed her eyes. She had roused only when they pulled into the Sedgemoor service area and Rose led her into the crowded vestibule.

Emily's head was still bandaged and she attracted curious glances, but she was oblivious to them all. When her aunt came out of the lavatory cubicle, she was leaning against a washbasin, staring expressionlessly straight into the eyes of her white-faced reflection. Rose's stomach constricted with concern.

"Come on." She put her arm round the girl. "Let's get something to eat. A burger? Yes, let's have a burger and chips." She had to raise her voice against the noise of the computer games being played nearby.

Emily shrugged herself free. "I'm not hungry, thanks. Rose?"

"Yes, love?"

"What happened to the others – his friends?"

"Well, they just sort of melted away, I think. Look, if you don't want anything to eat, let's have a drink. You ought to have something."

"I'm not thirsty." And Emily walked out, back to the van.

As Rose got in alongside her, she opened her mouth to speak, then, seeing the girl's shuttered face, closed it again and concentrated on driving through the heavy traffic which, as always, had built up around Bristol. Just occasionally, as a red car flashed past beyond the barrier, heading south, she did wonder if it was Daniel, with Leo beside him. She would be as silent as this girl beside her ...

She'd clutched the phone in the hospital office, almost too paralysed to move. She ought to ring Leo but the thought of actually talking to her, never mind telling her, was more than she could bear. And Leo would be alone, in that silent cottage. George and Angela? They were so good, so kind. No, Daniel. It could only be Daniel.

He'd answered the phone on the second ring.

"Oh, Daniel, thank God you're there ..." and she told him, as coherently as she could. "... and I don't know how to break it to Leo," she choked back a sob. "It'll kill her."

"No it won't. Leo is made of strong stuff, you know that. Don't worry. I'll go straight over now. I know she's there. I rang her last night to see if there was any news, and she said she was working at home today."

"Thank you, Daniel."

"She'll have to come down to Plymouth, won't she?"

"Yes."

"I'll bring her myself. I don't want her driving. What a bloody, lousy, stinking thing to happen."

"Yes."

"And how about you? And that poor kid?"

"They wanted her to stay in hospital overnight, but when she heard – about Jamie," Rose swallowed, "she insisted on going home. So I'm taking her."

"Now listen, Rose. Put what's happened out of your mind, while you're driving. There's nothing you can do for Jamie, and you and Emily must get back safely. In fact, look – let me hire a car for you."

"No. It's very kind – but I'll be glad of a few hours' driving ..."

"All right. I'll ring you to let you know what's happening."

"Thank you." Her voice was almost inaudible.

"And listen to me. You are not to blame yourself. It was an accident."

"But if I hadn't –"

"*No.* It was an accident – a ghastly accident. And nobody's – *nobody's* – fault. Believe that, Rose. Hold on to that."

Believe it, believe it ... hold on to that, hold on to that ...

She turned off the M40.

"Nearly home, love."

Emily, staring dry-eyed through the windscreen, did not reply.

The front door opened as the van stopped and Roddie stood, waiting for them to approach. Rose, who had not seen him since the christening, was shocked. He had lost weight, all of that rather teddy bearish little paunch had gone, and his face was gaunt. He even seemed slightly stooped.

Emily stopped in front of him.

"Hello, darling."

He made as if to embrace her, but when she made no response, his arms fell back by his side and he stood rather awkwardly. Over her head he looked at Rose and she saw that there were tears in his eyes.

She gently propelled Emily into the hall and kissed Roddie.

"Hello, girls," as she became aware of Abigail and Cordelia, standing silently in the kitchen doorway, watching them. "Here we are, safe and sound."

They too looked thinner, their faces solemn, as their eyes went from Emily, to their father, to Rose. She was reminded, all at once, of scenes she had watched recently on the TV News. A bomb had exploded in an apartment block somewhere, the dazed survivors were wandering among the ruins ...

A rather austere-looking middle-aged woman, in a neat pink overall appeared behind them. The redoubtable Miss Lathbury, no doubt. She took in the scene in the hall at a glance.

"You must be Emily. Hello, my dear." She took the girl's hand and patted it. "I've just put a hot water bottle in your bed, and laid out a clean nightshirt for you."

"Where's Mum?"

It was the first time Emily had spoken and as they all stood, as if frozen, Rose thought, Oh my God, I should have told her – but I forgot. I forgot about Susan.

Miss Lathbury put her arm round the girl's thin shoulders.

"Come along, my dear. I'll help you upstairs, then bring you a nice hot cup of tea – yes, you do," as Emily murmured a protest. "And Abigail and Cordelia, you'll have lots of time to see your sister later, so go and finish putting the buttons on those gingerbread men, please, then Emily can try one with her tea."

The girls turned away obediently and Roddie and Rose stood in silence, watching the other two go off upstairs.

"I'm so sorry, Roddie. I just – well, I forgot – about Susan."

"That's all right, Rose. I quite understand."

He looked down at her but his eyes were blank. He's in shock, Rose thought with alarm. She wanted to hug him to her, will him to be his old expansive, smug, opinionated self, instead of this drained, grey-faced shadow.

Through the open door they heard a car pull up on the drive. They both turned, to see a taxi, the driver opening the door for a woman. Blonde hair piled up on top of her head, skimpy pink dress showing off a superb tan, teetering on high-heeled gold sandals. She left the driver to get out her luggage and came down the path. Halfway along, just for a second, she seemed to falter, almost turn back, but then, chin jutted, she came on towards them.

She stepped into the hall, screwing her face up against the dim light, then took her dark shades off.

"Roddie, dear, would you pay the driver, please? I don't seem to have any money on me just at the moment. Hello, Rose, whatever are you doing here?"

Her brother-in-law seemed incapable of movement, of thought even, so Rose said, in a shaky voice, "Susan! You've come back."

"Well, Josh had an offer he couldn't refuse," her voice was ultra-casual, "and there didn't really seem to be much point in staying on alone. In any case, I was bored with the Bahamas – so flat, you know. Just like Southwold, in fact. Oh darling, don't look like that. We can still go to silly old Southwold, if you really want to – there's heaps of time before the girls start school, I'm sure. But did you hear what I asked you? Would you pay the driver, please?" And Roddie went.

"Well –" Rose began then stopped, unable to continue. Just as Roddie wasn't Roddie any more, so Susan had turned into a glamorous, beautiful woman. Just for a moment, she even felt a touch of pique.

"Well, Rose," Susan smiled kindly at her, put her tiny gold leather bag down on the hall table, "and what have you been doing with yourself?"

"Oh, this and that ... Er," she gave a quick glance outside but Roddie was still talking to the driver, wallet in hand, "what was this offer that Josh couldn't refuse?"

"Oh," with her handkerchief, Susan wiped a non-existent smear from the hall mirror, "he had this phone call from his agent. He's got a part in some new soap the Beeb are doing. A marvellous chance for him – he couldn't possibly turn it down."

"No, of course not. Um – what sort of part?"

"He gets shacked up with this super-rich divorcee. He's her toy boy."

"Oh." Rose stared at her, fighting down hysterical laughter. One thing at least had not changed in the new Susan – poised, defiant, maybe – but still a total lack of any sense of the ridiculous. A toy boy. Maybe that was what Josh had been auditioning for all along – rehearsing his role so that when the opportunity came it would be already honed to perfection.

The kitchen door opened and Abigail and Cordelia appeared again, with floury hands. They too stared at their mother.

"Hello, darlings," Susan said brightly. "I'm home."

She kissed them both.

"Tarquin's got a teething rash," said Cordelia.

"Oh dear."

Upstairs, a door banged. Emily, in a Pooh Bear night shirt, stood on the landing, Miss Lathbury behind her.

"Mummy! Oh, Mummy!"

Racing down the stairs, Emily hurled herself into Susan's arms, crying loud, wrenching sobs, as if her heart was tearing in two.

"My, my, what a fuss. I'm back now, sweetheart." Susan held her eldest daughter to her. "And whatever have you been doing to your head, you silly girl? Come in here and tell me all about it."

And the sitting room door closed behind them.

CHAPTER TWENTY-TWO

It was the evening of the next day when Daniel rang.
"Rose, we're back." He sounded very subdued.
"How did it – how did you get on?"
"Oh – all right. We managed to sort everything out in the one day."
"That's good."
"How are you?"
"Oh, fine." With her fingernail, she was tracing around the pattern on the cover of her phone book.
"And Emily?"
"Well, you know. But Susan's back. She arrived while I was dropping Emily off."
"That's something, I suppose. What about Roddie?"
"Well, I rang this morning to see how they were, and, I can hardly believe it, but he's getting his wish about something, anyway. They're all going to Southwold on Saturday, apparently – including the home help." Was home help quite the right word for Miss Lathbury?
"But surely?"
"Yes, I know. But, oh, I can't explain, Daniel. Susan has changed so much, and poor Roddie – he's just a total zombie. And Emily doesn't seem to care where she is, so –"
"I think it's a good idea. Give them a chance to sort themselves out a bit. And it'll be as well if Emily isn't around – we don't want her deciding she must come to the funeral."
"To be honest, I don't think she's even thought of it." Remembering Emily's white face and haunted eyes, Rose doubted very much that anything beyond the scene in the lane was occupying the girl's thoughts. "When is it, the funeral? Do you know?"
"Next Monday."
"In the church, I suppose?" Although Leo had never, to Rose's knowledge, set foot in the village church. As for Jamie – a cracked laugh escaped her.
"What's the matter?"
"Oh, I was just remembering that time when Jamie let loose Ratilda."
"His pet rat? During a deanery Mothers' Union service,

wasn't it?"

"That's right."

"What you might call rat among the pigeons. And he was in the choir at the time, wasn't he?"

"Yes. Not for much longer, though. But I'm sure Mr Davies – you know, our vicar – forgave him long ago."

"Of course. But in any case, the funeral isn't at church. Leo thinks that Jamie would have wanted a green funeral. There's a place quite near you, apparently."

"Yes, there is. There was quite a fuss about it at first, a lot of people didn't like the idea, but Mike and Sally have gone ahead with it. Oh, Daniel, it's a lovely place; an old meadow, down a narrow lane, and there's a tiny wood, with primroses and bluebells in spring, and wild orchids."

She bit her lip, remembering suddenly how she and Leo had gone to see it when the idea was first mooted. Leo had surveyed the little field, then said, "This'll do for me, Rose."

"I must go and see her," she said abruptly.

"Well – I'd leave it a while, if I were you."

"But of course I must."

"Rose –" she heard him hesitate "be a good girl. You know Leo – she'll want to be on her own. Give her a day or so."

"But I've got to see her." Even though she quailed at the thought. "In fact, I'll go now."

"At least wait until tomorrow – promise me. Rose! Are you listening?"

"Well – all right," she said, a shade huffily. "I suppose you're right. I'll go tomorrow."

"If you must."

"Yes, I must. And thank you, Daniel, for all you did."

"It was nothing. But –"

"Yes?"

"I'm glad it was me you rang – that we're still friends enough for that."

"Of course we're still friends." At the mere thought that Daniel could even consider that they might not be friends, Rose's heart jumped a beat. "Of course we are," she repeated. "I mean, you and I –"

"We go back to our prams," he completed, with a shade of irony in his voice which she did not quite like. "I know. Bye, Rose."

Leo's gate was firmly closed. Rose opened it, and carefully relatched it. She stood for a few moments on the path, trying to compose herself, then went round towards the back door.

It was open and she could hear the low murmur of voices. Leo and Angela. They were sitting at the kitchen table and as she hesitated in the doorway Angela saw her.

"Oh, here's Rose."

Leo looked up. Only her features were the same; everything else had changed into the grey mask of a stranger.

"H-hello, Leo."

"Well, come in, then."

Rose put a hand on her shoulder and bent to kiss her, but Leo drew back.

"I've brought you these." She laid the huge bunch of flowers on the sink unit. "I'm sorry they're only from the garden."

In fact, she had spent a long time systematically stripping her borders of all the best blooms, including every one of her pink lilies.

"Oh, Rose, they're absolutely beautiful," Angela exclaimed. "Aren't they, Leo, dear?"

"Very nice. Thank you." But Rose knew that she had barely glanced at them.

She stood, rather awkwardly, and it was Angela who said, "Do sit down, Rose. Leo has been showing me all these lovely things. Look at this – isn't it sweet?"

As Rose slid into a chair, she held up a small cardboard chicken, covered with moth-eaten yellow cotton wool. The half of its red beak that remained proclaimed, 'Hapy Easter, dere Mummy'.

"Jamie was only five when he did it." Angela turned to Leo. "He was, wasn't he?"

"Yes."

"It's lovely." The chicken blurred and swam in Rose's vision.

"And just look at this."

Angela handed her a heart-shaped card, painted red. It had a grimy white ribbon glued across it. On the back, she read, in uneven lettering:

> Roses are red
> Violets are blue

Sugar is sweet
I love you
Happy Valentine dear Mummy
"And there's this."

From a crumpled piece of tissue paper, Angela drew out a small wooden silhouette of a rabbit, one ear longer than the other and a very oddly shaped tail, but lovingly smoothed and polished. On the bottom was a neat label with 'Christmas 1990' in Leo's writing. Rose held it, turning it over and over in her fingers, feeling her throat tighten up with grief.

"It's beautiful," she managed to say.

Angela glanced from one to the other of them.

"I'll go now, love." She got up then put her arms round Leo, hugging her to her for a moment. "Chin up, my dear, and if you want anything, anything at all, you know where we are. Goodbye, Rose." She clasped her hand for a moment, then went.

There was silence in the room. When Rose looked at Leo, her eyes, wide open but lifeless, were fixed on the opposite wall.

No words, nothing at all, would come to her. She picked up another card, from among the mounds of old tissue paper. A Father Christmas climbing out of a grubby-looking chimney. She put it down again, unable to read another message. It was all here, she thought. Twenty years of a life. Twenty years of a relationship. A relationship which to any outsider had seemed frail, almost non-existent, and yet Leo, whom Rose had always thought the toughest, least sentimental of women, had kept every single token given her by her son.

An empty cup stood at Leo's elbow.

"Would you like me to make you some coffee?"

"What?" Frowning with the effort, Leo removed her gaze from whatever it had been fixed on, turned it to Rose.

"Shall I make you a cup of coffee?" repeated Rose.

"No, thank you."

"Oh, Leo –"

Leo's thin hand rested on the table. She put her hand over it but Leo withdrew hers sharply, as if the contact had stung her.

"Just go, Rose, will you?" she said in a toneless voice.

"But I –"

"I said, just go." With a violent movement, Leo pushed back her chair, which rocked and fell with a clatter, and leapt to her feet. "Get out of my house."

Rose, too stunned to move, stared up at her, as Leo banged her palms down on the table.

"Get out, I said. Get out! I don't want you – or any of your fucking family in my house ever again. Do you hear me, Rose Ashenby?"

As Rose got slowly to her feet, she went on, her voice rising shrill, "What in Christ's name were you doing in that bloody lane? Oh yes," as she saw Rose's expression, "I know all about it. I made Daniel take me out there, to see it – to see the place where he – What business had you to be there? What business did you and that simpering niece of yours have, ruining my life? You stupid, stupid bitch – you've ruined my life. Do you hear me? So get out – and stay out, will you? And take your flowers with you."

As Rose, her face as deathly as Leo's own, half turned, Leo clapped her hand to her mouth and ran from the room. Standing like a statue of ice, Rose heard her going upstairs. A door banged open, and when she went through to the hall she could hear sobs.

She put one foot on the stairs then stopped and stood for several minutes, irresolute, before going back into the kitchen.

Almost mechanically, she wrapped in their tissue paper all the cards and little offerings, the tiny strand of fair hair, the pair of small, worn shoes, and replaced them very neatly in the plastic box which stood on the table.

She was nearly at the gate when she collided with something large and solid.

"Hey, Rose."

A pair of hands took her by the elbows and she looked up into a half-familiar face.

"It's Steve – remember?" He gave her elbows a little shake.

"Oh. Oh, yes. Hello, Steve. I thought you were in," she frowned, "in Scotland."

"I'm on my way to Heathrow. I just called off to get those drawings Leo promised me."

"Oh, yes, she's finished them, I think. But –"

"Yeah, I know about it – her boy, I mean. I just met Angela. She told me. Where is she?"

"Upstairs. She – she sent me away." Rose pressed her lips

together in the effort not to break down.

"Oh, honey – don't look like that." Steve gathered her and the flowers to him, holding her to his warm bear's chest for a few moments. "Don't take it personally."

"How else can I take it? She said she never wants to see me again."

"Oh, honey, hush. Listen to me, Rose." He held her away from him. "It's natural at first. You just need to lash out, to blame somebody, to simplify the whole terrible thing in your own mind. Believe me, Leo will come round."

"I don't think so. She's right, you see – it *was* my fault."

"No, it wasn't. Just as it wasn't my fault when Lindy died, along with our child she was expecting. I spent three years blaming the truck driver, blaming myself, blaming the whole world – even blaming Chrysler for making the goddamn car in the first place. And in the end, I came to realise, as Leo will, that there's no point in doing that. These things – well, they just happen. Always have, always will. You cling to that, my dear."

"But I've left her upstairs, crying her heart out."

"That'll do nothing but good, I promise you." He smiled down at her, his eyes warm with concern. "Go on home, now. I'll stay with her. After all," his face twisted, "I know what she's going through. Who better to help her? Go on now." He gave her a little push.

She was halfway down Middlefield Lane when a car stopped just behind her. She turned as Daniel got out, made an instinctive movement as if for flight, then stood motionless, the bunch of flowers dragging against her knee.

As he came up to her, she said, "You were right – what you tried to tell me. Leo says she never wants to see me again."

"Oh, Rose." He shook his head. She looked deathly, hollows in her face that he'd never seen before. "I told you to give her a bit of time, for both your sakes."

"Yes, well – anyway, Steve's come back. You know, that American –"

The one who'd made it so obvious that he was sweet on Rose. "Yes, I remember him."

"He lost his wife in a car crash, so he understands ... He's going to stay with her for a time, I think – if she lets him, that is," she added, with a rueful grimace, then thrust the flowers at him. "Have these for the gallery. I took them to Leo, but she said – she told me to get out of her house, and take my flowers too."

"Oh, my poor darling."

"No, please don't, Daniel." She felt her fragile composure begin to crack. "Here you are." She put the flowers into his hands.

"I'll run you home."

"I'm not going home. I shan't be able to work, and I can't just go back and sit around. I'm having a walk."

"Have you been on the back road lately?"

"Through to Hamley? No."

"In that case, I've got something to show you."

He steered her across to the car, put her in, then got in beside her.

As he went to switch on, she said, "But the gallery. You should be there."

"Oliver's perfectly capable of running the place without me breathing down his neck. In fact –"

"Yes, and of course he's got Lucy to help him." She managed to keep her voice totally neutral.

Daniel looked at her. "No, he hasn't. Lucy doesn't work there any more. I fired her a couple of weeks ago."

"Oh."

"And what's 'oh' supposed to mean?"

"Nothing." But as he put his hand on the ignition again, she went on in a small voice, "Daniel, I'm sorry. About Lucy, I mean. I had no right. I am sorry."

"So am I," he said sombrely.

"And we are still friends?"

"If that's what you want, Rose."

His dark eyes were very close to hers. Such lovely long lashes. She'd always teased him about them. She made a funny little sound, half a laugh, half a sob.

"You know, your eyelashes are ridiculous on a man. It's not fair."

"So you've always told me."

They smiled at each other, the *frisson* of tension between them gone, and he drove away.

CHAPTER TWENTY-THREE

They were both silent as they made their way through the winding lanes, Daniel apparently absorbed in driving, Rose wrapped in her own unhappy thoughts. She roused herself only when they pulled up alongside a hedge, on the far side of which was a field full of maize.

"What've we come here for?"

"You'll see. Come on, out you get."

He locked the car and steered her through a gateway. Just inside was a trestle table, and a wicker chair under a faded parasol. A hand-painted sign said: 'Admission £2, children under 12 half-price', another: 'Back at 2.30. Go on in'.

Daniel dropped a five-pound note into the tin on the chair. Seeing Rose's puzzled face, he grinned at her.

"It's a maze – the Amazing Maize Maze. Haven't you read about these mazes? They're all the rage. Well, the farmers don't seem to be able to make much of a living any other way these days – and at the end of the season he'll be doing 'pick your own sweet corn'. It's a great idea, don't you think?"

"Oh, yes." Rose tried her best to look enthusiastic. "Yes, it is."

A well-beaten path led towards the entrance, the tall corn curved like the horns of a Bronze Age tomb. They stepped in and the maze enclosed them, over Rose's head, so that all she could see were silky tassels and leaves which rustled stiffly as they passed. The track broke into several narrower pathways, all identical. Daniel stopped.

"Which way, then?"

Rose pursed her lips. "I read once that you should always keep turning left in a maze."

"Did you? And where was that, I wonder – in *Tammy*?"

She laughed, in spite of herself. "No, it wasn't. And how on earth do you remember that my favourite bedtime reading was *Tammy*?"

"Oh, I remember everything about you, Rose," he said lightly. "Now, are you quite sure you're turning left?"

"Absolutely. At least, I think I am."

"In that case – beat you to the centre."

And Daniel turned sharp right and was lost round a bend in the path.

Rose's route followed a long, curving trail and she was still looking out for the first turning off to the left when she came up against a solid green wall. She retraced her steps, and this time she did come to a left hand turn. This was more like it; surely, she was heading straight for the middle. No – she was heading for another blank wall of maize.

The sun was beating down on her head, and she had had almost no sleep the night before. Every path she took turned a blind corner and petered out. Finally, she rounded a corner and found herself back at the entrance. She kicked the nearest maize stem, stubbing her toe, then set out along the path Daniel had taken.

At last, long last, she reached the centre. She knew it was the centre because Daniel was already there, reclining in one of the two old deck chairs, which someone with a sense of humour had placed there, along with a small potted palm tree and a Union flag on a stick. He was leaning back at his ease, arms linked behind his head, looking cool and unruffled.

"What kept you?"

"You – you've been here before." Rose could have kicked him as well.

"Well, I just might have come a couple of weeks ago." He stood up. "But I did suggest the right hand path, if you recall."

"Yes, you did – but I still think you cheated." She wiped her arm across her sweaty forehead.

"Sit down. You look all in." He took her hands. "I shouldn't have brought you, not today. It's just that on the spur of the moment I couldn't think of anything else to take your mind off things. My poor Rose."

She looked up at him, his face warm with concern for her. Then, like a sailor drowning in a green sea of maize, she clutched onto his hands and flung herself against his chest, weeping – for Emily, for Leo, for herself, and most of all for Jamie.

Daniel did not speak, simply enfolded her, until at last the sobs died and, apart from little shuddering snuffles, she was silent. He held her a little way away from himself.

"Better?" His own voice was rather shaky. Rose's sufferings had cut him open, raw, without anaesthetic.

"Y-yes. Sorry, it's just –" Her voice faded away as she rubbed the back of her hand across her eyes.

"I know, I know. But like I said, you mustn't blame yourself. Leo will see that, in time. She'll come round, I promise you. And there was always something about Jamie – I don't know –" he shook his head "– a kind of fey quality – his hold on life never seemed to me to be very strong. Believe me, love, if it hadn't been this way, it would have been another."

"Maybe you're right." She gave him a pale little smile. "I'm sure you are – you always are."

"Not always, no." His mouth twisted. "Sometimes I do the most bloody stupid things imaginable."

His face was cast in shadow by the overhanging maize but, perhaps because her senses had been honed and slashed in the last weeks, and because she too was lonely and distressed, needing to both give and receive comfort, she sensed in him a deep pain. Poor Daniel – he must really have loved Lucy.

"Oh, Daniel," she said softly, and drew him to her.

At first, she felt his resistance, but then he relaxed and they stood, tightly locked, each hearing the other's heart beat. When they drew apart, they looked into each other's eyes, feeling the other's breath on their skin. Then she put her hands one each side of his face and, drawing it down, kissed him on the lips.

They moved back together again, looking into each other's eyes once more, as if searching for an answer to an unspoken question.

"No, Rose – please." Daniel's voice was tense.

In response, she placed her palms flat against his chest, until she felt his pulse beat begin to flicker erratically. She smiled up at him, then, with growing confidence, undid the top button of his shirt.

"Oh, Rose."

He pulled her roughly into his arms and began pouring kisses over her hair, her face, her neck, his lips scalding. She clung to him, breathless, and together they sank to their knees, pulling off their clothes until they were both naked. Their adult bodies were strangers – and yet they were their other halves.

They kissed again, this time gently, then slowly lay down, watching the other's face, as though for the very first time, pale limbs and olive-brown ones twining, straining every tissue in the desire to be a part of someone else, until joy and rapture such as neither had ever known filled them both.

Daniel was the first to recover. He opened his eyes, gazed blankly for a moment at the green canopy over his head, then turning, saw Rose beside him. She lay in total abandon, arms and legs flung wide, her palms open and trusting as a baby, her face half turned towards him, her eyes shadowed by her lashes. One of her pale, gingery curls lay beside his hand. He softly twined his finger in it. How would she react, this prickly, thorny Rose of his? Surely, he could not have told her more clearly in words about his feelings?

Far away, at the periphery of the world, he heard a car door slam, voices. He looked at his watch. Half past two.

"Come on," he said softly. "Time to go."

Rose half rolled over, yawned, stretched voluptuously then lay still again, her eyes almost closed. There was a shifting pattern of leaves and sunlight against her lids. Her body felt languid, wrapped in a deep peace.

Something was tugging gently at one of her curls. As she moved her head, a voice said, "Come on. Time to go."

Her eyes flew open and she saw Daniel, propped on one elbow, looking down at her. His lips were curved in a smile, but his eyes were serious, brooding even.

The mood of delicious languor vanished instantly. What had she done? When, instinctively, she'd turned to Daniel for comfort, just as instinctively she'd felt him try to draw back, to hold her at arm's length. He'd known better than she had, and now she'd blown it. She'd ruined everything – at least, the only thing which really mattered to her, the best thing she'd owned, which was Daniel's friendship. She'd smashed it, like one of those precious, fragile ceramics in his galleries.

For a moment longer she lay, feeling black misery engulf her, then she leapt to her feet. Her back to him, she began scrambling herself into her clothes. Behind her, she heard Daniel get to his feet. She had just scuffed her feet back into her sandals when he took hold of her shoulders, turning her to him.

"I'm sorry," she whispered miserably.

He looked down at her bent face. She looked distraught, on the verge of tears but, far more than that, it was as if she couldn't even meet his eye now.

"I'm sorry," she repeated. "I was a fool."

"It's all right." His voice was devoid of any expression.

But she knew it wasn't all right. It would never be all right again. Biting her lip, she ducked from under his hands, caught up her bag and plunged into the green tunnel.

Daniel stood motionless, his arms limply by his sides. He wanted to shake her, crush her fiercely to him, shout into her face, I won't let you go this time – do you hear me, Rose? But a lifetime's habits were too strong. He followed her, caught up with her, and without a word steered her down the right paths.

At one turn they came face to face with a dispirited looking young couple, towing two sulky children.

"For God's sake, is this the way?" panted the man.

Unable to trust his voice, Daniel jerked his thumb behind him.

"Thanks, mate." And they went on.

A young girl was sitting beneath the parasol. When they came up to her, she said, "Was it you who put the five pounds in the box? You need a pound change."

"Forget it." Daniel barely glanced at her.

Rose was waiting beside his car, but when he came up to her she said, still not quite meeting his eye, "Look, I think I'll walk home – it'll do me good. I'll take the footpath."

"Rose."

"What?"

When he did not go on, she forced herself to look up into his face, which was strained and weary.

"Oh, Daniel, I'm so sorry."

Without another word, she crossed the lane and ducked through the narrow kissing gate which marked the dusty footpath to the village.

From the depths of a hazel tree, a thrush's song pierced Rose to the heart.

"Ashes to ashes, dust to dust ..."

It seemed as though half the village was there. Rose looked round the little field, starred with buttercups and white campion, bathed in morning sunshine, the women like more colourful flowers – for Leo, via Angela, had asked that there be no black. George and Angela, Mike and Sally, of course, Zoë, Jenny and Roger, Lettie Johnson, in the same outfit she'd worn to the party that night, when Jamie had come home, two of her dogs with her.

Leo, was wearing the bright red dress, which surely had been a fierce gesture of defiance, and which only showed up more clearly her pallor and thinness; Steve, right alongside her, towered over her. His expression was bleak, far away. Was he at this moment remembering that long-dead Lindy, their baby, who had never even had a life, only a funeral? And Daniel, standing just beside her, so close their arms brushed. His face, above his pink shirt and flowered tie, was grave. She'd heard nothing from him for a week, then the previous night he'd rung, told her he was taking her to the funeral. When he arrived, it had almost been the same as before – almost, but just not exactly.

Lettie's were not the only dogs. The young man whom she had last seen outside that squat in Edgbaston, the one who didn't split on his mates, had brought his dog, which didn't like people but sat at his master's feet now, chin on paws, watching everything. Beside him was a young girl. When she'd first glimpsed her, Rose's stomach lurched, for she was slim, had long blonde hair; but this girl was older than Emily, her face thinner, surely the same girl who'd been holding that baby to her when she'd seen her last? Other dogs with another group of young people – the Animal Rights activists, perhaps, but there were no placards today, no drum beating, for Daniel had told her Leo had insisted that there should be no demonstration, no turning of her son into a martyr for their cause.

The short service was almost over. Rose saw the young man take a recorder from his pocket. He began to play, very softly, *Amazing Grace*. The thin, reedy notes echoed eerily round the field and the trees which edged it, and Rose's mouth went dry as, just for a moment, the image of a little Jamie came into her mind, sitting at the kitchen table, struggling to learn that same piece for the school service next morning.

"I once was lost, but now am found." Gritty-eyed, she stared hard at the trees.

The notes died away, he took a breath then began again. This time, the girl joined in, quite unselfconsciously, her hands clasped in front of her. She had a lovely, rich contralto voice which dipped and soared above the recorder in the old Negro spiritual, *Going Home*. And when the last reverberation of her voice died away, it seemed to Rose as if the whole world had been holding its breath.

At the end, she hung back, watching Leo in the little gateway, greeting people with Steve, her shadow, just at her elbow. Half of her hoped that Leo would go then, so that she did not have to face her. But Daniel put his arm round her waist and silently propelled her forward. Her hands clutched tightly on her bag, she saw the two men exchange glances, then she was in front of Leo.

They looked at each other for a long moment. Then Leo put out her hand.

"You'll come back to the cottage, I hope, Rose."

She clasped Leo's hand. It felt dry and brittle like a bird's body, as if it could be crushed with a single squeeze, so she just held it.

"Thank you."

She stood aside and waited, while Daniel said a few murmured words to Steve and kissed Leo. Then the four of them left the field together.

CHAPTER TWENTY-FOUR

Rose carried the scarecrow down the path and carefully deposited him in the back of her new, second-hand estate car. He sat there, smiling benignly out at her from under his black velvet hat. Richard the Third. He'd been much the hardest of all her scarecrows so far, the clothes themselves a nightmare until one morning, after delivering, to yelps of joy, Cassie's scarlet-tunic-clad Mountie, she'd finally tracked down a superb black and gold doublet and hose and a sword in a shady backstreet shop in Birmingham. She hadn't even tried to haggle with the even shadier owner, just paid the exorbitant price, grabbed the outfit and run, before the theatre at Stratford could discover that one of their costumes had gone walkabout.

And then Richard himself. Her immediate thought when Mrs Broome had rung her was of an Olivier lookalike, complete with large hump and jovial 'I've just been smothering my nephews in the Tower' leer. But that wouldn't do at all for Mr Broome, who was an ardent member of the Richard III Society. Richard Plantagenet had been much maligned; he'd loved his little nephews to bits, while his hump was no more than over-developed muscles in his sword shoulder.

"Well, Richard," Rose smoothed down one black tress of hair, "you look pretty good to me. Let's hope Mr Broome approves."

A wasp blundered into the car. She flapped it out and it zoomed off towards the fallen pears in her front garden. As she went to get into the car, she saw a long V formation of geese, flying very high up. Going south for the winter? Far more likely heading for the nearest town park with a lake, to mug the resident ducks; she knew that, but it was more romantic to imagine them flying away to the sunshine. Rose watched them until they wheeled away and were hidden by trees at the back of Angela's garden.

As she approached Leo's cottage, she saw a removal van parked on the verge, with two men easing a Welsh pine dresser in through the doorway. A youngish woman with a harassed expression hovered alongside them, while a man was throwing open the window of the bedroom that had been Leo's.

The new tenants. Angela had told her that they were moving in today, but she'd forgotten. Rose felt a vicious jab of pain. Of course, it was only temporary, Leo had told her, the evening before she flew out to Washington with Steve, and she'd be coming back in November – for the inquest, though neither of them spoke the word. But her furniture was in store, she'd cancelled all her garden commissions, the book she'd begun had been put on hold, and Steve had asked her to design his mother's new garden at first hand. Rose suspected sorrowfully that the book would be on a very long hold.

Until that evening, there had been a constraint between them but then, just when she was leaving, Leo said, "Take care of yourself, love", and something in her voice made Rose turn and hold her to her. They'd stood for a long time, without speaking, then she'd kissed her and left, before the tears began. She seemed to be doing a lot of crying these days.

As she drove past the cottage, across the garden wall she saw a little boy, standing rather aimlessly, swishing a stick at a clump of Michaelmas daisies. Small, fair hair, solemn-faced. Rose's mind jolted her back – was it ten years? No, more. She'd just rented George and Angela's cottage and studio, and was lurching past in the ancient Renault 4 she'd had in those days, when she saw a little self-move van drawn up on the grass. A tall, thin woman and a little boy were struggling to manoeuvre an old armchair through the garden gate. She'd braked, leapt out and gone to help them.

Back in the present, she waved to the boy, who only stared at her rear seat passenger, and drove on. She'd call on the new family soon, but not today.

As she drew up outside Susan's house, she saw that her parents' car was parked in the drive. Rose hesitated. She wasn't really in the mood for anyone this afternoon. Strange really – Mr Broome had been in raptures over his Silver Wedding present, the fat cheque was, literally, in her bag, she'd had a call from Adam on her new answer phone while she was busy putting the finishing touches to Richard's shoes; and yet, all she felt was a kind of leaden ache which had for days, weeks even, been creeping through her. It was a strangely unpleasant feeling, not sharp like toothache, but dull and unremitting; there when she went to bed, there when she woke.

She had to ring the bell twice before the door opened.

"Oh, hello, stranger." The sisters kissed, then Susan said, "Sorry to keep you – I've just been changing Tarquin."

"Oh, is it – what's she called? – Miss Lathbury's day off, then?"

"No." Susan's face tightened. "She's gone."

Gone? The formidable Miss Lathbury? Not the same way as Birgitta, surely?

"Anyway," Susan went on, "we're outside. Come on through."

Although the glorious summer weather had broken, they were still getting the odd mellow day, and this afternoon it was sunny and warm on the little terrace. Her mother was nursing Tarquin.

"Good heavens," she exclaimed, "look who's here. It's your Auntie Rosemary, darling."

"Hello, Mum, Dad." She bent to kiss them both, then ruffled her godson's chicken-down head.

"We haven't seen much of you lately," continued Mrs Ashenby. "Where have you been hiding yourself?"

"Oh, well, I've been quite busy – lots of work on, you know."

"I really do think, dear," her father resumed his conversation with Susan, "that that's quite the wrong place for your extension. Don't you agree, Edna?"

"Oh yes, it would spoil those lovely French doors."

"Are you having an extension?" asked Rose. "But weren't you thinking of moving to a larger house?"

"Well, we're not, actually." Did she imagine it, or was that expression on Susan's face again? "Roddie is –"

Her voice tapered off, and her mother broke in firmly, "Jeremy has decided that Roddie is too young to be a partner – utter nonsense, of course, isn't it, dear?"

"Absolute rubbish," grunted her husband.

"So Roddie is leaving and going to set up on his own, working from home, at first, before he finds suitable premises in town. And you mustn't worry, darling," as a shadow passed across Susan's face, "he'll give Jeremy a run for his money."

"Of course he will," added Mr Ashenby. "All his old clients will be flocking to him, you mark my words."

It was unreal. Rose felt, as she so often did with her family, that she was watching a play in which all the actors were entirely word-perfect. A few months ago, she herself would have taken it all as offered to her. Now, she remembered *dear* Jeremy, her fellow godparent – a mean little tight-arse, Daniel had called him, barely out of earshot. Prim, straight laced; alongside him, Roddie had

194

seemed like someone out of *Men Behaving Badly*. And that was it, of course. Roddie – and Susan – *had* behaved badly. And since no whiff of scandal must ever touch the firm, Roddie was out on his ear.

"Don't worry, dear," her mother repeated. "Everything will be all right, I promise you."

And everything would be all right, because it always was within this charmed circle in which, Rose at last realised, she had no part. She had an eerie feeling that Emily, Birgitta, pants-off Roddie, Susan – "Well, yes, the dear girl needed a little break" was how she'd heard her mother describe that particular escapade to one of her village cronies – none of it had happened, except in her own imagination.

"Oh, by the way, Rosemary, there was something in yesterday's *Telegraph* that might interest you."

Holding on to Tarquin, she dug a cutting out of her bag and handed it over. Mrs Ashenby's first – often, only – reading each morning was the Court Circular, followed by the Births, Marriages and Deaths announcements, and holding the scrap of paper, Rose read: Forthcoming Marriages: The engagement is announced between Christopher, only son of Mrs and the late Mr John Mallory of Fenton Curlieus, Oxfordshire, and Candida Lucinda, younger daughter of Mr and Mrs Peter Latymer-Dasset of Brandon St Mary, Northamptonshire.

So Mrs Mallory had finally won.

I dislike them intensely, Candida most of all. Oh, Christo, what have you done? But perhaps they'd reach an – what was it? – accommodation, and go their separate ways.

"I thought you'd be interested," her mother repeated.

Was there a hint of reproach in her voice? If there was, Rose didn't care. Be happy, she willed him silently. Try to be happy, my dear, lovely Christo.

"Yes. Thank you." Keeping her voice and face expressionless, she went to give it back.

"No." Her mother waved it away. "I was going to post it to you, but as you're here, you can keep it. What are you doing round this way, anyway?"

"Well, I wanted to see how Susan was –"

"Oh, she's absolutely fine."

"– and to deliver a scarecrow a few miles away."

"That reminds me. Daphne saw one of your scarecrows the other day."

"Oh, yes? Which one was it?"

Her mother gave a faint shrug. "I can't remember. She did say, but –"

Their eyes met and Rose thought, she's waiting for me to ask if dear Daphne – another of her little chums – liked my work. She wants me to, so she can put me down. Well, she could deny her that pleasure.

"Talking of scarecrows," she said brightly, "I've had some good news today. A friend of mine is doing a children's series on TV. It's built round scarecrow characters, and he's had the go-ahead for me to do the puppets. It's Sky TV," she added, when no-one said anything.

"Sky? Good God." Her father stared at her in horror. "You're not working for that appalling little Australian, are you? Oh, dear, Edna," he shook his head sadly, "whatever next?"

Rose looked at them both. Instead of pleasure – relief, even – that after years of near insolvency, bumping along the bottom of the money pond, she might actually be on the verge of prosperity, there was almost a hint of chagrin on their faces. All at once, she thought, they don't want me to succeed, to break out of the place they've set for me. No, more than that – they're jealous. Susan's going through a bad patch and, almost as if I'm someone else's daughter, I shouldn't, for the first time ever, be doing better than their own beloved child.

Once, not long ago, she would have been deeply hurt. But not any more. Never again need she look to them for their approval, their support. She was free.

A door banged and Emily came through the house and out onto the terrace.

"Hi, everybody." She tossed down her bag.

Rose had not seen her for weeks, and now she was astonished. The girl looked exactly the same as before, in jeans and blue sweatshirt. Except –

"Emily!" Her grandmother almost squawked and Tarquin, chewing frantically on a plastic ring, jumped and the corners of his mouth turned down. "Whatever have you done with your lovely hair? Oh, *darling*." For Emily's long blonde hair had been chopped short, and there was now a wide henna streak running from front to back.

"Susan," she turned to her daughter, "how could you?"

"I had no say in it, Mummy," replied Susan, a shade less sweetly than usual. "She just came home like it. You're back early, Emily."

"Yeah, well, the last lecturer's absolute –" she caught her mother's eye "– ly awful, so I got the early bus."

"How's the Sixth Form College?" Rose put in quickly.

"Oh, all right, I s'pose." Emily shrugged then dropped into a chair. "Hi, Fatso." She chucked her brother, none too gently, under the chin and he beamed at her.

"Darling, I do wish you wouldn't ..."

Rose sat, as the bickering flowed around her. Nothing, no-one had changed. Even Emily had been totally untouched by the events of the summer. For a moment, she almost hated her niece, then thought; well, the young are so resilient, and surely it's better this way.

"What's for tea? I'm starving. I hope you remembered those veggie pies I wanted."

"Yes, I did," Susan snapped. She turned to her mother. "Honestly, Mummy, as if life isn't difficult enough at the moment, Emily has taken it into her head to go vegetarian. She calmly tipped her lamb casserole in the bin one day and announced that she was never eating meat again."

As her grandparents took a sharp intake of breath, Emily's eyes met Rose's. They exchanged a long look then, to forestall the storm which was about to break, Rose snatched up her bag and got to her feet.

"I must go. I want to get to Stratford before the shops shut. Bye, Susan. Mum, Dad, see you all soon. Bye, Emily."

But the girl got up too. "I'll see you off."

She said nothing until Rose opened her car door, then, "Rose."

"Yes, love?"

"They just won't talk about it – about him. It's as if he never existed."

Out here, close up, there were dark shadows under her eyes, her mouth pinched. Fury towards the rest of the family surged through

Rose. This wasn't her job. Someone in that house should be doing this.

"Listen to me, love." She put her arms round Emily, drew her close. "You will never forget Jamie. He was a lovely, gentle boy – and he loved you – and he would be glad to know that you're alive because of him."

"Oh, Rose, I wish I –"

"Don't cry, my love. Jamie wouldn't want you to. But you'll always remember him, and whoever you love in the future – yes, you will," as a muffled protest came from Emily, "he'll always be very precious to you."

She kissed the top of the shorn head, then held the girl away from her.

"All right?"

"Yes, thank you."

"You know, Emily, nothing lasts. The good and the bad things, they all pass. Hold on to that – and remember, any time you want to talk about – anything, just pick up the phone."

"Can I come and stay with you at half-term?"

"Of course you can."

"And Rose –" She hesitated.

"Mmm?"

"Will you take me to see it – the grave, I mean? Oh, it's all right. I know all about it, how – how Jamie's buried in a field. I heard Mum and Grandma talking – Grandma said that Grandad said it was disgraceful, no better than a pagan funeral, and he didn't know what the vicar was thinking of, taking the service. It wasn't disgraceful, was it, Rose?"

"No, it wasn't. It was lovely. It was – exactly what Jamie would have wanted. And before she went to America, Leo planted an ash tree beside him."

"Will you take me?" Emily repeated.

"One day I will, I promise, but not quite yet."

"Well, if I buy some flower seeds, will you – would you mind planting them on the grave?"

"Of course I wouldn't mind. And it's a great idea. They'll have to be wild flowers, though. In fact, I tell you what, love – buy some poppy seeds. Jamie loved poppies. I know he'd like that."

"Thanks, Rose." A smile broke through the girl's strained

features. "I'll get them tomorrow and post them to you."

As she drove away, the small figure was in her driving mirror, until she turned the corner into the main road.

CHAPTER TWENTY-FIVE

"No. I think just a little closer will be better. Ye-es, that's it. Do you see how the lines of the bowl pick up the curves of the jug now?"

The two men, Oliver Paige and a younger man she did not know, looked round as Rose shifted her carrier bags slightly.

"Why, hello, Rose," said Oliver, "you're quite a stranger."

She had been standing rather hesitantly in the doorway to the gallery, but now came further in.

"Hello, Oliver. How are you?"

"Oh, fine – fine. It's good to see you, my dear." He shook her hand. "I was only saying to Daniel the other day that we rarely see Rose these days."

"Oh – oh, well, I'm rather busy at the moment."

"Yes, I hear you've launched into a new career."

"What did Daniel say?"

"That your scarecrows are doing very well – a great success, apparently. I know that he is very impressed." He smiled kindly down at her.

"Oh? Oh, good." Rose had always been fond of the shy, rather bumbling Oliver Paige, and on an impulse she went on, "If you'd like one, I'd love to make you a scarecrow for your back garden."

"Oh, how kind, how very kind, my dear. Thank you." And he seemed genuinely touched. "But I'm leaving my little house, I'm afraid."

"Oh, no. I am sorry." He and Sasha, his Siamese, fitted into the red brick terraced house in Old Town, with its cosy, book-lined study, snug dining room, the window framed by an ancient wisteria, like a foot into a comfortable slipper. "I'm so sorry," she repeated.

"Yes, well, the lease is expiring and my landlord really wants the house for his daughter. She's an actress, you know – a very fine one, by all reports, though to my mind her Viola does not bear comparison with dear Judi's. Anyway, she's doing a season at the RSC next year, and so I have to move on." But in fact, he sounded remarkably cheerful. "Yes, it's amazing, isn't it, how things always seem to work to our good?"

"Do they?"

"Oh yes. Oh, I'm sorry, my dear, I'm forgetting my manners," as the young man shuffled his feet. "Rose, this is Toby Hayden. Toby – Rose Ashenby, a friend of Daniel's and mine. Toby's my new assistant."

Lucy Smith's replacement – and a distinct improvement to Rose's mind.

"I hope you'll enjoy working here," she said, as they shook hands.

"Oh, I'm sure I shall."

His face lit up. How young he was, barely past his middle twenties, yet already another edition of Oliver. Tall, slightly stooped, the same shy expression, he even wrinkled his spectacles up his nose in the same way. It was quite uncanny to think that one day, quite soon, he would turn into a fully-fledged Oliver Paige.

And yet Oliver himself, she thought suddenly, was different today. Hard to put her finger on it, but he was, well, different.

She smiled at the young man.

"I like that arrangement you've done." She pointed to a low plinth, draped in black, where were displayed three large earthenware platters, underglazed in a bold swirling pattern of orange and pink orchids against a background of bamboo stems, and a pair of tall, oval jugs with dark blue clematis splashed boldly across them. "They're gorgeous." She gently ran her fingertips across one of the platters. "Absolutely beautiful."

"They are, aren't they?" Toby exclaimed enthusiastically. "Oliver found him – the potter, I mean."

"Yes, my first real discovery." Oliver almost visibly preened himself. Yes, there definitely was something different about him. "Quite by chance, Rose, as all the best discoveries are made. I was in Wales for a few days with my sister some weeks ago. One day, I followed a rough sign 'To Pottery' up an even rougher track, and found this young potter – his name is Mark – working in an old cowshed. Daniel is delighted with him – as you know, he's always keen to encourage young craftsmen – and he's suggested that next spring we hold a big exhibition of his work. Quite like old times, eh, my dear? Remember when we arranged that show for you, when you were first starting out?"

"Yes, I remember." In fact, that had been another time when she'd never finished what was planned as the centre-piece, and Daniel had been angry with her. "Well, I'll leave you both to it. Is

Daniel upstairs?"

"Yes, he is." Then, in a lower voice, "Try and cheer him up – he's a bit down. Well, I suppose it's only natural in one way, even if it is so exciting."

Upstairs, the door to Daniel's flat, which was usually wide open, was closed and Rose hesitated on the landing before knocking. When there was no answer, she opened the door.

"Oliver, could you come through for a moment?" Daniel's voice came from the bedroom.

"It – it isn't Oliver. It's me."

"Rose?" He appeared in the doorway, a large cardboard box in his arms which he carefully set down before coming towards her. His lips just brushed her cheek in a cool kiss.

"Hello, Daniel. I was just passing, so –" For the first time, her brain took in what her eyes had registered the moment she opened the door; that the room was in total chaos. "If it's not inconvenient–"

"Of course it isn't inconvenient. I'm glad to take a breather from this lot. Sit down, I'll make some tea." He took the carrier bags off her and put them down in the corner of the room. "Don't tell me," he gave her a smile which was faintly rueful, "more scarecrow gear."

"Afraid so."

"What are you up to now?"

"Oh – you know, various things." Now that the moment had come she felt, not triumphant, as she would have been a few months ago, but strangely reluctant to tell him. "Actually – I'm almost certainly going to do some telly work."

"Good heavens." He laughed. "Tell me all."

He went into the tiny kitchen and she steered a path through the boxes, to lean in the doorway.

"You remember that scarecrow festival I went to?" For a moment, their eyes met in shared recognition of the events which had followed. "Well, I met Adam Harding there. You've heard of him?"

"The children's author? Of course."

"We got talking and he was looking for a new idea for a TV series – and he's decided to do one based on scarecrows."

"And he wants you to do them? That's brilliant – congratulations, Rose."

He came across to her, gave her a hug. "What's the matter?" He stood looking down at her, his hands on her arms.

"You don't mind?"

"Mind? Of course not. Why should I? Oh – yes, I see what you mean." The kettle whistled and, releasing her, he made the tea. "Actually, I was out of order that time." He paused. "It's nothing to do with me what you do. Just so long as you're happy, Rose."

Actually, I'm not happy. Actually, I'm bloody miserable, if you really want to know. Actually, what she longed to do was bang her fists against the wooden lintel and jump up and down and yell, Don't be like this, Daniel. I want you to mind what I do.

"Biscuit? Or I'll send Toby out for some cakes for you."

"Oh, no thanks – nothing for me."

He was loading the tray, and as she turned back into the sitting room her eye fell on the box he had put down. On top of a pile of clothes lay a small painting. She picked it up and carried it across to the sofa.

"Good grief – I haven't seen this for years."

She sat down, still holding it.

"What's that?" He set down the tray. "Oh – that."

Rose went on gazing at the painting, feeling strange emotions stir in her. So long ago it had been, her second, no, her first year at Art College. She'd been rereading one of her favourite childhood books, *The Phoenix and the Carpet,* at the time. Daniel had come down to see her that weekend – they'd spent most of the Saturday in the Tate, where they'd both been entranced by the Turners. She'd spent most of the next week working on the painting, and when she'd given it to him, Daniel had called it a Turner in miniature. She'd never seen it from that day.

"I didn't know you still had it."

"Why shouldn't I still have it?" There was an angry vibration in his voice which she retreated from.

"Oh – well." She looked down at it. The phoenix, just visible through the flames, was a bit lopsided and she hadn't at all managed to catch the impression she'd been striving for. "Really, it isn't very good." She grimaced. "Thank goodness my Turner period didn't go on for long. Let me do you another one. Would you like me to?" when he did not reply at once.

"I like this one."

He took it from her, holding it as she had done, looking down at it. That weekend, the new boyfriend – he'd met him for a few minutes, and conceived an instant loathing for him – the first of all Rose's dire men – then, fortunately, the swine had left them, after a kiss, walking away surprisingly lightly, loaded down as he was with so much hatred. He and Rose had gone to the Tate. She'd stood, entranced, in front of the Turners, while he had stood, entranced by her, her face tilted to the paintings, so that the light had seemed to pour off them, illuminating her pale, translucent skin.

Abruptly, he got up, laid the picture face down on his desk, then took up his cup.

"Drink up – it's getting cold."

"Are you spring-cleaning?" Rose looked round the boxes.

"No. Clearing things. Sorting out what I'll leave, what I'll take."

"Take?"

"To New York. And what I leave, I'll cram into a couple of cupboards. Oliver will want to bring his own stuff, and God knows, he's got enough of it. I mean – five thousand photographs of Dame Judi, for starters." He laughed wryly, but when Rose only stared at him, he went on, "Didn't he tell you? I thought he would have done."

"Tell me what?"

"He's moving in here. Well, it makes sense – he's losing his place."

"He told me that."

"And it'll be a weight off my mind to have someone reliable actually living over the shop, so to speak. Toby seems very promising, but he's rather young for the responsibility. And," he went on rapidly, "the thought that he's going to be in charge seems to have worked wonders for Oliver's confidence. He's a different man, don't you think?"

"Oh yes – yes, he is. But I don't understand," she went on, very slowly, knowing that she did not want to understand. "I mean, I knew you were going to New York – you told me that – but I thought you were just going for –" Her voice tailed away. "You aren't, are you?"

He got up again, took some photographs from his desk and dropped them in her lap.

"This is my new gallery. Not much to write home about – it's an old warehouse, down by the river."

Rose shuffled through them. A huge, vaulted space, a beamed ceiling, a broken window, with a view down to a wharf, the river beyond. The points of light coming off the water danced and blurred in front of her eyes.

"It's very nice," she said in a low voice.

Was that all she could find to say? He felt a twinge of resentment at her muted reaction, but he merely said, "Well, it will be, I hope. It'll take time, of course."

Up here, under the roofs of Stratford, twilight was setting in early, and he switched on his desk light. Rose's head was still bent over the photographs.

"And it'll be better for me to be there," he went on, "on the spot, if anything goes wrong."

"You aren't coming back, are you?" Rose, who could barely get the words out for the weight of misery on her, was busily arranging the photographs into a neat stack. "You're never coming back."

"Never's a long time. I shall have to come back sometimes, of course, with the gallery here and the one in London."

He was sitting opposite her but his face was thrown into shadow by the lamp and she could not read his expression. She handed him the photographs.

"It'll be lovely, I know." She managed a faint smile. "Everything you touch turns out well."

"Not everything, no."

Rose felt as though a giant hand was slowly, painfully settling its grip on her lungs, until she could hardly breathe. She took a sip of lukewarm tea, the cup rattling as she set it down.

"When are you going?"

"Sunday."

So soon. "And – you *were* coming to see me – before you go?"

"Of course." But the slight hesitation had already answered her. Unable to sit any longer, she got to her feet.

"I must be going. Unless I can do anything to help you here?"

"I think I've broken the back of it, thanks."

"Well, I'll – I suppose you'll be quite near Leo and Steve."

"Not that near. But we shall see each other, I hope."

"I forgot to tell you. The family who are renting her cottage moved in today."

"Oh yes? That's good. It's not nice to have empty houses in a village."

"No." And as Leo won't be coming home either –

"She'll be back in November, of course, so you'll see her then."

"At the inquest, yes."

There was silence between them. In the distance, a clock chimed, while downstairs, faintly, they could hear Oliver's and Toby's voices.

"Rose."

"Daniel."

They both spoke together.

"Sorry." He opened his hands. "You go first."

"Nothing. Just – I must go." But she didn't want to go. Outside this door dreary loneliness was waiting to pounce on her, sink its claws into her, devour her.

"Well." He moved towards her, and for a moment she thought he was going to kiss her. But he only took her hands, holding them tightly between his. "Rose."

"Mmm?"

"I'm just at the end of a phone, you know – if you ever need me."

He crushed her hands until she almost cried out with the pain, then abruptly released her. Turning, he picked up her carrier bags and gave them to her.

"Good luck with these."

"Thank you – and you."

She couldn't look at him. The next moment, she had gone.

He heard Oliver's voice again, then Toby's; the gallery door banged. Crossing to the window, he looked down. A moment later, into his oblique view, she appeared. She was moving quickly, almost running, her hair a halo from the light of the setting sun reflecting off a shop window. He watched as her slim figure wove through the crowds on the pavement. When she was sculpting, he'd always secretly marvelled how something so slender, so fragile could ever conceive of, never mind create some of the massive sculptures she had worked on.

He saw her stand on the edge of the pavement, turn her head as if towards him for a moment, then she darted across the road and was lost to his sight.

CHAPTER TWENTY-SIX

Rose, who had been crouching for hours, straightened up, easing out her back. She surveyed her handiwork – a line of half a dozen quarter-size scarecrows propped against her studio wall. Adam would be pleased, she was sure, when he came to see them next week.

Glancing at her watch, she saw to her surprise – and relief – that it was gone two. That was what she liked; a large chunk of the day sliding past unnoticed. A cold burst of wind came under the studio floor and she shivered. Reaching for her sweater, she opened the door.

Dead leaves were eddying around the yard and Bugsy, his fur standing on end and transformed, as he always was by wind, into a kitten again, was chasing some wisps of straw. When he saw her he stopped dead, then, very dignified, came stalking across to her.

"Hello, Bugsy darling."

She picked him up, squeezing him to her. Laying her cheek against his soft fur, she felt the faint charge of animal electricity, then carried him in her arms across the yard. As she reached her gate Andrew, the boy from Leo's cottage, rode past on his mountain bike. He waved and she waved back, then went indoors.

When she'd made and eaten a sandwich and poured a cup of coffee, she switched on her answer phone. A brief message from Adam: Yes, he was definitely coming next Thursday and yes, the producer would be coming too. She listened without emotion. She'd done the job, and done it well, but she felt no pleasure in the thought. She was hollow inside.

She turned the tape right back to the beginning, to the message she always kept. But something had gone wrong this time, there was only a blurred jumble of sounds then Adam again. Of course, it didn't matter in the least – she knew the words by heart, but somehow losing his voice – slightly hurried, as though he didn't really want to speak – was the straw which, if she wasn't careful, would break her.

"Dear Rose, they say parting is such sweet sorrow, so I'll keep this brief. All packed. I'm off first thing tomorrow. This is all for the best. Since that day in the maze I've known it couldn't go on like this. I'm freeing us both –" a long pause. "My dearest Rose, no-one will ever mean as much to me as you do. Be happy, my darling girl –" another, even longer pause. "Remember the old song, *Whistle and I'll come to you* –"

The house was silent when Adam's message ended, even though Daniel's voice still echoed in her mind.

She could not face working any more that day. Putting on her jacket and woolly hat, she plunged into the network of old footpaths which crossed and recrossed the fields and spinneys behind her cottage, until she stood on top of the hill, beside the ruined windmill. She leaned against the stonework, her collar turned up against the bitter wind, her hands jammed in her pockets. Overhead, grey clouds scudded along; below her, the countryside was spread like a living map.

In the entire landscape nothing moved. Rose had never in her life felt so alone. The cheerful little fields had turned into a bleak, empty wilderness which mirrored the emptiness inside her. She shivered, went to move, then stopped.

Far beneath her was that field. She recognised it, even though the crop of maize had been gathered weeks ago and when she'd driven past there'd been a sign: 'The Amazing Maize Maze – now closed. Reopens next August'. The faint patterning had survived the harvester, and she followed the twisting paths until her eye reached the centre.

Huddled against the base of the mill, she gazed at that centre for a long time, her eyes wide open and staring. And with no fanfare of trumpets, no roll of drums, silently her own heart told her the truth.

She loved Daniel. She loved Daniel. She'd always loved him. It was just that, knowing him as long as she had, she'd been a fool – a blind fool, who'd always looked not at him but past him. He'd been such a part of her she hadn't realised that if he was cut away from her, she would bleed. Now she was bleeding. And it was too late.

Whistle and I'll come to you. But she couldn't whistle – it was too late for that, too late for words. She had to show him. What would bring him back? For long minutes, her thinking was so intense that she held icy hands against her temples.

Then she relaxed, even smiled a little, as inside her a candle flame sparked into life, flickered, then burned up fiercely. She would do a sculpture, a huge piece – the biggest she'd ever made; and people would say that it was Rose Ashenby's finest work to date.

It would be a giant phoenix – not lopsided this time, but rising true from the flames, reaching upwards in ecstasy, straining every gilded feather in the joy of life. It would be a phoenix because that way Daniel would know exactly what it was she was trying to tell him, without a word being spoken. The phoenix would bring him back to her.

A toy tractor had turned into the field. It began to plough, cutting a deep furrow. As Rose, laughing out loud, ran down the hillside, a flock of white seagulls wheeled behind it, then swooped over the chocolate earth.